Fang and Bone

Text Copyright © 2023 SL Thorne, Mae Baum, A.J. Jensen

All rights reserved under International and Pan-American Copyright Conventions.

No part of this book may be reproduced or transmitted in any form or by any means, graphic, electronic, or mechanical, including photocopying, recording, taping, or by any information storage or retrieval system, without the permission in writing from the authors.

This book is a work of fiction. Names, characters, places and incidents are products of the author's imagination or are used fictitiously. Any resemblance to actual events or locales or persons, living or dead, is entirely coincidental.

ISBN: 9798385502554
Imprint: Thornewood Studios

FANG AND BONE

EDITED BY
S.L. THORNE

DEDICATION

To the insistent, nagging figments and eidolon of characters, their tragic pasts and all manner of horrors begging to be inflicted upon them. Those things which might otherwise go bump in the night but made it to paper instead. This is for those characters who would not go away, but refused to stick around long enough for a whole book.

Within these pages you will find six short stories of the monsters of the night that most often haunt our psyches. Mostly their becoming. Some their destruction. At least one is just mad.

Well, anyway, go on. Don't forget your torch and mind your step. And for heaven's sake, be *careful!* Not everything in here shuns the light.

Table of Contents

The Birth of Stormcrow -S.L. Thorne...1
Death Wishes -Mae Baum..13
Right Behind You -S.L. Thorne..31
Pride Goeth -S.L. Thorne...89
The Wolves of Vinland -A.J. Jensen..167
Casefile: Thornewood -S.L. Thorne...205

The Birth of Stormcrow

S.L. Thorne

It was a late summer evening, the weather clear and just south of muggy. The cicadas were thrumming in the brush and the birds were coming to roost for the night. Lan was a young man already, tall and reedy, a well-muscled young buck. His dark hair hung wild around his face as he crouched in a tree, the blue eyes peering through the leaves incongruous with the copper tone of his skin, with his strong Indian heritage. He watched the slightly younger boy in the distance running cautiously through the darkening forest, looking for any sign of him.

Matthew was all of sixteen, a light-skinned, darkly red-haired Irish boy who practically worshipped the ground his adopted brother walked on. The five years between them didn't matter, neither did the full knowledge that Matthew would likely follow in his father's footsteps and grow into a powerful werewolf and that Lan would not. Lan was not kin or kine, but like any of the strays werewolves took in, their connection ran thicker than any accident of blood. They were blood brothers as well as legal ones, and that ran deeper than anything else in the boys' minds.

Matt squinted in the dim light and paused, trying to get his breathing under control, to find any sign of Lan's passing. The forest

The Birth of Stormcrow

litter all looked the same to him. Though there was a broken branch over there. He crept over to it to check how fresh.

With a loud war whoop, Lan leapt out of the tree and tackled him, and the two boys went rolling, laughing as they wrestled. Lan had to admit the boy was growing stronger. He let Matt pin him. Matt grinned down at him. "Thought ye had me, din't ye? I'm not so weak now, eh?"

"Yeah, you're sprouting a few muscles," he conceded. "But your senses are as dull as an old spoon. If I'd had a knife and a mind, I'd have scalped ya!" he cried, flipping the smaller boy off of him.

They faced off like two football players on opposite lines of scrimmage. Matt played for the high school as Lan had before him, and Lan knew the boy would be a very imposing opponent by his senior year. "Hardly fair," Matt panted. "It's getting dark. I kin barely see m' nose."

Lan laughed and thumped his nose. "What happened to those werewolf senses you keep bragging about, eh? Must be all the fire water you keep sneaking out of Pa's cabinet."

"Hey!" he cried and tackled. "Well if yer so keen in th' dark, why don't ye track me?"

"Be harder to follow a bull elephant," he taunted as they struggled.

"Prove it!"

Lan tightened his grip, wrapping his legs around Matt's pinning them, and pulled the boy in closer. "Fine," he said with a wolfish grin. "You've got... fifteen seconds.... No, make it thirty," and he let him go.

It took Matt three of those seconds to grasp the situation before he threw himself off of Lan and bolted through the woods. Lan rolled onto his stomach and laughed. "You're going the wrong way, white boy!"

He heard the retreating footsteps shift direction, and he counted off the seconds before he got up and trotted off after him. He loped along at an easy pace for a little while, still able to hear the pounding and sliding of sneakers through the old leaves. "You make a great deal of noise, wolf-boy," he teased, then smiled as the footsteps got quieter.

"I'm not the one who woke up a sleeping bear last winter," Matt countered.

Lan turned his head. The forest made his voice echo strangely, hinting at a slightly different direction than the footsteps had shown, and he adjusted his tracking accordingly.

Before long it was full dark and a low-hanging fog had rolled in off the creek. Lan grew worried. The thickness of the fog meant they were closer to the water than he had thought. All teaching games aside, it was now too late and too dangerous to be horsing around. Father Pafford would have his hide, grown man or not, if anything happened out of carelessness.

"Matt! Game's over. It's too dangerous. We're too close to the creek!"

Matthew's laughter rang out through the mist, light despite the heaviness of the air. "Givin' up?"

He used his grown-up voice. "Matt, I'm not kidding. We must have gotten turned around 'cause we shouldn't be this close to the water."

A chill ran up the back of his neck. Some inner sense was warning him that something wasn't right. He stopped and listened. The world was wrapped in a blanket and he could barely see. The moon showed dimly through the canopy and made the fog glow eerily while obscuring all details. He could barely tell one tree from another. Unable to trust his eyes, he listened. Off to his left, he heard the brief rattle of a snake's tail and the scream of a dying rabbit. Up ahead and a little to the right, he thought he heard a branch break, leaves rustling. He held his breath. There was no splash, so Matt had not fallen into the creek. Still, it was all he had to go on, so he began quietly walking in that direction, his eyes constantly in motion.

Every few seconds he'd hear the noise again, a foot sliding against the forest floor and then it would stop, but always in the same place. "Matt?" he called softly.

The Birth of Stormcrow

A strangled cry was the only response. He moved faster. If Matt was hurt...

Ahead, he caught the glimpse of red light and approached with more caution. The trees thinned a little, and the light became two red eyes and Lan stopped. Fog formed an unnatural ring around the owner of the red eyes and the soft glow gave off just enough light to let him see Matthew pinned against the tall, dark body and the long, pale talons pressing against the boy's soft, white throat. The area reeked of loam, moldy soil, and old blood.

"Welcome to the party, Lan," came the gravelly voice. "We've been waiting for you. I've been waiting a long time."

Matthew struggled in his grip, but the man lifted him off his feet with one arm as easily as if he were a toddler and the talons tightened on his neck, one piercing the skin. The man sniffed the air at that, lifted the nail and peered at it, then sucked it clean. "Oh, how careless of me."

"Matt, stop," Lan warned. He did not know what this man was or what he wanted, but he knew that his adopted family had many enemies that were less than natural. It was clear this man, this creature could snap Matt like a twig if he chose.

"Smart. But I knew that," the man purred, setting Matt back on his feet. He lowered his face close to his neck, took a deep, shuddering breath, and smiled, revealing a mouth full of pronounced fangs. "Vampire," Lan spat. He watched Matt's whole body stiffen, his widened eyes betraying both fear and hatred at once. The Pafford family had a long, well-fueled feud with the undead in general.

The vampire chuckled. "Perceptive, too. Already half-educated. Self-sufficient... just what I've been looking for. Waiting for."

Lan narrowed his eyes. "Waiting for?"

"Oh yes," he smiled, a mad grin. "A long time. Well, by your standards. By mine, it was only a breath, really. But long enough to know what I want."

"And what is that?" he asked warily. Instinct told him to keep the creature talking. He had to find a way out of this for Matt, and at the moment, he couldn't see one. The Paffords had waited a long time for a child of their own, to the point of adopting Lan before they had finally had Matthew. He would allow nothing to happen to the boy now, not if he could do something about it.

"You," the man said in an exaggerated, conversational tone, "You see, I've always wanted a boy of my own. A son to take after me and follow in my footsteps and fight the good fight...." His grin was far from friendly. His dark red tongue flicked across Matt's skin, licking up the blood on his throat. The boy shuddered with revulsion. Lan's muscles coiled, ready to attack, but the vampire moved even more swiftly, talons once more pressing into Matt's neck, not yet breaking the skin, but painful nonetheless. To his credit, Matthew did not even cry out.

"Ah," he warned. "Not so hasty, my boy. You see, you have a decision to make. I can only have one of you. As it stands, one of you gets eternal life and the other a shallow grave. However...," he looked back down at Matt, the red eyes gazing hungrily at the exposed throat. "I might be convinced..."

Lan waited as long as he could stand it before he asked, "Convinced of what?"

The eyes flicked up at him, and the look made his skin crawl. "To let one of you live."

"And what would convince you?"

"Ah, now we bargain!" he exclaimed with sadistic delight, loosening his grip on Matt's throat to wrap him in a hug. In the next heartbeat, he set the boy on his feet, grabbed a fistful of unruly red hair, and set the razor talons against the artery below his ears. "Either you submit to me, agree to become my childe, and obey me implicitly until I choose to release you or I will slaughter him right here and now. Then I will embrace you anyway and feed you his oh-so-sweet young blood for your first meal. Or I could be really evil and make you kill

The Birth of Stormcrow

him in your initial blood frenzy. How would that sit on your conscience? He really is quite tasty."

Lan forced himself to rein in the rage that threatened to blind him. He knew from experience how much strength it took to hold Matt still and this man, this... thing, did it with such ease that he could probably fend Lan off without exertion. So fighting would only get both of them killed. "And if I go with you?" he asked, hating the choice.

"NO!" Matt yelled, was immediately silenced by pressure on his throat.

"Agree and I'll let the wolf's brat live."

His eyes widened. "You know what he is? What he could be?" he choked.

He chuckled. "Oh yes, and you know... thinking about it... he might make a better choice than you, though he'll need a bit more schooling." The fangs brushed close to Matt's neck again. Matt choked at the smell of his breath.

"Wait!"

The vampire stopped, blinked innocently at him. "Yeeees?"

"If I agree, you'll let him go?"

"On the condition he keeps his mouth shut. I know where he lives. If you betray me, go back on your word or displease me in any way, and I'll return here and slaughter not only the boy but the parents as well."

Matt's struggles were useless. Lan was conflicted. He wanted to save his family, the only family he had ever known. But saving them meant losing them. What he would become was everything they despised and fought against. He could never return home again. But if he didn't, they would all die, and this thing might take Matt instead, and that would be worse. He saw the way Father Pafford watched his son, the way friends of the family looked at him and nodded knowingly, as if they expected greatness from him, a change... a change he would be denied if this thing...

"Fine."

"No," Matt growled through clenched teeth. He managed to get an arm free and clawed behind him for the face of the beast.

"You swear on your little brother's head?" he asked, ignoring the fingers scrabbling for his eyes.

"I do."

He threw Matt at Lan's feet. "Then make him understand. I assure you, play me false, and catching him will be easy. And your mother will not die in her sleep..." he threatened.

Matt landed in a heap and threw himself to his feet again, ready to lunge back at the vampire, but Lan caught him, and turned him to face him. He shook him to get his attention, to still the rage burning behind his pale blue eyes. "Now is not the time, Matt!" he said firmly. "Now is not the time. You heard him. He'll kill mother too. Father would kill me if anything happened to you."

"But ye matter too, Lan. Ye can't just sacrifice yerself..."

"I can and I will, if it means I get to see you grow up and become that which you were meant to be. If I refuse... I can't even think about the consequences. You have to go home."

"What will I tell pa when I come home wi'out ye? Clawed up like I am? He'll come after ye. He'll be honour-bound t' kill ye too!"

"Then you don't tell him. Tell him we were attacked, and you got away while I fought. Tell them I was kidnapped. Anything but the truth." He pulled him into a smothering hug, hiding the boy's sobs of anger and sorrow. "We can't win this one, Mattie. It's the only way out. I don't, we'll all die. Just know I'll always be there for you." He held him just a moment more before pushing him away. "Now go home, Matthew. And don't look back."

Matthew hesitated a moment, stared back at his brother with tear-stained eyes. Catching sight of the monster again, he ran. Lan listened to the footsteps fading into the fog but knew they had not gone far. The vampire was just behind him. He could feel the man's fetid breath on the back of his neck. His muscles tightened as he got control of his fear and temper. "Remember this, vampire. That boy and his family are hostage against your word. Anything happens to them and I will turn on you in a heartbeat," he promised through gritted teeth.

"Agreed," he hissed. "Kneel."

Lan ground his fists, resisted the commanding voice.

"I said kneel! ...It is not too late to go after him..."

Though it went against every ounce of will, Lan slowly sank to his knees in the loamy earth. The body behind him was cold, as were the hands that grabbed the collar of his shirt and yanked it down over his shoulder. A taloned finger ran lightly along his skin, from the base of his ear to the arch of his collarbone, seeking out his pulse. "If you relax, this might even be pleasant for you," came the low, grating voice.

But Lan did not want this to be pleasant. It wasn't a pleasant thing. He was a sacrificial lamb on the altar of his family's safety. He was the stag giving up his life so that others might live. That did not mean he had to make this easy. His arms remained at his sides, hands balled into fists, every muscle rigid as one hand set onto his shoulder, holding him easily in place, and the other seized his hair and violently tipped his head.

Pain lanced into the side of his neck like a snake bite and ten times more acute. Tissues tore as the curved teeth ripped their way into his artery and began to suck the life out of him. It spread like a fire outward from the wound, set his heart pounding, his blood singing in his ears. Involuntarily, he raised a hand to fight back, but the wrist was seized in a crushing grip. The vampire adjusted his hold, jerking Lan's whole body back against him like a dog worrying over its prey, and Lan cried out as the fangs tore at him again. A long, deep growl emerged from the feeding beast.

He felt his blood drip down his chest as the widened wounds made the blood flow faster than the vampire could drink. His face was hot and wet from tears spilled against his will: for the family and happiness he had lost, for the hatred they would now bear for him. For the loss of daylight and the heat of the sun and the sweet taste of a girl's lips as her body pressed against his. Things he would never know again. His feet and hands went slowly numb with cold and he felt a strange weight settling upon his body, like a blanket of snow.

He could feel his heart slowing, and his breathing go shallow. His vision narrowed, not that he could see much in the growing darkness. He felt the teeth he had forgotten were there pull free and the stench of rotting earth and carrion was suddenly in his face. He tried to pull away, but his head moved only a few inches. His mouth was forced open and something thick and foul and salty was poured in. He could taste dirt and mould as the thick, oily blood slid down his throat. The hands holding him up pulled away, and he slumped to the warm earth. His vision began to fade with his heartbeat as the last of his blood trickled from his opened throat onto the forest floor.

"Yes, boy," he heard through failing senses. He struggled to hang on to life one moment more. He looked up, and what little he could see was suddenly razor clear. Matthew was standing just beyond the trees, watching in horror. Lan reached out his hand to him, to beg him to run even as he begged the Great Spirit to let him just die.

The vampire ignored Lan's death throes, all his focus on the sixteen-year-old boy not twenty feet away. "Yes, watch and remember, and run home to your family. But remember this: tell a living soul what happened here and you will be the last to die." Then he bared his fangs and hissed, snarling in the boy's direction. But Matthew remained frozen in place, struggling against the urge to fight for the brother who was dying in front of his eyes. "I'd go before he wakes. He will be hungry, and you are quite ...delicious."

It was Lan's voice that spurred him, a voice barely heard, speaking with his last breath. "Matt, run."

That alone put his heels to flight.

Matthew's retreating footsteps were the last thing Lan heard as he closed his eyes and waited for death to claim him, waiting for that bliss of nothingness, of being one with the universe. But something was interfering with that oneness, something that rose up like a wall between him and the rest Nature intended for all things at their end. It began as something that shouldn't be: pain. He should be beyond pain, beyond the crippling vice grip seizing his innards. If he didn't know that he should already be dead, he would have thought he was dying. His hands clawed at the earth, his body curling in on itself. It was like growing pains and hunger pangs attacking all at once. He writhed on the ground, grabbing his head in an attempt to quell the screaming he kept hearing, to block out the blinding light hammering its way into his skull. After a moment, he realized the source of the screaming was him.

He forced himself to stop, rolled onto his belly, aware that he shouldn't even be moving. Every muscle was rigid with searing pain, crying out for something he didn't have and didn't know how to get. He looked around him. The forest was dark and empty and the fog was gone, yet everything was as clear as daylight. He felt light-headed and dizzy, as if his brain wasn't getting enough oxygen, and then he realized he wasn't breathing. Lan took a breath. It didn't help. He couldn't concentrate. There was something he needed to do, but it was just out of his reach. The pain was becoming commonplace now, though it did not lessen its intensity. He tried to sit up. The world reeled, and he began vomiting. He could not stop until his stomach was past empty and found himself surprised to see no blood in it. But why should there have been blood?

He caught the scent of something in the air and looked down at himself, at his torn shirt and the blood smeared on his chest. He wiped it with his hand, brought it to his face... was immediately repulsed by the idea of licking it, yet that was what he found himself doing, dirt and all. He wiped up all he could, then began to suck the blood from the fabric.

A dead rabbit landed in front of him, its neck broken. He seized it on instinct and bit into it, suddenly recognizing the fire within him as hunger. He started to eat the rabbit raw, but the moment the blood touched his tongue, all he wanted was the blood. The thought of eating the rest of it revolted him. He drained the bunny dry and tossed it aside, looking for more, but there was someone in front of him, crouched, watching him.

As he moved towards him, smelling more blood, a taloned hand came up. "Not yet, Stormcrow. Now you must hunt on your own, but first, we must leave this area lest you force me to go back on my word."

"Your word?" he asked, his brain dull.

"Think, Stormcrow. Why are you here?"

"My name is not Stormcrow," he said, realizing what had bothered him.

"It is now. Now, why are you here?"

"Because..." He racked his brain. Flashes of wrestling with a young boy ran through his sluggish mind. The teen being held by the man in front of him. Some kind of bargain made. "Because I said... I would..."

"Obey. If not, I would..."

"Kill them." It was suddenly painfully clear. He had traded his life for his brother's, for his family. His life was over. And whatever this man said to do, he must. A coldness seized his heart that had nothing to do with the lack of blood in his system. Slowly, he rose.

"We must go before they come looking for you," he said, picking up the rabbit's body. "We'll hunt in another part of the forest."

Lan followed numbly, looking back over his shoulder only once, towards the home and comforts that had once been his, which he would never see again. In his heart, he wanted to throw back his head and howl his sorrow to the wood, but his body simply did not have the strength.

The Beginning

Death Wishes

Mae Baum

Vera waited for the life to drain from her victim's eyes. The young man slumped against her red velvet chaise. Her hands wrapped around his head, holding it, so she could see the exact moment that death took him. His black hair was cut close to his head, and his brown eyes were glassy and out of focus.

Her mind wandered back to her last kill. Hunting a witch had been fun, entertainment for a vampire who'd lived a long time. Vera smirked. But the death curse had been an unexpected problem. When Vera had drained the old bat's life, she'd cast it with her dying breath. *"You'll hear the last wishes of your victims and will be compelled to fulfill them,"* she'd said.

Pulling herself back to the present, Vera licked her fang and listened. This was the first death she'd caused since the curse. She'd found the handsome young man in her nightclub and hadn't been able to resist a taste. And as a century-old vampire, Vera was nothing if not curious. What form would the curse take? Would it be hard? She did like a challenge, but she was also spoiled. No matter what, things usually went her way.

I wish I'd kissed the girl, the young man's voice whispered in her mind before fading into nothing.

Death Wishes

Vera laughed and pushed the corpse onto the floor of her private lounge. It wouldn't do to get any blood stains on the velvet chaise. She stood, smoothing her short, black dress, and stalked towards the double doors leading to the club proper.

Faith jumped, as skittish as ever, her embroidery falling to the floor. "Madam, wait!"

"What?" Vera paused, glaring at the skeletal vampire companion. Unlike Vera, Faith hadn't taken to vampirism well. She didn't relish in the hunt like Vera did. Faith lived on Vera's leftovers, too timid to take a meal for herself. Vera smirked, wiping away a drop of blood sliding down her chin.

Faith wrung her hands. "Are you sure?" Her hazelnut eyes darted toward the club, and then she gestured to Vera. "You *are* covered in blood."

"My club, my rules," Vera growled, although she couldn't have stopped moving forward if she wanted to. The curse insisted on completion of the wish. She hadn't survived this long without learning how to be discreet, but the magic pulled on her, forcing action.

Vera pushed through the doors and out into the nightclub. The sweaty smell of humanity hit her nose, and she grimaced. She wanted to press her hands to her ears to shut out the techno music, but she resisted. She was the most powerful creature here. She wouldn't show any weakness. Vera squinted into the darkness, illuminated only by flashing laser lights. She spotted the girl from earlier, now dancing with a long-haired boy, their half-naked bodies entwined. They were surrounded by others, couples and groups, lost in what this generation called music.

Yanking them apart, Vera inspected the girl in the dim light. Blonde hair, blue eyes, and a well-shaped figure. No wonder the dead kid had wanted to kiss her. Vera grinned, knowing what a gruesome sight she made covered in blood. The boy swore, turned, and ran, while the girl stared at her with a mix of fascination and repulsion.

"Danny sends his regards," Vera whispered. Then she slid an arm around the girl and yanked her close for a kiss. Vera slid her tongue into the girl's mouth, knowing the second the girl recognized the metallic taste of blood by the way she bucked against Vera's embrace.

The girl's eyes bulged and she beat her hands against Vera's chest.

Predator instincts at the fore, the vampire in Vera enjoyed the girl's panic. Releasing her, Vera turned and left the dance floor with a grin pulling at her lips. She waved a hand at her bouncers, knowing they'd clean up her mess. Her manager already held the boy who'd run off and awaited her signal.

Throwing open the doors, she strolled back into her quarters. An elegant bar ran along one end, lined with crystal glasses and decanters of fine alcohol. Low lights and candles illuminated the space. She'd had the doors double insulated so no one outside could hear her victims and so she didn't have to tolerate the club music that frayed her nerves. Her furniture was deep mahogany and red velvet, in stark contrast to the industrialism of the nightclub decor.

Faith was already slurping what was left of the young man's blood. Even kneeling on the floor and bent over a corpse, she kept her high-necked, white gown immaculate. Her dark-brown hair was pulled back in a tight bun and she wore no makeup on her face. Remaining spotless and not killing her own meals was Faith's way of pretending that she wasn't a beast. But she wasn't fooling anyone.

Pursing her lips, Vera waited.

Her face strained, Faith wiped her pale lips with a handkerchief. "I'm so sorry, my lady...."

"I worry about you," Vera said, arching an eyebrow. "You should eat more."

As a former lady's maid, Faith had never given up her old-fashioned mannerisms. She gazed at the floor. "Yes, my lady. As you say."

Vera laughed, wondering who she should kill next. The old witch's curse felt so light. She'd been compelled to fulfill the wish, but

Death Wishes

the old bat hadn't specified how. Besides, humans were idiots and asked for the most ridiculous things.

This could be fun.

***

A week later, Vera drank from a pretty young woman. Vera stroked the side of the girl's face, watching the emotions run across it as she faced her impending death. Humans were such fragile little things. How did they ever expect to survive in a world of predators? Yet, somehow they did. The woman's luxurious brown locks reminded Vera of Faith's own hair when she'd been human. Not that it still wasn't beautiful if she'd ever undo it from that severe bun.

Faith was the prettiest of three sisters whom their pious father had called Faith, Hope, and Charity. Vera had so enjoyed breaking up the little trio by turning Faith. The father had, of course, tried to retaliate. But he was only a puny human. She'd allowed him to chase them for many years before she'd ended him. The surprised fury on the little man's face when Vera struck had been delightful.

The young woman's life slipped down Vera's throat, and a voice said, *I wish cancer wasn't killing my mother*.

Vera smiled. This was almost too easy. Leaving a few drops of blood for Faith, Vera stood and crossed the room. Taking a warm cloth from the bar, she glanced in the mirror behind it. She looked vicious, dangerous. Her short, black hair curled around her pale face, and blood was smeared across her chin. She smirked. Good thing the old story about vampires not being able to see their reflection hadn't been true, because this was a good look on her. It would have been a shame if she hadn't been able to see it. The old witch had been insane to think she could bring down a being as strong as Vera—even with a death curse.

Wiping the cloth across her chin, Vera said, "I'm going out."

"What did she say? What was her death wish?" Faith asked, looking up from her book. The pages were yellowed and the binding frayed. Her eyes betrayed her hunger as they fixated on the puncture wounds on the girl's neck.

Vera ignored the questions. Faith would see soon enough. Though the curse tugged at her, Vera frowned. "What are you reading?"

Red spots appeared on Faith's cheeks. "*Tess of the d'Urbervilles.*" Her gaze remained on the young woman's neck.

Curving her hand around Faith's chin, Vera yanked her face up so their eyes met. Faith's brown eyes were full of sentiment. Vera tilted her head, studying her companion. Faith trembled. If she'd had a heart, it would have been beating rapidly against her chest.

"Time to grow up, little Faith. You're coming with me," Vera said. Jerking the book from Faith's hands, she tossed it across the room.

Faith's face blanched. Her eyes strayed one last time to the corpse on the floor.

"Oh, finish it, then," Vera muttered, the wish still tugging at her. She needed to get this done. "But be done by the time the car arrives."

The vampire darted across the room and pulled the body to her mouth.

Vera sighed. At least Faith was meticulous enough not to make slurping sounds while she fed. The girl really needed to acknowledge that she was a monster so she could give herself over to it. And what had been the point of turning the girl, if she wasn't going to enjoy it?

After ringing for her driver, Vera pulled on a fur wrap over her modern black dress. The cold didn't bother her, but she liked the fashion. Unlike Faith, she adopted whatever was modern and fashionable. Her dresses were expensive and looked fabulous on her. Sliding into the limo at the door, she gave the driver the address that the girl's ID had so helpfully provided.

Death Wishes

Faith sat as far from Vera as she could, her face against the window. She wore a navy wool coat that, despite the old-fashioned style, at least made her appear part of this world. It also hid the worst of her thinness, thankfully. The humans tended to comment on it, most annoyingly, and Vera couldn't be bothered to compel their curiosity away. Especially with the curse pulling on her like this, insisting she complete it.

But Faith's shoulders were hunched and her eyes averted. Anger and hatred rolled off of her. Probably furious with herself, with her own beast.

With a shrug, Vera turned her gaze to her own window and watched the city streets roll by, crawling with life. Electric lighting had changed so much about the world, but especially the number of humans out late at night. It made fine feeding for vampires, but it was also a little more difficult to hide one's activities. Vera hadn't survived this long without being smart. The days of torches and pitchforks were not so far behind them. Still, the curse tugged her onwards. Even if the mother had been in the midst of a crowd, she couldn't have stopped.

But they saw fewer and fewer people as the limo rolled through the city and into a residential neighbourhood. Little white picket fences and backyard treehouses meant the people felt safe here. Vera snorted. These humans stoutly refused to see the monsters, even when they were on their streets or soon to be knocking at their door.

The limo pulled into a driveway next to a white, two-story house.

When the driver opened her door, Vera exited the limo, dragging Faith along with her. Her heels clicked on the sidewalk as she approached the house. Little flowers bloomed along the path. The blue light of the television shone through the windows, and Vera glimpsed two gray heads resting against the top of the sofa. Vera clucked her tongue. Humans were so dull. The night was for fun, for feasting, for death, and they spent it curled up in their dens.

Vera snorted and rapped on the front door. She glanced up and down the street, but it was late, and these people were all wrapped up in their boring little lives.

A woman answered, her back stooped with age and her hand curled around a wooden cane. She wore a sky-blue robe and slippers on her feet. The smell of vanilla and lotion surrounded her, and a clump of animal hair sat on her shoulder.

Vera sniffed. Yes, some kind of small dog. Wasn't that what these humans always did? Got an animal when their child moved out?

"Yes?" the woman asked.

"Hello," Vera said, pouring sweetness into her voice. "We're friends of your daughter's."

Peering at them suspiciously, the woman asked, "Jenny? Is something wrong?"

Vera verified no others were around. Then she shoved her hand under the ribcage and up into the woman's chest.

The woman's eyes bulged, and she sputtered, falling forward against Vera.

Faith squeaked, hiding her face behind her hands.

Vera yanked the bloody organ out. The body fell, and she pushed it back into the house. "Must have lost the heart for a fight," Vera said with a shrug. "But she didn't die of cancer." She smirked and studied Faith.

Her maid's eyes clung to the body, appearing torn between grief and hunger. Bloody tears leaked down her face, while her mouth gaped, fangs sharp and ready. She leaned against the wall as if it were the only thing in the world holding her up. Her chest heaved as if she was breathing. Vera handed her the heart and Faith grabbed it, biting into the flesh, her eyes wild.

A scream echoed down the hallway.

Vera waved a bloody hand at the man. The terms of the wish had been fulfilled. She stretched, free of the compulsion of the curse once more.

Death Wishes

The man ran forward to the corpse, gulping and trying to speak.

She'd intended to let Faith feed more, but this had gotten messy. Luckily, he was too distraught to pull out a phone and take pictures. Vera sighed in exasperation. She tore the heart from Faith's grip and tossed it on the floor. Then, pulling her companion behind her, she turned and strolled back down the path to her limo. The sound of the man's weeping followed her as she licked the blood off her fingers. Gesturing the driver toward the house, she slid into the vehicle.

He exited and headed inside to smooth things over. Having well-trained lackeys was important for any vampire. Vera waited.

In the far corner of the seat, Faith was keening. Her coat and dress were smeared with blood, and she'd had anything but her usual careful feed.

"Be quiet," Vera said, glaring at her. One would think that in the hundred years they'd been together, Faith would have gotten used to the violence. Would have gotten used to being a vampire, to fulfilling her own needs. Instead, Vera was constantly forced to give her lessons like this.

Quieting her whimpers, Faith curled tighter into a ball.

At least the girl listened to commands. As much as Vera tired of Faith's faint-heartedness, she had never been able to replace her. There were few attendants as loyal as a lady's maid from the 1900s, and if nothing else, Vera demanded constancy.

Tucked into the back seat, she tapped her finger against her chin. The death wish hadn't been triggered when Vera had killed the woman or when she'd tasted her blood. Was it because she hadn't drunk her to death? Vera filed the thought away. That would be important information if she ever became tired of this game. Of course, she didn't *have* to drain the humans to death in order to feed, but it did make it more entertaining.

Tsk. Tsk. The witch had been an idiot to allow for so many loopholes in her curse.

***

Several weeks later, Vera hunted an older man down the deserted alley. Around them rose the deserted architecture of old factories. Some of them had been converted into whorehouses and strip clubs, and that's where she'd found this guy, presumably a businessman by his cheap suit. He'd come down to enjoy the ladies, and now she was going to take her own pleasure. It seemed fair enough. Vera smirked.

This area had the added advantage that the residents of this part of town didn't look too closely at anyone, so Vera could enjoy this—the savagery of the hunt. The thrill of making grown men cry and piss themselves at the sight of a monster. Vera snarled, showing her fangs as she stalked after him.

His fear rolled off him in waves, and she licked her lips.

Grabbing a loose pipe, he swung around to face her. His sweat-soaked dress shirt clung to him, outlining his rotund form. His hair was balding, and his breath came in gasps from running—a fine specimen indeed. But it didn't matter to her what he looked like, blood was blood. And despite his lack of fitness, fear made him stronger and more of a challenge.

Laughing, she inched closer to him.

He lunged toward her, heaving the metal at her like a baseball bat, and Vera caught it in one hand. Pressing the pipe against his chest, she used it to back him up to the wall. Vera leaned into him. His breath was hot and fast against her cheek.

"Now, love," she whispered, "the dinner bell has rung."

She yanked his head to one side and bit into his neck. His blood spurted down her throat and she purred in satisfaction. The night around them was quiet, waiting on her pleasure. Taking her time, she sucked out every last drop of his life. The man's body sagged against the wall, only held up by her hands. She waited, her eyes on his lifeless face.

Death Wishes

I wish my wife didn't have to hear about my death in this filthy alley, the voice said.

Leaning her head back, Vera cackled in glee. She ripped his throat with her claws, hiding the bite marks. Then, she pulled out his wallet and dropped the human's body into the garbage pile. Flipping open the billfold, she scanned the address on the ID before she tossed it in after him and marched toward the mouth of the alley.

At the corner, her limo sat with the engine running. She slid inside next to Faith. "I left you some crumbs," she murmured.

Faith shook her head. Inspecting Vera's disheveled appearance, Faith murmured disgruntled noises. "Why must you hunt?"

"Because it's fun," Vera said, mulling the wish over in her mind. The compulsion of the curse was already upon her, but she knew just what to do.

Faith wiped Vera's face with a cool cloth. "There are plenty of discreet meals at the club."

Vera eyed Faith. Her maid was braver tonight, speaking more confidently. Her eyes glittered and her skin seemed plumper. *What might cause that? Had she eaten on her own?* Despite the pull of the curse, Vera needed to know.

"Have you eaten?"

"Yes," Faith said. Her voice had a note of hope that Vera had rarely heard and disliked intensely.

Vera stretched her lips in a false smile. "Did you see your family today, Faith, dear?"

Faith squirmed in her seat, refusing to meet Vera's eyes.

"Did you?" growled Vera.

Faith's sisters had gone on to marry and have large families after Faith's and their father's passing. While her sisters had passed many years ago, their children and grandchildren lived on. Vera grimaced. She should have eradicated the whole family when she had a chance.

Every few years or so, Faith got the notion to visit home. She fed off a few people—not to the death, of course—to give herself the appearance of health. Then she passed herself off as a faraway cousin and played human for a while.

Vera despised it. Vampires had no need for human ties.

"Yes," Faith whispered, looking down at her hands in her lap. "I missed them."

"I told you," Vera said between gritted teeth, "never again." She didn't understand why Faith wanted to cling to her human family. Being human had been a drudgery of following rules to Vera. Rules set by everyone but her. Now, she made the rules.

"But Augusta, my great-niece, is grown now." Faith smiled. Her whole face lit up as if she stood in the sun. "She loves to hear my stories."

Vera scowled. "Stories of vampires?"

"No," Faith said, twisting a ring on her finger. "She would hate me if she knew the truth."

"That's right, Faith. She would." Vera patted Faith's hand. "We're monsters. *You* are a monster."

Faith looked like she wanted to fight, but she sighed, and her shoulders slumped in defeat. They had had this same argument so many times before. Nothing had changed.

"Don't go back there again," Vera commanded. "I've warned you what would happen if you did. Do not test me."

Tapping on the window, Vera gave the driver instructions to her latest victim's home. How entertaining that the man hadn't wanted his wife to hear about the circumstances of his death, and what an easy wish to fulfill. If he hadn't been in a strip club when Vera had found him, maybe he would have had a better death wish. She smirked.

Dumb humans. No wonder they were prey.

***

Faith had given Vera the evil eye for days after the man's death. Vera hadn't been doing anything but lounging in the club's back room. She hadn't even eaten yet tonight. "What is it?"

"You tore that woman's ears off," cried Faith. "And then you dug out her eardrums." Her maid's eyes were wide and unbelieving.

"That's what this is about?" Vera shrugged. How could Faith still be so naive after all these years? "He didn't want her to hear about how he died. Now she won't hear anything." She turned back to the magazine in her lap.

"You're a beast."

Vera raised an eyebrow, looking up from an article that claimed to know the secret to an eternally youthful appearance. "As are you, my dear."

"No." Faith shook her head vehemently. "I don't kill people or rip out their ears!"

"And isn't that a sad fact?" Vera snarled. "A vampire who won't kill...."

Faith hissed at her and stormed off.

Watching Faith stride away, Vera sighed. Her maid was hungry and cranky. She'd get over it after a good meal.

Vera was starting to feel peckish herself. Time to find someone to eat. She pushed open the doors of her private quarters and sauntered into the club. The strobe lights still stung, but she maneuvered toward the bar.

The barkeep had a martini waiting for her, just as she liked it. Vera took the drink and turned to survey tonight's offering. The milling crowd had it all, any type of humanity she would want.

Vera spotted a white dress on the edge of the crowd. Faith rarely ventured out into the club. She must be furious. They'd lived together for so many years, fights were inevitable, but just the same, Vera would be glad when it was over.

Faith was talking to someone, a brown-haired girl in a short dress. *Curious.* Vera slipped through the crowd, as close to Faith as she could without being seen, and listened.

"I want to meet her," the girl demanded.

The young woman looked so familiar: brown hair, hazelnut eyes, and a sharp nose. Vera perused her features, trying to figure it out.

"No," Faith said. "It's too dangerous."

"Cousin!" The girl's hands were on her hips as if she could intimidate the vampire.

Vera blinked. *Who is this spirited creature?*

Faith shook her head and fled toward the back room.

The girl glared after her, and Vera laughed. Faith had been just as energetic when they first met. Seemed this girl had inherited some of that.

Vera approached her. "Who is it you want to meet?" Vera inquired.

Eyes widening, the girl blurted, "You."

With a grin, Vera took the girl's hand and pressed it to her lips. "My pleasure. I'm Vera."

"I know." The girl swallowed as if she regretted her bluntness. "I'm Augusta."

"And what else were you and your... *cousin* arguing about?"

"I want to become a vampire. Like you." The truth rolled off the girl's lips before she knew she had spoken.

Vera chuckled. Of course the child did. So many had come to her over the years, wanting to be turned. She rarely granted the request. Vera glanced in the direction Faith had gone. Would turning one of her precious relatives please Faith? Maybe Faith would feel compelled to look after the new vampire, prompting her to take better care of herself. Vera's maid could have a friend, and maybe the woman would gain a real playmate.

Giddy with excitement, Vera grabbed the girl's arm and dragged her to the back room. Faith was nowhere to be seen, but wouldn't this make a lovely surprise?

"What's going on?" Augusta asked.

"I'm going to make you a vampire!" Vera turned to her with a bright smile. "Isn't that what you wanted?"

Death Wishes

"Really?" Augusta seemed genuinely pleased.

What an odd sensation, to please someone. Vera hadn't made anyone happy in years, and she wasn't entirely sure she liked it. Still, if pleasing Augusta would help Faith, she'd do it.

"Yes." Vera sat down on the chaise and waved the girl forward. "Come here, child."

Without hesitation, Augusta knelt down on the floor in front of Vera. "How does it work?"

"I feed you my blood," said Vera. Taking a sharp nail, she punctured her wrist. "Then I drain you until you're dead."

At the sight of the blood, Augusta looked a little queasy.

Vera snorted. *Not all fun and games. Best to learn that now.* She wrapped her hands in Augusta's luscious locks and yanked her head back. Then Vera shoved her wrist against the girl's mouth. Augusta squirmed, fighting the force Vera used, and Vera held her tight. Once the girl had swallowed enough, Vera let her go.

Augusta jumped up, spitting and sputtering. "Disgusting!"

A cruel smile twisted Vera's lips. "Still want to be a vampire?" She poured a glass of champagne from the nearby table and settled back on the couch, sipping it. "Blood's your main drink for however long you live."

The girl shuddered and gestured to Vera's glass, gasping, "Can I have some of that?"

"No," Vera said.

Squeezing her hands into fists, Augusta growled.

Vera chuckled. For so long she'd only had simpering Faith for company. Augusta's spunk made her so happy. "Come on, girl," Vera said. "Let's finish this." She set her glass back on the table.

Augusta stalked over and plopped herself down in front of Vera.

Yanking Augusta's head to the side, Vera bit into her neck. The blood mixed with the champagne on her tongue, and Vera moaned. Her thoughts seeped away as she drank deeply from Augusta. Pure animal thirst took over, and Vera gripped Augusta tighter when she thrashed.

When Augusta's life force fled, the voice spoke in Vera's mind, *I wish you would die.*

Vera gasped, dropping the girl's lifeless body to the floor. What the hell had the girl just wished? I want you to die? The only being that could hear the wish was Vera. Had the girl intentionally made a wish? Vera clucked her tongue. That would have taken some serious force of will.

A scream came from the doorway. Vera looked up and met Faith's eyes.

Faith cried, "What have you done?" and barreled across the room to the dead girl on the floor. Bloody tears flowed down Faith's cheeks and splashed onto her white gown.

"She wanted to become a vampire," said Vera.

"So you made her one?"

Faith's tone sounded accusatory, not happy. Vera frowned. "I was sure you'd be pleased."

"Pleased!" Faith hollered, two red spots appearing high on her porcelain cheeks.

Vera shrugged. It had been worth a shot. See if she did anything nice for anyone again.

Pondering Augusta's wish, Vera stood and walked toward the champagne. Vera was already dead. She was a vampire. *So could the wish force her to die again?* Vera gasped, her hand flying to her mouth. *Or die a permanent death? Surely not.* There had to be a way around it. Vera thought back over the wishes she'd already granted. There was always another way to read them.

She eyed Faith, who was bent over the dead girl's form. Faith's shoulders shook with her weeping. Augusta had been gazing at the door when she died, well, as much as anyone could be looking at anything with that amount of blood loss. Maybe she'd seen Faith and the "you" in the wish meant her aunt. They had been arguing earlier in the club. Couldn't the girl have just been expressing some irritation with her elder? Vera nodded to herself.

After moving the champagne bucket to the floor, Vera snapped a wooden leg off the table. Carrying the rough stake, she approached her maid.

"I'm sorry old friend." Vera raised the stake and slammed it towards Faith's back, but it never struck. The curse wouldn't let it.

Vera heard the faint sound of the old witch's laughter as an unseen force wrapped around her fingers. The magic compelled Vera to drive the stake into her own chest. Pain radiated through her. She screamed as the tip touched her heart. Gritting her teeth, she forced her hand to stop. Vera stumbled to her knees and cried out, "Faith."

Faith straightened and gazed at Vera, her eyes cold and dispassionate.

"Help me." Vera hated the note of pleading in her voice.

Glancing at Augusta, Faith shook her head. "She did it for me, you know."

"Did what?" gasped Vera. Her shoulders and arms ached from the tension of holding the stake still.

"For a hundred years, my family has sought revenge for what you did to me and my father," Faith said. "And when I told them about the death curse...."

Fury roared through Vera. "You told them! You idiot!"

"I didn't think I actually *wanted* you to die," Faith continued, picking at a loose string on her gown. "Only punished." Her hazelnut eyes met Vera's. "For the evil you do to everyone."

Vera's arms shook and the stake slid in a little more. She wheezed and redoubled her hold on it. Vera whispered, "But you're my friend."

Faith snorted. "When have you ever been anyone's *friend*?"

Sweat made the stake slippery and it pushed in further. *But I don't sweat. I'm a vampire.*

Turning around, Faith strolled to her chair and sat down. She clasped her hands in her lap over her pristine white skirt.

"What are you doing?" squeaked Vera.

With a faint smile, Faith shrugged. "Waiting."

The End

RIGHT BEHIND YOU

S.L. THORNE

I hit the door of the fifth convenience store in the last hour. This was getting old.

The place was grimy, smelling of old food, stale coffee, and sweat. Even the radio blaring the newest Roy Orbison from behind the counter did nothing to bring up the atmosphere. I stood in line behind three other people, gave up trying to see behind the counter over their heads. Tucking my hands into the pockets of my worn bomber jacket, I eyed the curvy bottle of Coca-cola in the man's hand in the front of the line. I remembered when you had to go to a soda jerk for one of those. Glancing around the small, dim room, I sighed. Those places were cleaner, too.

The line moved as an older woman in a baggy dress took her brown bag of whatever rot-gut they sold here and shuffled off into the night. My eyes followed her even as I took a step closer to the counter and my increasingly futile goal. She looked both ways before stepping off the front walk of the corner store and furtively went left around the building. She might be good for a quick pick-me-up if I fed her, I thought. If I caught her before she'd gotten too far into that bottle, anyway.

Someone else walking past the store cut off my view of her, and I turned away. I was next.

I could now see the array of cigarettes behind the clerk around the woman in front of me, now that the man in the ten-gallon had left. I saw the characteristic white pack with the red bullseye on it and hope sprang up in my chest. There was a chance. At this point, I considered buying them whether they were filtered or not and just ripping the ends off.

The lady in front of me took her package from the counter and shuffled towards the door. I thought I heard a slight sniffle and smelled the salt of tears, but it was none of my business. Not tonight.

I glanced at the pimply kid behind the counter who looked like all early-night service workers these days: bored to tears and counting the minutes til clock off. "Lucky Strike, no filter," I said firmly, trying to keep the sound of my exasperation out of my voice.

"Lemme check," he squeaked, turning.

Both my hands crossed fingers where they rested on the counter, and I leaned forward on them, letting my head go slack for a minute. I needed a cigarette and a snack in the worst way right now.

There was a rustle of a paper bag near the door, which I foolishly ignored. There were only two heartbeats in the store right now, and I didn't give a damn about either of them.

The kid turned around with an empty carton in hand. "I might have another one in the back," he said. "I haven't had time to put the new shipment away. Want me to look?"

I lifted my head, giving him my winningest smile through the loose strands of my sandy blonde hair. "Please. I got all night," I added without a hint of the sarcasm I fully meant.

And that was my mistake. Actually, my first mistake had been to come back to Texas in the first place. I don't care if it *was* the 60's now. Some of the people I knew were still alive and breathing.

"Lily?" came an incredulous, middle-aged voice as the clerk headed into the back.

I tried to ignore the lady as if that wasn't my name. (Actually, it hadn't been for the last eight years, but I wasn't fond of this decade's moniker.) I half turned away, pretending to look at a display of Clark's Teaberry and Blackjack, while I glanced at the nearest reflective surface, trying to catch a glimpse of the person calling my name.

The sudden exclamation of "Bulldog!" brought a reaction I couldn't control.

I heard the bag of groceries hit the floor and turned when a hand touched the faded image on the back of my jacket.

The woman was in her forties and looked every year of it. Her once rich brunette hair was cut fashionably suburban, but starting to grey at the edges. Her eyes were the same greeny-brown, now dilating as she took in my ageless face. "Lorraine," I whispered, not even aware I'd spoken.

Fighting back a tear in her eye, she snapped to attention, giving me a sharp salute that looked out of place in her brown plaid dress with the little paisley scarf at her throat. "First Lieutenant Lorraine Fontaine, reporting for duty, Captain!"

I sank back against the counter, knowing there was no way out of this now. "At ease," I breathed, trying not to tear up or laugh at the joke we'd perpetrated back when we hadn't been considered military.

Lorraine started nattering immediately, the same old chatterbox, twenty years be-damned. "Where have you been? What happened? We thought you dead and here you are not looking a day!" she spouted. It sounded like it was all one breath.

I just leaned there, looking her over, deciding what I was and wasn't going to tell her. There was a ring on her finger, a dull gold band that was probably not solid. She looked care worn, and smelled like a cheap floral perfume, cheaper rye whiskey, menthol cigarettes, and ...baloney? I took another breath. No, a child. Damn it all to hell, Lori'd had a kid! The perfume hit me again as she shut up, just watching me take everything in and make whatever decision was percolating. It wasn't just cheap, now that I thought about it. Yeah, it was a drugstore fragrance, but something like a kid would pick out.

My mind made up, I moved away from the counter and her and the kid coming back with the cigarettes, headed for the freezer case at the back. She saw me aim for the ice cream and muttered a quiet, "Oh dear."

I looked over the weak selection. There was the usual vanilla and chocolate, Neapolitan. I reached for the pistachio and stopped, spotting a quart of rocky road just behind it. I grabbed that instead.

"That bad?" Lorraine gasped.

I gave her a wan smile as I went back to the register. She remembered our ice cream code. There was a hierarchy of flavours by which we could gauge just how serious, bad or good, a particular conversation was going to be.

The kid looked at me, then Lorraine, not sure what was going on. "H-h-how many you want?" he asked, holding the carton.

"Just give me the whole thing," I said, slipping him the money for the ice cream and cigarettes. God only knew when I'd find unfiltered again. Taking another deep breath, I smelled the faint scent of whiskey again. "And throw in a bottle of Cutty Sark," I added, laying out another twenty. What did I care? It's not like it was my money anyway, and I still had another forty in my pocket.

I grabbed my bag and turned back to Lorraine. "So where are we going?"

She picked up her groceries from the floor while I leaned into the door, standing against it to hold it open for her. "Arthur won't be home until six," she mused. "Tommy's asleep, so my house? I need to get back, anyway. He's alone. I wouldn't have left him but I needed bread and milk for tomorrow and this was the only time I could slip out to get it. I'm just a couple blocks."

I wondered why she was trying so hard to defend her choice. "How old?"

"Ten," she smiled softly.

I put the ice cream, cigarettes, and whiskey in the saddle bag of my Indian and put her bag in the other. I glanced down from my dark slacks to her frumpy housewife dress. "Can you ride in that?"

She put a fist on her hip. "I may have traded my commission for a white picket fence, but I still know how to ride," she huffed. Then she tipped her nose up and sniffed disdainfully. "Only now I can do it side-saddle," she simpered. She held that attitude for a remarkable three seconds before she cracked, making both of us laugh. Everything might be different, but surprisingly little had actually changed.

I threw my leg over the motorcycle and supported it while she got herself situated. She had to tuck in her damned skirts to keep them from getting caught in anything. Once we were set, I revved up and followed her directions.

Her house was a little yellow thing, with aluminium shades over the windows and a tiny carport. She had me pull my bike around the back, into the grass and leave it by the kitchen door. I carried her groceries for her and let her lead me into the sunny little kitchen. She stopped long enough to put them away and my ice cream in the freezer before she gave me the nickel tour.

The house was small. There was a living room only a little larger than the eat-in kitchen, and this was where the smell of menthol cigarettes and rye came from. It had a fancy sideboard with a decanter set filled with that cheap rye whiskey, and a well-used arm-chair facing a decent-sized TV. Hell, it might even be a colour model. There was a small chintz couch at an angle from it, but it clearly saw little use. There were a few toys neatly arranged under the coffee table. I noticed the heavy ashtray on the table next to the armchair had been freshly washed.

There was a short hall by the kitchen which led to the bedrooms and a bath. She didn't open any of the rooms or turn on the hall light, just told me what the doors were. "The WC is that first door on the right. Our bedroom is across the hall and that's Tommy's at the end. We'll have to keep it down so we don't wake him. He's got school tomorrow."

I nodded, following her back to the kitchen. It was clearly her favourite room. This was the only place that had any sign of her. The half shelf over the stove that was supposed to hold spices sported little nick-knacks and tchotchkes instead, most of them, I noticed, she'd picked up overseas... most of them while with me and the rest of our flight crew.

She pulled out two bowls, and spoons and doled out portions of the rocky road before putting it back and setting two highball glasses next to the now unbagged Cutty. She left it to me to pour. I was generous.

We sat at the little family table. I deliberately chose the chair her husband normally sat in, across from her, and watched her a long moment, taking a pull of the liquor that I didn't really need. I reached back into my bag and got a pack from my new carton, tearing it open, and, after inhaling the delicious, toasted aroma, began flipping them one by one, all but the last.

Lorraine chuckled as she watched me.

"What?" I asked.

"You still?"

"Every damned time." I started to reach for my lighter, then noticed there was no ashtray in the kitchen or lingering smell of smoke. I hesitated. "You mind?"

She shook her head, fetching a small one from a drawer. It looked like something you would keep for guests. I offered her a cigarette.

She looked at it, almost hungry for it, then shook her head. "Arthur doesn't like me to smoke. But you go ahead. I'll live vicariously," she grinned.

I lit up, letting the glorious smoke slip into my lungs and release, let it change the taste of my own stale air. I gestured with a finger to the ceiling, indicating the house. "So, this?"

She began with her ice cream, smiling with a mix of shyness and regrets. "Met him after we escaped France," she said. "He was a machinist; we just... clicked. After they shut the WASPs down and sent the bulk of us home, I joined the WAC for the rest of the war." She gave me a look of carefully shielded pride, "I actually made First Lieutenant. Arthur and I kept running into each other and eventually he asked me to marry him,... and I did. I left the WAC and became an Army wife."

"You still fly much?" I asked, finally tasting the ice cream.

She shook her head, "My licence has lapsed. Arthur... we couldn't afford to keep it up. He got hurt in '52 when a part broke off something he was working on and crushed his leg. He got a medical discharge, and we moved here to Corpus Christi. Not as nice as Baton Rouge, but... not bad."

"And Tommy? He's ten, you say?"

She nodded, happy. "Yeah, we tried for so long before we got lucky. He's my lucky star, that boy. He nearly killed me, but they caught the problem in time, by luck, really. Had to cut him out, but I don't mind the scar."

I watched her, spooning the ice cream into her mouth. There weren't as many wrinkles there when she spoke of him. "I'd love to meet him one day," I said, tasting a marshmallow.

She brightened. "Well, we go to the park every other Saturday. You could meet us there! We'll have a picnic!"

I set my spoon down and grabbed my whiskey. "About that," I said, taking a sip.

She froze, watching me as carefully as I had her. I knew Lorraine had grown up in Louisiana, all but breathed superstition and the supernatural. It was one thing to talk about it, read about it, halfway believe it. It was another thing altogether to be confronted by it. But, if anyone could handle the truth, it would be Lorraine. The trouble was knowing which way she'd run with it.

Her eyes narrowed, "This is going to be a whopper, ain't it?" I nodded once. "Worse than rocky-road and Cutty Sark?"

I shrugged, giving her my famous half smile, "It was all they had."

She gave a low whistle. "Fuck me twisted." I smiled. I had always loved her colourful turns of phrase. After a minute of just sitting there, staring at her melting ice cream, she topped off our drinks as if they were iced tea instead of heady alcohol. She raised her glass in a silent salute, waiting as I did the same. We sipped, and she waited on me.

I really didn't know how to begin.

I sighed. "Have I ever lied to you?" I asked.

She just eyed me, trying to read what had become unreadable, or so I thought. "Once," she said flatly.

I looked up at her, startled. "When?" I snapped defensively.

Her gaze never wavered as she lifted her glass. "When you told me you were right behind me."

I gave another small sigh, but smiled ruefully, tucking a strand of hair behind my ear. "Okay, so never." I lifted my blue eyes to hold her greeny-browns. "Remember that."

It was easy to remember that night, both what Lorraine had been there for and what came after. It was forgetting it that was hard, and God knows I've tried.

***

We had landed at some spit-in-the-wind airstrip in the backwoods of England with two brand-new Boeing B-17s for our boys some eight long hours before. It was our job, and we lived for it. We'd flown spitfires the week before and loved them, but it was those beautiful queens of the sky we adored most. We had been scheduled to stay the night at the airstrip before we were to be driven back up north to catch a transport to Reykjavik and start all over again. When we climbed out of the planes we were stopped by a single, very harried flight sergeant telling us not to leave the tarmac. The entire base had come down with a case of influenza and they were not letting anyone in or out. The poor man had been the first to be able to perform even rudimentary duties and was well over his head and he knew it.

"I'm not fevered," he told us, even though he kept his distance. "I'm well over the worst of it, but... best stay back."

Our attention was caught by a man staggering out a door, only to rush to the nearest bin to attempt to vomit. Poor soul had nothing left to spew and ended up suffering a case of the dry heaves. We politely turned away as the sergeant rushed to him. An argument ensued once the man could speak which ended with the sergeant coming back to us after propping the sick man against a crate.

"Completely unorthodox, but," the sergeant sputtered, "it's the only way I can get him to go back to bed."

"Do tell," Dorothy snarked, crossing her arms. She had captained the other B-17.

"There's a shipment of medicals that was supposed to fly out tonight for a village near Toulouse. Red Cross job. But the lads flying the run are sick as curs. Technically, the Captain over there outranks me," he sighed. "He says you can do it. Just a modified Lanc. If you can fly the Fortresses, you can handle the four Merlins on the Lancaster. All you have to do is fly the plane to the co-ords, drop the cargo out the bomb bay, and dash back. Shouldn't take more than five hours, but it absolutely must get there before midnight." He looked from one of us to the other, eyes flicking between Dorothy and myself, ignoring Lorraine and Mary. "That is, unless you ladies are whipped?"

I looked over at Dorothy, knowing it would be the two of us to decide. She shrugged, and I looked back at the sergeant. "Is it already loaded?"

"Yes, ma'am. The ground crews finished before mess. And then they were a mess," he groaned in not-so-fond remembrance.

Dorothy groaned, "The Lanc's a little tight."

I shrugged back at her, "Yeah, well, she ain't got a Texas-sized living room, but she's got moxie."

Next to me, Lorraine snorted, "You could fly that bitch home on one engine. Can't do that in a 17. Granted, she can't take the same pounding and still slither onto the runway, but it's a fair trade-off. I don't mind the cramped cockpit. Hell, one or two of us could probably catch a cat nap if we're of a mind."

Dorothy narrowed her eyes at her, "You too tired to man the instruments?"

Lorraine laughed, "Not this little white bird. I could fly all night! Maria?" she asked, looking around Dorothy looking for the small Hispanic woman.

Maria shrugged. "We've only been up eighteen hours and flying for eight. Spot us some java and we're good for another six."

I looked back at the slightly less uptight sergeant. "You got yourself a crew."

He asked us to make ourselves comfortable but to wait over in the hanger while he went to put the Captain to bed and get the flight information.

While he was gone, Dorothy and I haggled over who was going to pilot, and our co-pilots checked over the versatile little bomber.

An hour later, with our B-4 bags stowed and our own parachutes strapped on, Dorothy got us into the air and halfway to Brest while Maria and Lorraine got the navigation worked out. Lorraine was the only one of the four of us who could actually use the navigation equipment on the bombers and she had been teaching Maria when she could. She had saved my ass more than once with that skill. I had sworn I was going to have her teach me. Not that it ended up mattering. Dorothy switched out with me on the approach to the end of the French coast and I was the one who flew over Spain and slipped the German lines into the French Free Zone.

The mission was an easy success. We came in low over the French countryside, twenty miles southwest of Toulouse, found our target zone, and released six crates of much-needed supplies with their own little red cross parachutes. We turned around and headed back the way we had come. Everything had been perfect.

Then we got hit by a squall somewhere on the south coast. One minute we were flying easy, the next, black clouds rolled over us with sixty-mile-an-hour winds and St. Elmo's Fire playing off the wingtips. It startled us, but we knew it was harmless by itself. Then lightning followed it, striking close enough to fry the instruments Maria was using to guide us back.

Maria climbed out of the flight engineer's seat and began saying something in Spanish that sounded like prayers in between hollering for Lorraine. They swapped out and Lori did her best, but we were flying blind. All we had was a little hiking compass she kept with her for luck, and that was fighting the magnetics coming off the storm. It kept telling us that North was one way and Lorraine insisted it was the opposite. She was almost always right.

I took us as high as I could get, but the storm was worse up there, so I settled for low cloud cover, trying not to drift too far West and risk the anti-aircraft batteries on the coast. Dorothy was behind me, trying to get the radio working, and Maria... Maria was deep in prayer. I don't believe, but... who am I to question? We needed all the help we could get.

After about an hour, the storm seemed to slack off, and I decided we needed to risk going low enough to get our bearings. The storm ceiling was still out of the game little bomber's reach. Easing out of the clouds into the hiss of rain on steel, we realized just how deep was the shit we were in. Instead of miles of rain-silvered ocean as we had hoped, we were staring at miles of broad black land where the bright signs of non-rural life began winking out just as fast as other lights began to explode into being around us.

Dorothy gave up on the radio and began flashing our lights in the established mayday pattern, knowing it made us an easier target while trusting my skills to make us a harder one. We had no choice. We had no way of knowing if we had stumbled over English soil and were being fired upon by our own, or if we were knee-deep in German-occupied France.

Maria unclipped her parachute at something Lorraine had said, I didn't hear what and slithered down into the nose of the plane where the bombardier sat to aim. She scanned the rainy night below for anything that might give us a clue where we were. When one of the shells clipped an engine, causing it to sputter and die, she raced back into the cockpit, all but throwing herself back into her 'chute. Her rosary was wrapped so tight around her fist, it was leaving dents and her light brown face was whiter than mine. "Angers," she told us. "We're flying southeast over Angers."

I will confess. We panicked. We had to decide if we were better off trying to race for the French Free Zone and pray we could land, refuel and slip out through Spain before we caused too much trouble, or bank west and pray the storm lasted long enough to hide us from every anti-aircraft gun from here to the coastline. I made a snap decision, almost rolling the plane as I turned for the coast, and reached for the clouds. Lightning and a spray of 88 mm bullets set one engine on fire and perforated another. The fuel gauge, if it was to be trusted, might get us to the coast of Spain or just inside the demarcation line of France.

We watched the erratic spinning of our number three engine, praying it wouldn't stop. It and our Number one were all we had left. We held our breath as it caught, spun, choked, spun... then just stopped. We watched in shock as a piece of the plating fell away. This was it. We were on a wing and a prayer. I had the wing and Maria had the prayer for all of us.

Here was the difference between the British Lancaster and our American B-17s. The Flying Fortress had been safely landed with huge chunks missing, ripped tails and fragmented wings with most of the crew still alive, landing gear or no landing gear. But she couldn't fly on one engine. The Lanc could. The irony was, that if she had the dual control system of the Fortresses, she wouldn't be such a bitch to keep level on that one engine.

Just as we thought we were done for, we passed the reach of the artillery. They'd be scrambling fighters after us, if they weren't already in the air. We were spewing trails of black smoke and the one engine still on fire could be seen for miles in the dark.

"This is it, ladies. I'm going low and heading south. Going to get us as close to the zone as I can. Maria, open the bomb-bay doors and the three of you get your frilly asses back there." I knew there were escape hatches, I also knew they were narrow as hell.

Lorraine protested even as Maria pulled the bay release and began working her way back. "It's just a hundred miles!" She glanced at the instruments out of habit, guessing instead. "Twenty minutes! Twenty fucking minutes and we'll be out of the German's reach and can land her!"

"We don't have twenty minutes, darlin'," I drawled, my native Texan coming out for once. I knew this was goodbye, even if she didn't. I wished I'd taken the time to tell her I loved her. Now I couldn't even risk taking my hand from the stick to touch her in farewell. "We're losing speed, altitude, and fuel. Bird's gonna bite the dust in fifteen minutes if I can manage it. Ya'll are jumping in ten, 'cause after that, I ain't sure ya'll're gonna have enough time to pop your picnic blankets."

"I am not jumping out of this plane without you!"

"I will be right behind you, Lorraine," I told her, fighting to keep the bird from rolling and still send it where I wanted it. "I got a chute right behind me. I just want to limp this thing a little farther after you bail, misdirect the Nazis a mite. I don't know if the autopilot will hold with one engine."

"I'll wait until you're ready."

"I will be five minutes behind you. I promise. Just a few miles. When you land, find each other if you can, bury your chutes, and head south like the very devil were on your heels. Now GIT, Lorraine!"

With a sullen but determined expression, Lorraine obeyed, joining Maria hanging onto the cargo straps by the open bay, watching the French countryside blur by below in the dark.

Dorothy set her hand on my shoulder before getting up, knowing as well as I what this meant; we both knew the failings of this particular plane. It had almost been her in the pilot's seat but for a single toss of a coin. "May you find yourself in heaven five minutes before the devil knows you're dead," she said softly.

Unable to cover her hand like I wanted to, I protested. "Hey, ain't that supposed to be a half hour?"

She gave me a teary-eyed smile as she paused to kiss the top of my head. "I know how you like to cut things close."

"Lorraine is gonna try to be stupid," I said before she could leave. "Make sure the crazy fool makes it home in one piece. Cause if she doesn't, I'm gonna haunt some bitch."

"I'll make sure," she said, patting my shoulder as she left the cockpit.

The next eight minutes were filled with the drone of the single engine, the stink of leaking fuel, and the soft sound of Maria's prayers. It made me angry to think that, if we had been men, we'd be looking forward to full honours and military burials, but we weren't. We were women and civilians working for the military, doing our share of the war effort, and the military wouldn't even pay to send us home. It was

OK for me, really. I had no one to be sent home to, just an empty farmstead in a backwoods Texas town that the bank had taken the week I would have inherited it. Hell, they had snatched it up before the will had even been read. Not that anything had grown on it but rocks and stunted potatoes for half a decade. I'd heard they were going to build a shopping centre.

Snapping back to the present, I began manhandling the controls to get a little more altitude to give them room for their chutes. I heard Dorothy's comment to Lorraine, "I see why they call her the bulldog."

Lorraine choked back whatever emotion she was fighting with. "Once she sinks her teeth in something, she doesn't let go. She's better than any five marines put together, but they won't let a woman join."

I forced back a bitter laugh. She was exaggerating, but it was out of love and grief, so one could forgive it. I might be able to take three on, four if they got stupid or started off 'going easy on the dame'. Only way I'd take five was if they were drunk. And I had. It was how Lorraine and I had met. But that was another story, and it was time.

"Ladies," I called out, "I hate dropping ya'll off in the sticks, but it's time to take a powder! See you on the other side of the line!"

I spared a moment to glance back, saw Maria drop first, rosary in fist and B-4 bag clutched to her chest.

I heard Lorraine's voice telling Dorothy to go next, then an abruptly cut-off stream of Southern profanities as Dorothy pushed her. I glanced back again, to nod to Dorothy, saw her sit on the edge and salute before dropping into the night.

I turned back to the controls, fighting the Lanc like a tiring bronco still unwilling to give up. I turned her more north-easterly of the drifting parachutes, gunning the engine for all it would give me in altitude and speed, wanting as much distance as possible to confuse the Nazis. Every minute the Germans spent near the wreckage was a minute closer to safety for Lorraine and the others. And I had no doubts there would be wreckage. The only question was whether or not I would be in it. I'd always been one to shave the odds, but this one... this was one even I wouldn't call.

The trick would be to get enough altitude to buy me the time I would need to scramble to the open bay doors and pray I didn't get thrown back when she went into the inevitable nose-dive. If Lorraine had known about this little design flaw, she never would have left me. The pilots rarely got out.

Once I was as high as the bird would climb, I turned on the autopilot. I had maybe a minute if I was lucky. I scrambled from my seat, resisting the urge to look when I heard the lone merlin sputter. I clipped my parachute to my harness and began climbing down to the forward bomb bay. The autopilot failed just as I reached the open doors, and the plane immediately began to fall even as the engine died. I grabbed a spar and held on until she was fully tail up, then prepared to throw myself out of the hole, hoping I wasn't about to be batted into the wild blue yonder by a wing as the bird went into a tailspin.

Not even sure which way was up anymore, I decided it was now or never and crawled into the opening, fighting the rushing wind and inevitable dizziness. I was halfway out when the plane caught a burst of air under the left wing and bounced me. It was an odd sensation, and I wondered whether I had fallen out of the plane, or if the Lanc had fallen out from under me. I didn't even know which way was up, as everything was black but for the flickering of the flaming engine. The moment I deemed the wreckage was far enough away to safely deploy, I pulled my chute.

There was no way to tell how high I was or wasn't, to know if it was too soon or too late. I hadn't taken physics in school, didn't know squat about terminal velocity or wind-to-weight ratios or whatever it was they taught you that applied to parachutes. I just knew the hissing of fabric and cord as they slithered out of the pack and the snap of the silk canopy opening a blink before the wind was jerked out of me by the sudden stop. The lower straps jerked at the joins of my legs and the chest straps crushed the girls. Once I recovered, I paused to appreciate the view.

It was dark everywhere. Though I'd managed to escape the storm, there were still heavy clouds obscuring the starlight and the sliver of a moon. The plane fell away from me, spinning even further east as the wind drifted me west, which was a blessing. The flames had spread to the neighbouring engine, and the wing began trailing flames as well as smoke, becoming a macabre lantern giving me a glimpse of the sleepy French countryside.

I had no idea where I was or where the others were. I tried to look what I hoped was north and west, hoping to see three pale mushrooms hanging in the sky. I thought I saw a glimmer over a tree line some twenty miles back. It was all I could hope for. Below me, I caught a hint of a building and I craned my neck to see it better, to identify if it was sanctuary or damnation. I had just figured out it was two buildings instead of one when suddenly I could see it; then I heard the explosion, followed swiftly by a second as the twin fuel tanks blew one after the other. My guess was the plane had crashed some three miles away. Plenty of distance for Dorothy, Maria, and Lorraine, not so much for me. I would need to get out of Dodge fast.

Fortunately, the buildings below me were a half-destroyed farmhouse and barn. Somewhere in the last year, it had been shelled, leaving it an abandoned hulk. Part of the house had no roof, and it looked like a tank had driven through one side of the barn causing it to collapse over on itself. It was not so long ago that I could not still smell the decaying carcasses of the livestock that had been in the barn when it fell. It was a good place to land.

The light from the explosion was fading, and I felt the rough planks of the barn roof scrape the bottom of my feet as I sank lower. I managed to come to a stop near the top of the slope and forced the chute to collapse before it dragged me off. I was near the hay doors on the second floor and shoved my parachute and gear into the gaping hole. No one would look in there but wildlife scavengers. From the sound of it, as my chute pack hit, some of them were still poking around. Rats, I thought. Great.

I made a controlled slide down the wall of the barn. I might have been able to walk down, but I didn't want to risk it should the planks shift under my weight. I took a minute once my feet were on solid ground, not caring that it was muddy and stank of old pig shit. I looked to the sky, thankful I was alive and on the ground, but I missed the rumble of engines and the reek of air-fuel like a lost limb. Its absence was palpable.

Knowing I couldn't stay put long, I headed for what was left of the house.

The door had been kicked in and there were dark chips in the wall nearby, but I tried not to think of those poor farmers as I entered their home. By the light of my trusty Zippo, I found a lantern that still had some fuel, setting aside the broken glass chimney to light it. I didn't bother putting it back on.

I left the small front room, bypassing the large kitchen, and headed for the narrow staircase. Any bedrooms would be upstairs. I wasn't disappointed. I had seen feminine touches in the main room, so I looked for the same upstairs. They had all been thoroughly searched, drawers upended, mattresses flipped and slashed. There was evidence of resistance, small splatters of blood here and there. I tried to ignore it all, looking for something I could use.

Finally, I found clothes that would fit and not make me stand out. A simple frock in plain fabric and a scarf for my hair. There was a pair of sensible shoes that were only a little too big. I mended the fit with half a torn sleeve stuffed in the toes. I tried to ignore the bloodstains on the lapel of the shirt I had torn it from. As I buckled them on, I saw a scrap of a photo stuck between the floorboards under the bed.

Gingerly I pulled it out, checking first to make sure none of the boards lifted out to a secret compartment, but it had just gotten wedged in a crack. I glanced over the couple smiling in happier times. She wore a dress not unlike mine, though her belly was swollen in what must have been her seventh or eighth month, nestled back in the arms of the striking young man beaming proudly. Her hair was in a simple braid covered in a small, triangular kerchief, and my hand went to my own, tightly wound bun and my long fallen victory rolls.

Going to the dresser I found a broken brush and, swiftly taking down my hair, weaved it into a simple braid tied off with string. I tied the scarf as I had seen it in the photo. Confident I looked more like a French girl, I headed downstairs for the kitchen, hoping there was something there I could salvage to eat.

I got lucky and found a small, wax-dipped ball of hard cheese, a packet of stale crackers, a half jar of a dark jam and a bottle of home-brewed beer. I found a second bottle, empty, and filled it from the pump-handled sink, flipping the clever little stopper into place. Finally, I slipped out the door with a basket over my arm covered with a cloth to complete the picture. Should anyone stop me, I was just a farm girl walking to market or a relative's house; I hadn't settled on my story yet. Hopefully, I wouldn't encounter anyone while it was still dark and no one would ask me for my papers.

As I walked, I ate some of the crackers dipped in the jam, and drank a little of the water. I was fairly certain I was headed west, trying to remember where the demarcation line was from Angers and if I should go more southerly or just keep westward. In the end, I decided I would follow the road until dawn, at which point I would head into the fields and woods. I didn't like being unarmed in enemy territory, but then, I was only a WASP, and not supposed to be any nearer than thirty miles from enemy territory.

I still held out hope of finding the others, but I was counting on Dorothy to have a more level head than Lorraine. She would assure her that I would catch up at some known resistance point until she was safe. At least I hoped so. They would go until they found help. Maria might get them into Spain even though she wasn't from there. At least one of them would know the language. Dorothy was fluent in French; she would do alright until then. Me? I hung more hope on blind luck.

It had to have been four or five in the morning when I found myself approaching a house nestled into a hill in a curve of the road. At first, I thought it a typical one-level farmhouse. Then I noticed a handful of black cars parked out front and a light shining from the cellar stairway on the side of the building. From the sounds drifting from the closing door, the party was still going on downstairs. I froze for a half second, considered retreating and cutting behind the hill, but I had been seen by two coat-less German soldiers lighting a cigarette by one of the cars. One of them was drunk as a skunk, but the other exuded a smooth confidence that told me he was an officer at the very least. There was nothing for it but to continue on as if I had every right to be where I was.

I ignored them. You walk like you belong and, mostly, no one bothers you. A flyboy from New York had told me that once when he was trying to get into my girdle. To hear him talk, New Yorkers were like wolves. If you show fear, you get them interested.

Everything was fine for about fifty feet. Then I smelled him even as I felt his hand on my arm trying to pull me back towards the bar. I shrank back from him as I thought a good French girl might when assaulted by a drunk that early in the morning. I could hear him cajoling, calling me Fräulein and saying words I almost understood. I stepped back, shaking my head, saying "*non*". My French vocabulary was spotty at best, mostly learned as pillow talk from an old lover, but my accent was dead on Gascon.

He shifted to French, and his grasp of the language was worse than mine. He tried to put his arm around me while drawing the basket away, and I continued to resist. I glanced back to the cars, saw the officer just leaning lazily back against a sleek Renault smoking his cigarette as he watched, clearly bored. Finally, I'd had it. Still hampered by the behaviours of my disguise, I stomped on his foot to get him to pull back and slapped him, "*NEIN!*" I said. "*Comprendre das?*" I spat, deliberately mixing French and German.

He was stunned, his hand going to his face, then he grinned, babbling something in German, and lunged. The man ripped the basket from my arm and grabbed me, pinning my arms to my sides as he pressed close, backing me against a tree I hadn't even known was there. He attempted to kiss me, trying to get his knee between mine and I just saw red. If I had not been trying to play the helpless farm girl, he would never have laid his hands on me. I stopped trying to break his hold, knowing I couldn't now unless he made a mistake, and fumbled for what I could reach at his hip and belt level. My fingers found a knife. With a shift and a twist, I got the knife low between us and pulled it across as far as his grip allowed.

My hand was suddenly wet as he lifted his face from mine, looking more startled than when I had slapped him. He staggered back in shock, putting his hand to his crotch and then looking down at his spread fingers. It was a dark mess, the wetness there too dark to be anything but blood. He was dead even as he stood there blinking at me.

Before he could fall to the ground, the other man was between us, impossibly fast. His face twisted in anger as he spat, "*Du blyde kuh! Weißt du, wie lange ich gebraucht habe, um ihn betrunken genug zu machen?*"

I didn't have to know what he said. I didn't even need to see the faint red glow in his eyes and the gleam of unnaturally long teeth to know I was as good as dead. I rolled off the tree as I slashed at him blindly and turned to run.

He was too fast and too strong. I didn't get three steps when an iron band covered in a linen shirt wrapped around my face. He twisted the arm holding the knife behind my back, and, though I felt it dig into his chest where he crushed me against him, he didn't even flinch.

A long, cold-fingered hand grabbed my hair and forced my head aside. Those long, wicked teeth sank into my shoulder and felt like two spikes of fire. Somehow he let go of my knife arm and grabbed a firmer hold on me, lifting me off the ground and sucking me dry. It didn't matter how hard or where I kicked, what my free hand did to him: his grip held. I pulled his hair and clawed his face. Nothing fazed him. My life was gushing into his open mouth almost as quickly as it left the soldier lying under the tree a few yards away.

Finally, refusing to give in, refusing to just let him kill me, I bit back. His arm was across my face, cutting off my air, not letting me scream. But there are other things to do with open mouths than make noise. Like the bulldog Lorraine had named me for, I clamped down tight and refused to let go, not even when his thick, bitter, and sluggish blood filled my mouth and forced me to swallow or choke on it.

None of it was enough. I was dead three slow heartbeats later.

***

I felt like death warmed over when I woke. I sat up suddenly, coughing and retching all at once, trying to scramble to my feet and get my bearings, defend myself at the very least. Several things registered in those first three seconds. One, I wasn't on the ground outside some French bar but somewhere with hay; two, I was starved, numb, and freezing (in that order); and three, not alone.

Hands that did not belong to the blonde Nazi officer offered me a bottle of wine using soothing French words as one would to a skittish colt. I turned to follow the hands to the face and found myself distracted by the bottle. Without thinking, I took it from him and gulped it down. The bottle was half-empty before I realized it was warm and not wine at all.

Pulling it to arm's length, I glared down at the green glass. There was no label on it. I smelled it. It smelled coppery and salty and savoury, like the broth of Lorraine's beef stew, rich and fortifying. I drained the rest of the bottle and looked around me.

I was in a hayloft. Below me were livestock: a horse, a handful of sleepy cows, maybe a pig. It looked as if I had been buried in the hay and only just uncovered. Sitting in another divot in the loose timothy across from me was a small brown man. I focused in the light of the barn, realizing that he wasn't really small, just huddled to make himself seem unthreatening. He was wiry, lean, with creases etched into his face and hands that spoke of long, hard work in the sun. His hair was a shock of peppery grey, flying at all angles from static, making him look like a wild artist caught foraging outside of his natural habitat. He watched me with flinty grey eyes and a faint smile on his thin lips.

Hesitating, he dug another bottle out of the hay next to him and held it out to me, again treating me like some wild animal. I took the bottle, still craving whatever was in it, and he spoke more encouraging French. I had lifted it to my lips when I heard the word for eat, not drink. I pulled it back, resisting the urge to just drain it like the last one. That wasn't a mistake a native would use, and I studied him more carefully, wary; but he had the French look about him, the bone structure, the nose.

He must have noted a suspicious look in my eye as he hesitated.

"*Tu veux dire boire, oui?*" I asked him.

He grinned, shook his head, again gesturing for me to finish the bottle, saying, "Non, mange, mange."

I looked at the bottle again, frowning. I sniffed, dipped a finger into the mouth, and tipped til it was wet. It wasn't wine on my pinky, but blood: warm, sweet, life-giving blood. I was torn between horror and hunger. It smelled a little different from the last bottle, saltier, and I looked at him, my distaste and starvation warring in my expression. I didn't feel sick from the first bottle. In fact, I was feeling less numb, to feel the texture of the glass in my hand. If the first one hadn't harmed me, and I actually felt better... best to follow with the rest of the cure.

With a grimace, I chugged down this bottle, too. It tasted a little different too, and, once my mind set aside its prejudice about what it was, I found I actually liked it.

I set the second bottle carefully on the loft floor between us. Excited, he held up a third one, offering it as well, but I raised my hand, shaking my head. With a shrug, he sat back and drank it himself.

I simply sat there, watching him drink it, more slowly than I had, savouring it. He watched me with equal parts wariness and delight. Finally, I tapped my chest, trying not to notice the tears and bloodstains on my borrowed dress. "Lily," I said, with no trace of French accent. I had already exhausted most of my French and the smattering of other words and phrases I knew were ...not going to be applicable here.

He grinned, tapping himself, even as he folded his knees to his chest. "Jean-Baptiste. *D'où viens-tu?*"

Ok, there were a few more phrases in my vocabulary. But, I knew I didn't have the words to answer him fully. "Corpus Christi, Texas," I sighed.

He tipped his head like a dog with a slight frown. "Uoo es?" he said, and it took me a second to realize he had said US. I nodded. "*Comment?*" he replied, making it sound more like 'coo-maw'. I remembered that word, too. It meant how.

I decided to resort to a rough sign language, tapping myself, then making wings like a plane and engine noises. He shifted, his eyes widening in fascination as I mimed guns shooting down the plane, then myself trying to control it, then the crash and my parachute ride. He clapped his hands softly, then shocked me as he pointed at me and said, "Snoopy!"

"Repeat?" I said, knowing the French word was similar, but not remembering the right pronunciation.

He rolled onto his knees and began miming dogfights with both hands, making the sounds like a kid demonstrating this fascinating thing he had seen. "Red Baron! Sop-wit' Camelle!" he laughed. He pointed back to me, "You Snoopy!"

The man had not questioned that I had been flying the downed plane, had not doubted or called me a liar, or assumed I had been a passenger. But, what he had taken away from my ridiculous little demonstration was a Peanuts comic strip character. At least he had me in the right role. I couldn't help but laugh.

We laughed ourselves out within a few minutes. I clearly needed that. As I was getting my hysterics back under control by picking bits of timothy out of my braid, he surprised me yet again, this time by speaking English. It was broken, but understandable. "So, how did ze World War One Flying Ace end up Wolf-bait?"

I decided not to question his English, or correct his nickname for me. "Wolf-bait?" I asked.

He pointed at me, then his neck. "Man who killed you, name is Wulf."

"Killed me?" I stammered. "But I'm not..."

I stopped. His eyes flashed as he watched me, watched the realization spread from my brain to my face.

I felt thick inside, like I was stuffed with cotton batting like a damned mattress. I held my breath, listening for that soft tick-tick of my heartbeat that you can feel more than hear in utter silence. There was nothing. My fingers tried to find a pulse, but, though I could feel every seed in the tip of a stalk of hay, I could not find my heartbeat. I stared at him in horror.

He frowned suddenly, brought his finger to his lips as a light flared below us, nearly blinding me. I closed my eyes but froze, praying we would not be heard. A man came into the barn leading a stray cow and calmly berating her in rapid, soft French. I could hear them below me, and I cracked my eyelids. Jean-Baptiste was on his belly next to me with his eye to the cracks of the loft floor. As quietly as I could, I leaned forward to join him.

The man put the cow into the pen with the others, commenting on something on the neck of another one as he bent to inspect it. The too-bright light of the lantern he held flashed as it swung between the cows almost making me close my eyes again. I found myself wondering why he had a lantern in the already brightly lit barn, and then he was gone again, taking the light with him.

I looked up to see Jean-Baptiste's craggy face inches from mine, studying me intently. He was so close I could smell the blood on his breath. Breath he wasn't taking. I couldn't feel the movement of air from his nose though it was inches from mine... and I realized I had not taken one myself since I had tried to hear my own heart.

"I... I'm dead," I whispered.

He nodded solemnly, "Tu es mort."

"Is this hell?" I asked him. "Purgatory, maybe?"

He shook his head, sitting back on his heels.

"But I'm dead," I said, seeking confirmation. He nodded. "But I'm walking and talking and moving and not breathing... How? *Comment?*" I asked.

He shrugged. "*Comment?* I do na know. *Quelle?* Zis I know. You are... as moi, as Wulf. You are vampire."

"Vampire." Again, a statement that was really a question. "This is some grade-A, backwoods, Germanic Hollywood, Dracula horseshit!" I ranted, keeping my voice low though I really wanted to roar.

I wanted to scoff. I wanted to scream. I wanted to deny everything but couldn't. There was too much evidence in front of me. Wulf moving across forty feet of road in one step. The cold, inhuman strength of him. The glowing eyes and the elongated teeth that I had not imagined. Teeth that were a little sharper in my own mouth than they should be. My drinking two bottles of cow blood without throwing up, finding them not only palatable but tasty. My knowing it was cow blood. The fact that there was no hum of electric lights in the barn, and yet I could see as if it were fully lit.

I held my hands in front of my face and glanced through my fingers at the old Frenchman. "How much light is there, really?"

He shrugged, pointing at the roof, "La lune."

There wasn't much of that seeping in through the open loft window, but I could tell now.

"*C'est fascinant,*" he grinned, pointing at his own face, "to watch ze knowing bloom." He patted the hay next to him, pulling a fourth bottle from somewhere. "Come, sit. Tell Jean-Baptiste how ze wolf killed ze beautiful lily who falls from her Sop-wit' in ze dark."

Sighing, I sank into the hay next to him, breathing in his scent. It was wild, like new wine and earth and blood. There was the smell of green things, but death, too. I don't know how I missed the smell of death on him before. I took the bottle he passed me, taking a swig before handing it back as if it were an ordinary bottle of wine. In simple words, I told him what had happened to me, told him about the monster who had ripped out my throat and left me dead on the side of the road.

He chuckled when I was done, taking a swig and passing it back, waving for me to finish it. "He was piss you spill hez dinner."

"What?" I asked, horrified.

He nodded. "Wulf, he prefer hez food drunk."

"People are not food," I growled.

He laughed softly. "Just so. But to Wulf Alwin von Glasser... eh, people is tool or food. And he ez no respecting of females." He sobered, meeting my gaze without blinking. "You should be dead, but you are such a dog." I frowned and he explained, eager to not offend me. "You bite back. He bite you; you bite heem. You drink hez blood. *C'est comment* vampire ez made. You die bleeding. Vampire give hez blood. You wake vampire." He laughed again. "Wulf so piss, he na look if you get up. Left you for *le soliel*. But, he no look to see who see. His old enemy Jean-Baptiste find hez cast-offs where he t'rew behind hill. Jean-Baptiste will make Wulf's child a millstone for hez neck!" he cackled.

I narrowed my eyes at him. "So I am just a tool to you?"

He shook his head though he did not stop laughing. "Ah, *non*, not just my vengeance, *ma petit*. Remembre, ze bastard killed you. I would think zat would be wort' a little tooling."

I sighed, leaning back in the hay, grudgingly admitting he was right. I did owe that blonde bastard some payback. "So who's barn?" I asked, gesturing around us.

He waved a hand dismissively. "*Non un* we know." I merely raised an eyebrow at 'he and I' becoming 'we' so quickly. "It was near enough to le taverne to hide you before ze dawn."

I started to panic. "What?" I hissed. "We're near the… aren't you afraid they will search the loft looking for whoever killed that German officer?"

He chuckled and began collecting his bottles. "What German officer?"

I frowned, "Did you get rid of the body or did he?"

"Psh! What cares Wulf for mess he leaves? He only hides ze corpses if he needs to BE ze corpse!"

"Like the officer he was dressed as?" I asked, suddenly realizing that it would be next to impossible to remain in the German army, any army for that matter, if you were restricted to drinking blood and sleeping in a coffin.

He nodded, rolling the bottles in a scrap of dirty fabric so they wouldn't rattle against each other.

"So… how much of the legends are true?"

He paused from stuffing them into a pack he pulled out of the hay, thinking. "Ah, ze basics. Ah… *non soliel*. *Soliel* burn. Too much and Pfft!" he said with a 'poof' gesture of his fingers.

"How much is too much?"

He shrugged, continuing with his packing. "Depends. Age, strength, tolerance, blood… *Dieu seul sait*! Put hand out in sun, find out. Count: *un, deux, trois*. Zen judge. Just so! Now, eating. Blood only. Can sip or nip human food, wine, but very little. Will ...*vomir*," he said, miming throwing up in case I didn't know that one. "Only eat to hide what we are. Better yet, avoid nosy people!"

"Will those we bite become like us?" I asked, hesitating, standing to follow him as he crossed to the barn window, peering down at the small farmhouse.

"Non, I just tell you how you are made!" he scowled. "Are you Snoopy or ze Peppermint Patty?"

I was a little shocked. I think he had just asked if I was clever or stupid. "Fine, I'll be Snoopy," I sighed. "But... it's not too far to think both could be true."

He waved it off, went back to watching the light in the window of the house below. "*Voyon voir*," he muttered, trying to remember where he left off. "Ah, *oui*, tell no one. We live because zey do not know what we are. If others of us find out you are letting us to be known, it is you zey will hunt and kill. Maybe me for not teaching you better. Zat is it."

"That's all there is to being a vampire?" I asked, not believing it.

"Zat is not what I said. You ask trut' of legend. Zat is all... *pas de croix, pas d'ail, pas d'eau courante, c'est* Hollywood Dracula horseshit."

I held out my hand shaking my head. "No... crosses, no what?"

He sighed. "No... gahrlac? No run water?"

"So, we can cross running water, and garlic and crosses don't repel us?"

He nodded. "*Oui*. Only true belief, where God himself protects... but no one believes anymore." He waxed nostalgic for a moment. "Knew a *chevalier* once, mountain of a man, Hospitaler. For heem and hez littal Arab woman... for zem God meant business."

He shook himself as the light in the farmhouse went out. "We go."

"Where are we going?" I asked as I followed him down the ladder of the hayloft.

"You have much to learn."

"Yes, but where are we going?"

His grin was broad, toothy. "To give ze Germans Hell for stealing my country!"

***

Lorraine just sat there at the table across from me, staring into the bottom of the ice cream tub. For a moment she didn't say anything, then she poured what remained of her whiskey into the carton, swirled it around to get the last of the frozen chocolate from the sides, and drank it down. When she set the carton aside, I handed her a napkin, gesturing to the corners of her mouth where smears of chocolate had transferred.

She just stared at it for a second, then took it, wiping her mouth delicately. Then she reached for my pack of Lucky's and lit one up.

"I thought Arthur didn't like you smoking?"

She took a long drag, releasing it slowly. "Fuck him."

With a shrug of my brows, I reached for another myself, waiting her out.

"So,..." she began when she finally could speak. "The rest of the war?" she asked.

I shrugged. "Jean and I worked for the French Resistance. My French got better, as did his English. I learned a good bit of German. Never found Wulf, though. Not yet, anyway. Left him a few surprises here and there across Europe."

A hurt look crossed her face. "And after?"

I sighed, reaching out to take her warm hand in my cold one. "I was dead, honey. What would have been the point? I certainly couldn't just tell you, not then."

"But you can now?" she demanded, her voice cracking.

"I'm not supposed to be telling you now," I conceded. "But I've seen a few of us in the last twenty years who have select humans who they trust enough to let in the know." I shrugged, "You deserve to know. It's not like I can go back in the closet now," I breathed. "I mean, there are some of us who could make you forget you ever saw me, but... I can't do that. It's not something Jean-Baptiste taught me."

"What... what did he teach you?"

"You really want to know?"

She nodded mutely, pouring us more from the bottle. Perhaps remembering what I'd said about eating, she only gave me half a shot's worth.

I stretched, leaning back in the chair. "Mostly physical stuff. I'm fast- I can outrun a racehorse. I'm strong..."

"Can you bend steel?" came a small voice from the door behind me.

Lorraine's head snapped up, and I slowly turned in my chair. I should have heard him, smelled him, but I had been too preoccupied with his mother. "Tommy!" she exclaimed. "You're supposed to be in bed!"

I smiled at the dark-haired little boy in plaid pyjamas staring at me with his mother's eyes. "Hello, Tommy," I said quietly.

He shook his hair out of his eyes. "Well, can you?"

"No, I can't bend steel. I'm not faster than a speeding bullet or more powerful than a locomotive." His entire body showed his disappointment. "But, I can probably outrun your dad's car, and most likely stop a bus if I had to."

He stepped into the room, coming to stand next to the table. He was on the small side, I thought, but what do I know of ten-year-old boys? Lorraine seemed frozen across from me. I don't know what was going through her head, whether she was worried about what he'd heard or what I might do to him. Nah, she was probably not concerned about his safety. Whatever was running through her mind resolved itself, as I heard her get up and cross to the refrigerator. "I do have super hearing though."

He seemed to brighten slowly. "How super?"

I thought about it. "Oh... super enough to hear a mouse fart in the neighbour's yard." He giggled, wiggling himself into what I took to be his chair. "I have a super nose, too. Good enough to tell your mom to throw out that broccoli casserole."

Lorraine froze again, this time in the midst of setting a glass of milk in front of the boy. "You... can smell that?" I nodded. "But it's in Tupperware!" she all but whined.

I shrugged. "From the smell of it, it's been in that Tupperware about three days too long."

"One day is too long," Tommy mumbled into his milk. Lorraine scuffed his hair at that but he was grinning.

She sat back down in a huff. Finally, she caved. "Tommy, this is Lily. She was my best friend in all the world before I met your daddy."

I held out my hand to him. "Lillian Merideth Blankenship, pleased to meet you."

He took it with equal solemnity, trying to act like a man. "Thomas Lawrence Fontaine. A pleasure."

He studied me a minute before deciding I wasn't making fun of him and went back to his milk.

"I used to fly planes with your momma during the war."

He nodded, swinging his feet under the table. "I know, ma'am. She showed me pictures when Daddy wasn't home. You're dead."

I blinked, and glanced over at his mother who'd gone white-eyed. "What do you mean, Tommy?" I asked.

"She showed me. You and her and Miss Dorothy and Miss Maria and Mrs. Jessup?" he looked at her for confirmation. She nodded. "Yes, and Miss Jennifer."

"Jessup?" I asked, not remembering her.

"Elsie," Lorraine said, resigned. "Married Colonel Jessup in '44."

"Oh."

"Yup," he continued. "She told me that Miss Dorothy moved to Alberta. Miss Maria back to South America, where she was killed by gorillas." I flinched at this news, but he didn't notice. "Guerillas," his mother corrected. "I said gorillas," he complained. "Mrs. Jessup is in Tokyo, and Miss Jennifer died of sumpsus last year."

"Septicaemia," she whispered.

"And what'd she tell you about me?" I asked, almost afraid to.

His eyes flicked to me over the rim of his cup. "You died in France when mom's plane blew up. You didn't get out."

I took a deep breath, I didn't need, trying to maintain some semblance of life for the boy. "Well, I did get out. And the plane didn't blow up until no one was on it anymore."

There was doubt on his face as he set his cup down. "She said that was a Lancaster," he countered and began rattling off the statistics from the engine specs down to the escape hatch dimensions. "Only 17% of pilots ever escaped when shot down. She was pissed at Miss Dorothy for years 'cause she'd known."

"TOMMY!" Lorraine snapped, her hand flicking out to pop his shoulder. "Language!"

He picked his cup back up, even though it was empty. "Well, you were."

"Tommy," I began, trying another tactic. "We weren't shot down. We were shot up. Your mother and the others bailed before the last engine went out. I was already out of the plane before the engine fire reached the tanks."

"You're still dead," he said matter-of-factly.

"What do you think I am, then?" I asked him, taking a draw on my cigarette. "A ghost?"

He shook his head. "Ghosts aren't strong. They don't smoke or drink Dad's whiskey."

"This is not your father's rye," Lorraine said quickly. "This is Miss Lily's."

"They can't protect you when things get bad."

That shut us both up. I looked over at his mother who jumped up, taking his empty cup and ushering him out of the kitchen. "Ok, young man, you've had your milk and met Aunt Lily. Now it's time for bed."

Aunt Lily. I ...kinda liked the sound of that.

I sat there in that bright little kitchen, smoking my Lucky stamp-end first while I listened to the hushed whispers from the end of the hall. Lorraine didn't know where he got his ideas from (or so she told him), but I had a clue, and I didn't like what it was adding up to. That kid was scared of something and it wasn't me, and he heard more than he was letting his mother know. There had been a look in his eye as he watched me until his mother had gotten him out of the kitchen.

I sipped the whiskey, just enough to get the taste in my mouth, and waited for her to get back.

She bustled into the room and began putting our dishes immediately in the sink. "So, you know how I ended up here. What brings you to Texas?" she asked brightly.

I sighed, leaning back in the chair as she started washing the ice cream bowls. "I really haven't the slightest idea. It was a bad idea, especially Corpus Christi. But... like an idiot, I thought 'it's a big town' if I stayed out of the areas where I grew up there was less chance of running into people I knew, especially at night." I eyed her over my cigarette. "We see how well that went."

She made a small huff. "Well, I am glad you did. I don't care if you are a blood-sucking creature of the night. ...I missed you."

My dead heart gave a painful beat. She missed me? For twenty years? She was just my co-pilot on bomber deliveries, a fellow pilot when we flew the fighters. It didn't matter what we'd been through: in the air, or huddled in a London bomb shelter, or how *I* felt about **her**. To her, I had just been a friend, and you don't pine for friends for two decades. I was getting my hopes up. Besides, she was married with a kid.

"Shame we can't do that picnic," she sighed, rubbing longer at the bowl of a spoon than she really needed to. She'd waxed thoughtful. "We have a beautiful park. Maybe we could do a night one?" she ventured, but from her tone I could tell she was already finding issues with the idea.

This was starting to spiral into something I should avoid. JB had always warned me not to get too close to the living. Make friends, sure, but distant friends. Drink with them for camaraderie once in a while, keep them favourable, but don't spend too much time too often. There were those of our kind who bound humans to them, using their undead blood to control them until they were little more than cows or slaves, but neither he nor I believed in taking away their free will. Yes, our blood could make them tougher, impart our strength and speed for a little while, keep them young, but it also created a false love within them, and a dependency I refused to foist on her. JB had called them *goules*, even though they did not haunt graveyards and eat people. They did tend to hang around corpses (us), but they were more likely to be the eaten than the eaters. I had never liked them.

I rose, putting out the tiny stub of my cigarette. There were benefits to being dead. I could smoke them shorter. I emptied the ashtray into the trash and carried it and the glasses to Lori at the sink. "Thank you for the company. You have a wonderful home and a brilliant boy, but I should go. I still have to find something to eat and at this hour I'm going to be lucky to find anything sober."

She paused in setting a bowl on a spread towel, looking at me with something akin to desperation. "Do you have a place to stay?"

There was a quiver in her voice I didn't like and yet somehow craved. "I'll find a spot before dawn. I saw a couple places out Old Brownsville way where I might curl up and die."

She put a wet hand on her hip. "Those old factories?" I nodded. "Some of them are still damaged from Hurricane Carla! They're apt to be miserable!"

Right Behind You

I shrugged, sliding on my jacket and pulling my hair out from under the collar. "Miserable means less people poking about in dark corners. I don't mind the damp or mildew. God knows I've slept in worse places in the war," I breathed. "Hell, I've slept in a makeshift grave more than once."

"We all had to suffer deprivations in the war, Bulldog, but that's no reason to suffer them now. It's the sixties, for Christ's sake! I have a basement...."

I held up my hand to stop her. "Lorraine," I warned. "Even if you have no windows down there, what about Arthur? He'll see my bike."

She gave a weak, one-shouldered shrug as she dried the bowls and put them away. "I could hide it behind the potting shed. And Arthur never goes into the basement. He can't take the stairs, and Tommy and I do all the yard work."

I narrowed my eyes. "Because he works nights?"

"His injury," she said quietly as she washed the ashtray. She grabbed my glass and drank what was left, washing it, too. "It still gives him merry hell, especially when the weather's bad."

"Lorraine, what about Tommy?"

She looked up at me, her eyes full of wilful innocence, hurt, and desperation. "What about him?"

I softened my voice. "What are you going to do when he goes down there and finds my corpse?"

She gave me a dismissive huff and turned back to drying the ashtray. "He's not going to find a corpse, you're just sleeping. His father sleeps like the dead, too."

I took her by the shoulder and turned her to look at me. "I don't 'sleep like the dead', Lori. I *am* dead. D.A.A.D. Remember that?"

"Dead As A Doornail," she whispered. She was quiet for a long minute, then brightened. Setting aside the towel and ashtray and headed for a pair of doors on the other side of the kitchen. She opened one and flipped a light switch, her shoes beating a rapid tattoo down the wooden stairs.

Reluctantly, I followed.

It wasn't a huge basement and only a little crowded. There was an automatic washing machine in a corner but no dryer. Just a basket with clothes-pins clipped to the edge sitting on top. The rest of the room held the usual suburban detritus: shelves holding spare bulbs and tools, cleaning supplies, tinned vegetables and jars of home canning; boxes of things to be saved like baby stuff and wedding mementos; a bicycle I doubted the boy got to ride much seeing as the tires were dry-rotting.

Lorraine was in a corner under the stairs at a large locked cabinet fiddling with a key. I got to her as she opened it, setting the key on top of it and pulled out her old flight suit. She paused to breathe in familiar scents overlain with lavender. Then gave a nostalgic sigh and draped it over a box, turned back to the cabinet to remove her WAC uniform. As she added it to the growing pile, I ran my hand down the front of the dark jacket.

"I bet you looked sharp in this," I whispered.

I heard a laugh and looked up as she turned towards me, fitting her garrison cap on her brown curls. "Boy howdy!" she chirped.

Spinning, she began pulling out flight boots and her military dress shoes. "It'll be tight, but I'm sure you'll fit," she said, began looking for a box to put her memories in. "The lock can be manipulated from inside, so you can lock yourself in and get out without worrying about someone opening it on you or you getting trapped." She showed me the press lever inside that the simple key operated. "Just flick this and Bob's your Uncle."

I looked it over. For a locking cabinet, it was badly made and easily picked if you had even half an idea how, but it would serve as a coffin in a pinch. I was still reluctant. I shouldn't be doing this but the look in her eyes... I couldn't resist them.

"Fine," I sighed. "Only for a few days!" I added as she expressed her joy. "But I've got to get something to eat, OK?"

She hesitated. "Does it hurt?"

I softened further, reaching out to tuck a curl behind her ear, "No, honey. Not if I'm careful. But I'm not going to taste you. I haven't eaten in two days," I said a little louder to stifle her protest. "And I'm not sure I want to go there with you. I've never fed from someone I... cared for. Let me go out. I'll find something and come back. Would be easier in farm country, though cattle isn't as sustaining. What time does Arthur get home?"

"Six fifteen."

"I'll be back before then. Leave the kitchen door unlocked and I'll lock it when I come in." I brushed a hand on her warm cheek. "Just go to bed like normal. I'll... see you tonight."

I fled then, using my unnatural speed to get away from her and everything her reaction to my hand had promised. She wasn't like that, I told myself, pushing my bike down the road until starting it wouldn't wake neighbours. I would have known years ago if she was. I didn't want to read my desires into her reactions, didn't want to confuse things any more than they were. Worry was why I was staying, but hope was partly to blame, too.

***

I found that homeless woman under an overpass and traded her a sandwich and a bottle of orange juice for a nibble. I couldn't take enough to satisfy a two-day hunger from her and wandered until I found a couple of rowdies harassing a diner waitress trying to go home after a long night of work. They wouldn't remember my feeding, but they'd remember the bruises I left them with. I stopped short of breaking bones, though I wanted to.

I put my bike behind the potting shed like Lorraine told me to, and I could see why no one would notice it between the shed and the tall, wooden privacy fence of the house behind them. I slipped into the kitchen as quietly as only I could and locked the door behind me, finding the pantry door in the growing light of dawn. I'd cut it a little close, having to push the bike the last block.

Two steps into the basement I heard a heartbeat thrumming away in the darkness. Closing the door to the kitchen, I crouched peering below the level of the floor that served for a ceiling. Huddled by a row of boxes in his plaid pyjamas, holding an old flashlight to his chest as if it could protect him, was Tommy. The flashlight was still warm. He must have turned it off when I opened the door. His heart was racing, but I didn't smell fear. Well, I'm sure the lad was terrified of getting caught, but I didn't think he was scared of *me*.

"Tommy, what are you doing down here?" I asked softly.

I heard his heart skip, then slow. I was not what he had been worried about.

He took a breath, perhaps to lie to me, then let it out, and I knew what he was going to say would be the truth. "I wanted to talk to you without mom."

I came further down the steps, and sat on the third from the bottom. I didn't turn the light on, wanting to keep him off balance. What he was doing was dangerous, and I wanted him to be reluctant to do it again. I certainly didn't want him bringing friends down to see the 'vampire mommy keeps in the cellar'. "Why?"

"I... I know what you are," he whispered.

"And what is that?" I wished I had a cigarette, but the smell would alert the soon-to-return husband. He only smoked those nasty menthols.

"A v...v..v.vampire," he said, so softly a human would have only heard mumble.

"And you are not afraid of me?"

He shrugged. "Why should I be? You're my mom's friend."

"You hear more than you should, little boy."

He sighed, twisting his flashlight in his hands. "Tell me about it."

I cocked an eyebrow at that, but I didn't have time to find out more. I could feel the pull of the sun even now. JB could stay up an hour or so, get up early, but I was too young still, or so others of our kind said. JB had other ideas, something about the strength of the blood, but that is neither here nor there. "I will want to talk to you later, but I have to go to bed right now. I can't leave a corpse on the cellar stairs for your mother to deal with. You cannot come down here during the day unless it is something you would normally do, do you understand? I can't do anything while the sun is up. And if something were to happen to me... your mother would blame herself."

He nodded. "I just wanted to see if you were staying. ...And hold you to your promise."

I frowned. "What promise?"

He came carefully closer, feeling ahead with his feet and stopped when his toe hit the bottom step. He leaned forward as if he could see me in the darkness, trying to intimidate me as he narrowed his eyes and screwed up his face. I tried not to laugh. It didn't help that he was 'glaring' at my left knee, but his soft words fixed that problem. "*I'll be right behind you.*"

If I were still a breather that would have stopped both breath and heart. "She told you that story?" I asked, barely able to get it out. "Or did you hear me tell it tonight?"

He stood straighter, nodding once with an assurance older than ten. "She told me a lot of things. I'll let you go to bed now. I have to get back in mine before dad gets home. I'll... come see you... after mom goes to bed," he said. I wasn't sure if it was a promise or a threat as he reached out for the banister and climbed the steps in the dark towards the pale line of light below the door above us. It was clearly something he had done many times before.

I sat there watching him go. The light in the kitchen was enough for him to see by and for me to remember to get to my 'cabinet'. As the door closed, I heard an engine pull up and cut off. Only I heard the soft but hurried patter of feet racing for the room at the end of the hall, and the sound of springs as he bounded onto the bed. I opened the cabinet to the sound of the kitchen door unlocking, closing it on the sounds of heavier feet entering, dropping things on the table before going down the hall. The last sound I heard was the screaming of the pipes and the rush of water in the boiler as someone started the shower.

Talking to me wasn't a thing that happened. I rose the next evening and silently climbed the steps. I listened at the door counting heartbeats in the house. There was only one, and it was in the kitchen. I carefully cracked the door and peeked, found only Lorraine standing at the sink washing the ashtray from the living room. She carefully rinsed it under the water and set it on a towel to dry next to the rest of their dinner dishes. The kitchen reeked of homemade lasagna.

I leaned against the door frame and groaned, remembering how her lasagna tasted, even using Spam when there hadn't been any other real meat. The woman was a marvel at making scraps taste like chef-made.

She jumped at the sound of my voice, splashing sudsy water all over her frilly, Mrs. Cleaver apron. She set a hand over her heart and took deep breaths.

I leaned my head back against the sill and smiled at her. "Forget I was down here? Thought perhaps you'd dreamed me?" Hell, if I'd not come back last night, made off with all the evidence, she might have, I thought with sudden regret. But I couldn't do that to her, leave her wondering the rest of her life.

She let the water out of the sink and dried her hands, turning away from me. "For a couple hours, yeah," she admitted. "Hell, I even went into the cellar after Arthur went to bed to check. When I saw my uniforms out of the cabinet, I knew you weren't a ...psychosis." Something in the way she said it made me wonder if she'd been accused of having one of those. It wasn't uncommon in soldiers.

We called it Shell Shock. Twenty years before it had been called Cowardice. Amazing what a difference a couple of decades makes.

"Where's Tommy?" I asked, drifting over to the open Tupperware container on the table harbouring the remainder of the pasta. I ran a finger along the side to swipe up some of the sauce, licked it, and groaned. It was better than I remembered.

"A friend's," she said, appearing beside me with a fork. "Jimmy Meyers got a new tent for his birthday. He and Tommy are trying it out this weekend in their backyard. They have a pool."

I took a single forkful, mindful of the waste, but damn it, it had been twenty years! I just let it sit on my tongue, deconstructing it, taking in every nuance. It was real beef, real cheese... hell, the only thing in it that was probably store-bought was the noodles. I could smell the lingering fragrance of her having cooked the sauce all day. Turning to wash the fork, I noticed several jars in a pot on the stove. She had canned the rest.

She took the fork from me, washing it herself. "As good as it was in Reykjavik?" she asked without looking at me.

"Better. You had real ingredients this time." I chuckled. "Though that mess you made in that flat in London with wafers, Kraft cheese, and canned tomato paste was nothing short of magical."

She tried not to laugh, but couldn't help herself. "That mess only tasted good 'cause we were starving!"

"Maybe."

"Maybe, nothin'!" she growled, slapping her towel down over the back of a chair. Then her voice became sheepish as she added. "I know 'cause I tried it again."

I could have choked. "Really? ...And?"

"Whole thing tipped right in the trash. It was disgusting!"

I shrugged. "Maybe starvation *is* the best seasoning."

She gave me a small smile and picked up the towel again, began drying the dishes, and put them away.

"Can I do anything?"

She nodded her head towards the lasagna. "You can put the lid on that and slip it in the icebox if it's cool enough."

I nodded, fumbling with the lid. I'd heard about these things but never held one. It felt strange in my hands, and I knew there was a trick to it. "Better the next day anyway," I muttered.

Her soft laugh told me she heard and agreed.

"AHA!" I crowed in triumph as I pressed the lid in the right places and heard the snap of it locking into place. I put it away for her.

Turning around, I saw her coming in from the living room, presumably having put the ashtray back, taking off her apron, and hanging it beside the towel on the oven handle. Suddenly, she went to her pocketbook on the counter and fished out a key. "Here. It's a copy of the kitchen door key. I had it cut at the hardware store today. So, what do you want to do tonight?" she asked me as I stared down at the small piece of metal she'd placed in my palm, stunned for a moment.

Determined to process this later, I put it in my pocket and looked her over. She had on a little bit of makeup. Her hair was nicely styled if a bit too suburban for me, and she was wearing a plain blue dress with white lapels and white heels. She looked like Miss Suzy Homemaker 1960. I had an idea but wasn't sure if she'd go for it, or if I even should. I leaned back against the table, arms crossed. "I'm betting it's been years since you've been out to a dance." I saw the glitter rise up in her eyes. "And I do remember you loving to cut a rug."

"You know a place?" she hedged, clearly trying to think of where I could mean.

I started to get cagey. "Well, we don't want to do anything local, in case your neighbours like to party."

She waved that thought off. "Psh, they're dull as dishwater out here."

I cocked an eyebrow. "I wouldn't bet on that. I'm pretty sure the people at 1463 are swingers."

"What?! Betty and Finster? NO!" she gasped.

I liked the way she lit up.

"But I know a place no one will recognize you, but... it's not... traditional..." I hedged.

"I don't care," she suddenly declared, reaching for her purse and gloves. "It can't be worse than half the places we danced in England."

I chuckled. "It's no bomb shelter under fire, but it's nice. And, I promise to have you home no later than four AM."

"Well?" she asked, gesturing to the door. "Are we going or are you just going to stand around teasing me?"

I shook my head and went to get the bike as she locked up. I would get to the bottom of whatever was bothering Tommy soon enough. Tonight I was going to show his mother a great time and let myself dream just a little.

***

Fancy's was a hideaway, really. A place out in the boondocks of Corpus Christi where those whose gender preferences were less than acceptable and, in a lot of places, illegal. It was also a vampire-owned bar that served as a Gateway for the city. Every major city has one. The wise vampire stopped in on the way in and out of town (unless you didn't want anyone knowing where you were going, that is). It was a place to get the gossip on who controls what, where to avoid, where and when the local Gathers were if you were inclined to get involved with the machinations of our kind. You could also buy information for information, especially on places you were planning on going. It was helpful if you were looking for someone, and invaluable if you wanted to avoid certain... entanglements.

Fancy was an androgynous individual who dressed as whatever sex caught his (or her) fancy at the time and most of the breathers had no clue half the folks they were dancing with weren't exactly alive. I'd already been through here several days ago (he/she'd had no word on Wulf, sadly,) and when I came in tonight, they painted something on the back of Lorraine's hand that reacted to special lights in the hallway to the 'private areas'.

I was worried at first how Lori'd take it, walking in and seeing men dancing with men and women with women, but I shouldn't have been. There'd been times between flights when we had put on records and danced with each other in the barracks, sometimes as many as a dozen of us when there were reasons we couldn't go into town. She was glowing like a neon sign as she took everything in from the Wurlitzer jukebox playing Green Onions by Booker T. and the M.G.s to the svelte Hispanic in a magenta beehive hairdo and slinky sequin dress who was tending the bar. She took it all in stride.

When the box began playing Wipe-out, she dragged me out onto the floor to dance. She was still as wild as I remembered, not caring a wit about the two guys snogging in a corner booth. She was more up on modern music than I was, as far as dancing went, but from what I could tell it was a lot less structured than when I was alive.

When I went to get her a drink, she had apparently fed the jukebox because when I came back with a French 75 for her, she had that cat-bird look on her face. It lingered as she sipped and swayed to the end of a Patsy Cline until I heard the strains of trumpets leading into one of my favourite Andrews Sisters. This time I was the one dragging her out to dance. We cleared half the floor with our wide swings and leg slide twists. I had always taken the lead when we girls danced alone in the barracks, mostly 'cause I was one of the few strong enough to do the lifts, so it was like old times.

Lorraine was breathless when the song ended, and we found ourselves having to take a bow. I feigned a similar state so the breathers that surrounded us didn't suspect something was off. Then Moonlight Serenade came on, and she was stepping in close to dance instead of going back to the table as I had expected, and suddenly I found myself feeling breathless and heart-racy even though neither were possibilities anymore.

Her eyes never left me as we swayed in each other's arms, our feet remembering the steps for us. I was just a bit taller than she, even in her heels, her forehead coming up to my chin. But it was perfect for her to set her head on my shoulder as she held me close and just breathed me in. My lack of heartbeat had to be disconcerting, but it didn't seem to faze her. Finally, I gave in, pressing my cheek to the top of her head, memorizing this moment to sustain me when the illusion shattered come dawn.

We were dancing to Sentimental Journey when the lights went off and on again. Lorraine was startled when I spun her into the arms of one of the men to the left of us, and I turned to his partner without missing a beat. She caught that this had happened all over the bar, with every couple safely heterosexual and holding each other like they were the only two people in the world.

Lorraine gave me an asking look until she noticed the three official-looking brutes at the bar talking to Fancy.

The song ended, and she went to a table with her new partner and I brought mine to our table, sharing a sip of Lorraine's drink with him. My smile was for Lorraine, but the cops' eyes wouldn't see that. They left after Chubby Checker started playing, and the dance floor became just a mob of bodies, never minding partners. The lights flashed twice, and suddenly we were ignoring our heterosexual partners for more homogeneous coupling.

***

True to my word, I got her home by four, giving her plenty of time to shower out the smell of perfume, smoke, alcohol, and the sweat of dancing. I watched her bustle about with quiet aplomb that fascinated me. By five, the washing machine was done, her hair was dried, and she whisked about making sure everything was perfect. She stopped in front of me wearing a sweet little pink peignoir that I knew wasn't intended for me.

"Do I smell like I've been out?" she asked, a little worried.

I leaned forward, smelling her hair and the join of her neck and shoulder. I smiled a little as she shivered at that. "All I smell is homemade tomato sauce, laundry soap, and sleepy housewife."

She took my hands in hers. "Thank you for tonight. I imagine Fancy rules a doubly secret kingdom." She smiled at my incredulous look, tapping the side of her nose. "You could have stepped into the back for a bite if you had needed to. I would have been perfectly fine with Henri and Michael. Man, those *omi-polone* can swing!"

I gave her a happy smile, giving in. "Maybe next time."

She drifted backward towards the hallway. "I'll see you soon. Arthur is off tomorrow and we're going to go out for steak and a picture. So, wait until you hear the car leave. We should be back no earlier than ten. He tends to be up all night," she said with an apologetic look. "Just... be careful."

"I can count heartbeats," I assured her. She nodded and headed to bed.

I stood at the end of the dark hallway, my fingers turning the key in my pocket, listening as her breathing and heart eased, then raced, and eased again until she was finally asleep. I could easily imagine why. I know I would have been lying there for hours, reliving the night over and over again until dawn. But the sun would not afford me that luxury. Hell, I'm not even sure if I dream anymore. I certainly don't remember any, good or bad.

***

The next night I woke to an empty house and went out for a little while to think. I caught a young rat molesting some of the homeless near the overpass and was able to take out some of my frustrations on him as well as get in a good meal. I long ago had noticed that if you drag off some asswipe that had been bullying them, the homeless looked the other way no matter what you did to them, even if you were barely sheltered by a dumpster. As long as you didn't feed off one of their own against their will, no one would tell a soul. It was heart-wrenching that there were more vagrants these days, and even more so once I realized there were vets among them, mostly shell-shocked, once the military had decided they were done with them. I used to get angry at the treatment of post-war soldiers, but now it just made me sick. I never saw this in Europe.

The creep had nearly fifty dollars in his wallet. I left him alive, but so beaten up and scared he wouldn't remember the night straight. Twenty went into my own pocket for gas and cigarettes, and the rest bought hot food for the overpass. I know how to cultivate urban feeding grounds.

It was barely nine when I pushed my bike into Lorraine's driveway, but the car was there, and I could hear voices raised inside. The engine was still warm. When I heard something glass shatter, I ran to the backdoor with lightning speed, pausing with my hand on the knob, ready to break it, the key already forgotten. Looking in the window, I could see Lorraine's horrified face in the living room. In that instant, she saw me. I don't know how. The kitchen was dark and the living room dim, but there must have been just enough moonlight on my face.

With so small a motion that only I registered it, Lorraine's head shook me off, her fingers flying in our old signal to wait. That alone stilled me. She stepped into him, pleading, "Arthur, it's not what you think!"

"Then what is it, Lorraine?" Arthur snarled. I decided in that moment that I didn't like his voice. It carried exhaustion, frustration, anger, and middle-aged disillusionment, a general disgust and blind willingness to believe the worst. "Willy at the hardware store tells me you get a key cut, and I find a bottle of whiskey that's *not my brand* in the trash! What else can it be?"

My hand covered the lump of the key in my pocket. I had done this to her. JB had been right: we only hurt them more if we go back to them. Slowly, I walked back to where I'd left the Indian, unable to not hear her protests.

"Damn it, Artie! I had to get bread for Tommy's lunch the other day. I saw the empty bottle by the fence and got... nostalgic. Thought I could do something with it. Remember you and me, out of uniform, in the supply shed right before Omaha?"

"The Sark candle holder?" She must have nodded. "Then why was it in the trash?"

"Second thoughts. I know how you don't like to think about the war. I just got lost in the memory, you know? Not all of it was bad times..."

I didn't want to still be hearing them, but I couldn't tune it out. I stiffened as I heard a shriek, but it was followed by more amorous noises. As I stood there by the car, resting my head on my arms on the roof above the passenger door, I fought down my jealousy as I heard furniture shifting. Either he decided to put the small couch to use, or there'd be rug burns. I could smell them from here, but that could have been my imagination. I shouldn't have been able to smell her drugstore perfume and his cheap aftershave mingling with the musk of sex and menthol cigarettes through closed windows and doors.

I looked down at the not-so-closed window below me and leaned closer, taking in a deep whiff of the car's interior. It smelled like Lorraine's fragrance, but something was off. Timing myself with the sound of bumped furniture, I opened the car door, inhaling deeply as I sat in the passenger seat. The waft of air that rose smelled most recently of Lori and her make-up and perfume. But, beneath that, beneath her scent under all that, was the same perfume laced with the sweat of another woman. It was well-hidden beneath her, but still as fresh as Thursday night.

I began to snoop.

The evidence was beneath his seat. A half-empty bottle of Emeraude was tucked away beside a tissue that had Lorraine's lipstick on it, but not her scent. I stopped myself from breaking the bottle, putting it back where I'd found it. The bastard was good, having his girlfriend wear his wife's perfume and lipstick to keep from giving himself away. I sat there in the car, elbow on the sill, lit up one of my Luckys, and watched the windows of the living room. I was furious. How long had the piss-ant been having his cake on the side while grinding my Lori down?

Hell, she had never been this fastidious, to the point of washing ashtrays nightly. I had assumed the Army had done that to her. It had never occurred to me that her husband might have pressured her into that Harriet Nelson/Donna Reed ideal she put herself forth as. I was used to Lori in slacks, out-dancing, out-drinking, and out-cussing sailors, not perfectly manicured in ruffled aprons and white gloves.

I knew why she hid her uniform away. I had lived through that time too, but back then it didn't matter to us that we were viewed as 'loose' for what we did. (Some of us were, but not all.) Like the women who took over baseball during the war, WASPs and later the Women's Auxiliary Army Corps, faced shame and ridicule for stepping into what were traditionally men's occupations. We were single and most of us, at least Lorraine and I, let it run right off our flight jackets. A married man might want something different for his wife. I got that, but to bury it privately? To erase that she had been an accomplished woman... I suddenly wondered if not having the money to maintain her pilot's license was merely a lie to curtail any freedom she might have enjoyed.

Lorraine was chained to this house and a child by apron strings and a man's control of the checkbook. Hell, I remembered other ladies in our group talking about saving their pin money so they had access to little things their husbands didn't know about. I wondered if Lori was doing the same.

Field stripping my cigarette out the window, my anger rose again as the faint sounds (though loud to my ears) of climax drifted through the walls. That he accused her of cheating when he had been doing it himself for long enough to know the tricks of not getting caught boiled my blood.

Rolling out of the car, I eased the door shut and pushed my cycle into its place behind the shed. I had been going to leave and not come back, but now... now I would have a word first. I wasn't sure yet who with, I was so mad. Huddled in the dark next to the shed smelling of gasoline and rusting tools, I lit another and waited.

An hour went by and I heard the tv come on, and the sounds of studio laughter and the voice of Johnny Carson cut into the neighbourhood quiet. I heard the sounds of a broom and glass falling into a dust bucket. Lori's voice carried, almost artificially, through the house, husky with post-intimacy. "I'll just dump this in the can outside and start a load of laundry."

"I don't want to hear that damn thing while I'm trying to sleep!"

I think she kissed him from the sound of things. "It'll be done before we go to bed. I want to be able to hang it before Tommy gets home."

A few moments later she came out the back door wrapped in a less revealing bathrobe than the night before, carrying a bucket rattling with the broken glass. She looked around, and found me by the glow of my cigarette which I had deliberately not hidden. She rattled with the trash can as if having issues opening it. I crossed the yard in a second. She stifled a gasp, not having expected me that fast, then she took in my expression and turned away, dumping the shards of the Cutty Sark into the can.

"Lorraine," I began softly.

"Don't say it," she whispered. "Just... don't."

Her robe slipped from her shoulder as she wrestled with the can lid, and I caught sight of a reddening mark at her collarbone. I pulled it down further and felt my fangs beginning to ache, seeing the faintest outline of a hand. There'd be a bruise tomorrow.

She pulled back, covering it up again. She read my mood and sidestepped to put herself between me and the door. "No," she hissed. "Not for me. Not this." She gestured for silence and for me to follow her and went back into the kitchen, loudly putting her bucket under the sink.

"Will you keep it down in there? I can't hear Jonny," Arthur complained. I could smell menthol and cheap rye. "Hey, they got Danny Kaye tonight!"

"Let me just get the laundry started," she said, opening the basement door as she collected a laundry basket from the table. "It won't take a minute."

"Hurry up! You don't want to miss it."

"Be right back," she called sweetly.

The bastard never once turned around. When Lori flipped the cellar light on, I was already downstairs, leaning on the sorting table beside the washing machine.

She took her time, shaking the clothes out one by one and dropping them in. She never once looked me in the eye. "He didn't hit me," she said. "Just grabbed too hard."

"Why?" I asked, my voice hard.

"It's not your fault. We ran into Willy at dinner, and he made a joke about lost keys. I didn't know Arthur'd found the Sark bottle."

"Not that 'why'."

She paused, fingering a loose button, then decided to drop it in anyway. "Because I love him. And, it's not always like this." She shrugged, "Most times it's... comfortable. Then it's nice, and then it's not. Everyone goes through disagreements, Saint June of Cleaver to the contrary," she added with surprising vehemence.

"If he ever hits you..." I began.

She turned on me at that, held a finger just under my nose. "No. No, you won't. Not for me."

"That's the second time you've said that."

"Mother fucking greaseballs, Bulldog," she hissed. "I need you to let this one go. I won't have my boy fatherless!" She softened just as suddenly. "We were so in love, Lily. I still remember that, the times before he got hurt. It's the pain. The whiskey he drinks for the pain... it's everything. A man can only take so much disappointment before they're crushed."

"Same goes for women, Lori." I was only half talking about her. I kept my eyes on her lips, the best gauges of her mood, then and now. "But if he ever *hurts* you," I added, leaning in. "One day you're gonna wake up and he's run off with some floozy from the plant, and you're not going to ask me what really happened."

I let that sink in. When I saw the light go on behind her eyes, I moved with all my speed to my cabinet. It was closed before she could finish blinking.

"Hurry up, Lorraine! They're introducing him!" came muffled through the ceiling.

I heard her "Coming!" as she turned on the washing machine and walked away. I heard her quietly repeat herself at the top of the stairs, "Not for me."

The rest of my evening was pissy, sitting on the floor in the open cabinet playing Clocks with a ratty old deck I'd found, listening to Johnny Carson through the ceiling. When the Tonight Show ended and the station went off air, they turned off the TV and went to bed. From the sound of things, Artie-boy was a vigorous lover if nothing else. Kind of amazing for a guy with a bum leg when you think about it. I shrugged to myself, maybe Lorraine did the riding.

I climbed back into my cabinet as the sun rose, locking it carefully and making sure the key was inside with me before I died.

Right Behind You

***

I didn't get out at all the next night as Arthur spent the entire evening in his chair in front of the TV. It was a good thing I had eaten well the night before. Lorraine bustled about, trying to keep herself awake from the sound of her see-sawing heart rate and breathing. When she finally did fall asleep on the couch, I clearly heard Arthur's unkind mumbling about her laziness. It was all I could do not to go upstairs and teach him a thing or two, but I held myself still for her sake. It was outrageous for the man to expect her to be up during the day doing the housework and still stay up all night with him on his nights off. It didn't help that I had kept her up most of Friday night, which did even less for my mood.

I killed the time by going through the wedding box, looking through photo albums and mementos trying to understand why she had fallen for this man, to see what she had seen. They looked happy, at least in the early years. From the dates on the pictures, he had gotten hurt seven months after she fell pregnant, and Tommy had been born shortly thereafter, two months early, probably brought on by the horror of nearly losing her husband.

By the photos, Tommy'd never been a vigorous boy, small for his age, but bright and quick. I could also see the light slowly dying in his father's eyes as he grew, never quite reaching his sire's robust frame. The disappointment was clear. He'd wanted a son to live vicariously through and had gotten a weak slip of an early child. While I came to understand Arthur more, I didn't hate him any less for it.

Lorraine never got the chance to come down that night. I died that morning trying to see her as the blushing bride she'd been and trying to reconcile the man upstairs with the happy groom in the pictures.

***

I was dreaming. I had to be. Sounds were muffled and had that distorted quality I remember from dreams.

I was in my coffin, waiting to be buried. But a young boy opened the lid and tried to pull me out, begged me not to be dead, that I had to stop something. I was his Superman. Not his Wonder Woman: his *Superman*, and I had to help. I was dead, and I couldn't. His tugging at me only spilled my corpse onto the floor. There was a different thump, from above, and he ran, angry, an old, oversized flashlight in his grip like a weapon.

It wasn't until I heard the sound of a boy's voice shouting, "Leave my mother alone, you bastard!" that the fog began to lift, and I realized none of this was a dream.

There was screaming from upstairs, the door to the cellar open and the reek of broken perfume drifted down with the stink of fear and rage and pain.

I made myself move, not with the lightning quickness of my vampiric blood. The sun was still too high for that. It was like trying to walk out of the ocean quickly, the waves and the weight of your body trying to pull you back in, getting heavier with every step. I crawled up the stairs, hearing more clearly Lorraine's plea to leave him alone, and Arthur's snarl of: "If the boy wants to act like a man, I'll treat him like one!"

I got to my feet in the door frame, staring at the lethal slant of sunlight coming through the windows of the back door. There was too much. Beyond the bright kitchen, the living room was blissfully darkened by curtains. The fight was down the hall, the boy's room I thought. I had to get to them, sunlight be damned.

I remembered what JB had told me and cautiously reached my hand out of the cellar, palm up, counting. "*Un, deux, trois, quartre, cinq, six, sept, huit...*" I pulled back as the pain grew too great, examining my hand. It was burned, not smoking, but as badly as if I'd set it on a grill for eight seconds. Apparently, the younger you were, the more you could take. JB could only get to *quartre*.

I flexed it, expending a little of my precious resources to heal it before pulling my collar up over my ears and forcing myself to take that first step. The sound of something hitting a dresser and the resultant screams made me drop my collar and just move. Four steps to the living room. Three to the hallway. Six to the open door at the end and Lorraine crawling across the bed to the boy by the dresser to protect him, and one more to the monster standing just inside the room.

The boy's face was pale, but he smiled as he saw me, cradling his arm. Lorraine followed his gaze, and her horror at what had happened turned to fear for what was going to. Arthur, alerted by the changes in them, spun. "Who the hell are....!" But his demand was cut off as I grabbed him by the shirtfront and threw him behind me into the hall. I slammed the bedroom door closed on Lori's protests and turned to the bastard trying to grab his cane and get to his feet.

I stalked toward him, letting the monster inside of me have full rein. He swung the cane at me in desperation, breaking it on my thigh. His anger melted to shock and then to fear as I picked him up with one hand and pinned him to the wall, just off his feet.

"What are you?" he gasped, clutching at my hand wrapped in his shirt.

"Your reckoning," I snarled.

"Don't... don't hurt my family," he pleaded, clearly thinking I was some monster come to prey on the house and not just retribution made flesh.

I pulled him to my face, letting him smell death and old blood from deep within me. When angered, I knew I smelled like the carrion I was. "You have no family, small man. You hurt them yourself. And now you are done."

He paled. "Don't... don't kill me," he begged. And any respect he'd earned by trying to protect what lay sobbing beyond the door was lost.

"Only because Lorraine asked me not to," I hissed, showing my fangs. The sudden, sharp stink of urine pleased me. I threw him into their bedroom, shoving him into the closet door. "You will pack your bag. You will leave this house and go to whatever Jill you've had in your car wearing your wife's perfume," I punctuated this by throwing the remains of the green bottle from the dresser at a point three inches from his head, pleased that he flinched, "wearing her lipstick. You will run away with her, and never look back."

He started to protest, but I stalked forward like a beast on the prowl and he fell to the floor. "Every time you even think about that woman or that boy in the next room, you will see my eyes staring into your soul and remember the fear you feel right now. If you ever come near her or contact her again, I will suck you dry and crush your dessicated carcass like an empty beer can."

He shrank even further back, more shivering his affirmation than nodding it.

I crouched before him with a hungry grin, ignoring the discomfort of even the indirect sunlight hitting me through the window. "I am going to take your son to the emergency room. He will boldly tell them who did this to him. I will make sure your wife is seen, too. And if you are here when they get back, I am going to eat you slowly."

I stood, turned my back on him and the stink in the room, and closed the door. I did not hear any movement for a long time, just him holding his breath and trying to slow his heart and not be noticed. I paced to Tommy's room and opened it, staying back from the red and orange light of the sunset. I knew I had to look wild, but neither of them was afraid... not for themselves, not of me.

Lorraine had the boy on the bed, checking his arm, broken where he'd hit the dresser. There was also a bump on his forehead. Her eyes flicked behind me to the hallway, asking. I gave her a minute tilt of my head, telling her not to worry and not to ask. "Get your bag and put him in the car. You are going to the hospital. You will tell them everything that happened, and you will not make excuses."

Lori nodded, carefully ushering Tommy past me. I didn't like the boy's colour, but he caught my hand in his good one in passing, pulling his mother up short. He smiled at me, "My Superman," he breathed.

I gently squeezed his hand and made him go, following them to the end of the darkening hall. They only glanced as they passed Lori's bedroom at the sound of drawers scraping open. I stopped in the middle of the living room.

Keys clattered and scraped as she opened the front door, and turned back to look at me. The purpling light of the on-coming night was beautiful in her dark hair, the sun safely behind the house, but not yet far enough below the horizon for my safety. "What about you?" she asked, her eyes glistening with loss and love and emotions I didn't know how to read. "Will you at least be here when we get back?"

I smiled, buoyed by all the love in my heart that I felt for her, whether she felt the same kind of love or not. "Lori, I will be right where I always have been," I said softly. "Right behind you."

Pride Goeth

S.L. THORNE

November 23, 1853

Lady Arabella March lay patiently in the bed as the doctor bent over her, listening to her chest. He straightened, began putting the instruments into his bag. "Nothing to worry about," he smiled. "A touch of the vapours is all, and the cough is not uncommon this time of the year. I'll leave her something for the cough. But everything is going to be fine." He rose and gestured for the lady's husband to accompany him into the hallway.

Arabella watched the two men carefully as they left the room, Tilly, her maid, closing the door softly behind them. There was something in the doctor's reassuring manner that she did not quite believe. Quietly, she climbed out of the enormous bed and crept to the door to listen. Just outside she could hear the doctor speaking to her husband.

"Thank you so much for coming out on such short notice, Doctor. She has had me worried for days with that cough. I am glad it is nothing serious."

The doctor's tone when he spoke again was very different from the one he had used with Arabella. "I'm very sorry to mislead you like that, sir," he said. "I only said that for your wife's sake. I'm afraid her condition is quite serious."

"What do you mean? She's not..."

"Going to get well? No. ...She has consumption." There was a small gasp, presumably from Tilly. "There is nothing that can be done except keep her comfortable. She should be kept warm and unexcited, and should be confined to bed when she weakens."

"How long?" Thomas asked, barely above a whisper, his voice weaker than usual. The question came out almost as a whimper.

"That all depends on her Ladyship. Some last a few weeks, some can hang on a good month or more, maybe even as much as a year. Though in this weather...."

Arabella straightened up, moved slowly and mechanically across the room, and sank into her chair. She stared, stunned, into the fire, watching the demon-like tongues of flame dancing in the grate.

'Consumption,' she thought. She fished through her mind, trying to remember what little she knew of the disease. It was a lingering, wasting illness that reduced its victims to husks before taking their lives. Arabella was proud of her beauty and took every precaution to preserve it. At thirty-two, she should have been rounder in the hips from childbirth, something she had been spared of altogether. Her face should have begun to crease around the mouth and eyes, her hair to lose its lustre But she had taken care of herself, and her skin was just as unblemished and perfect, her hair as soft and black as the morning of her first wedding.

She looked down at her hands. She had always been proud of them, her long, graceful fingers. She never wore more than her wedding band, so as not to detract from their slender beauty. Now they seemed to take on a skeletal effect, almost withering as she watched them. They felt brittle and old. She gave a small, satiric laugh. 'All these years pass me untouched, and now this. Age alone could not take me down. So disease sets in to do what time could not. How ironic. How infuriating!'

Thomas quietly entered the room, saw her staring into the fireplace, unmoving. "My dear, what are you doing out of bed?" he gasped.

She turned her head, looked at him with cold flashing eyes, assessing her husband critically. His cravat was poorly tied and crooked, hanging loosely at his neck, his shirt dishevelled like his hair and nearly as limp and lifeless. His hands were trembling ever so slightly, as they always seemed to lately, whether drunk or sober his hands were never still anymore. "What is it, Thomas?" she asked, measuring her words. She would not let on that she already knew. "What did he say?"

He smiled, but she was not fooled. "Nothing, dear," he assured her. "Just medicine and fees."

Her gaze hardened. "Don't lie to me, Thomas," she said, her voice steady and firm.

"Lie to you, my love?" he asked innocently, but already his mask was crumbling away.

"You don't know how to lie to me. What did the doctor say?" she repeated.

All his composure suddenly fell away. He turned from her, hung his hand. "You are dying," he whispered, his throat too tight to speak any louder.

She leaned her head back against the chair, sitting perfectly straight as she stared forward at nothing. "Speak up."

Thomas took a breath. "You have consumption. How much time we have left together he could not tell me."

"Do you think me a child, Thomas? That you had to lie to me? That I could not handle the truth? Did you?!"

He turned to her, "I... I didn't...," he stammered, fighting to find the words, to face her piercing green-grey eyes. He gave up, looked down at the floor between his feet. "I am sorry, my dear. I should not have tried to deceive you." He looked over at her, his misery all too apparent. "God, I wish I had your strength. How can you sit there so calmly?" She did not answer him. She had turned away and closed her eyes. There were times like this when she was almost a stranger to him, like a cold and silent angel simply occupying space within his house. She had always been the stronger of the two.

He crossed to the window, leaning his head against the iced glass, watching the cold, winter squall tearing through the courtyard below. He watched the carriage horses fretting on the drive. The doctor was still down in the kitchen with Tilly and the cook, giving instructions on diet and medicine preparation. "Shall... shall I inform your brother, Jason?" he asked after a time.

"You will do no such thing," she answered in her usual tight tone, without even opening her eyes. "He would more than likely send you a letter of congratulations."

He glanced at her over his shoulder, "Oh, come now, dear. You underestimate him. He is, after all, your only remaining blood relative. I don't think he could be as boorish as all that."

"It is because he is my brother that I KNOW he is 'as boorish as all that'," she snapped.

"Still...."

"What is the matter, Thomas? Can't you even handle a dying woman?" she growled. "The answer is no. You will not inform him, or anyone else, of my condition. I have no desire to have those mindless gossips at Worthington come to gawk and gape and pretend consolation when all they are really after is something new to discuss over their tea. I want no visitors."

He sighed, hung his head as he watched the doctor finally dashing out of the house out to the waiting carriage. "Whatever you wish, my love."

***

A week passed. The house was quiet. The servants filled their duties with only a minimal amount of noise as if they were trying hard not to disturb Lady Arabella. She sat in front of the piano in the parlour and pecked at the keys. Thomas had gone to London, leaving her behind due to her fading health. She was furious with herself for allowing the collapse which had promptly cancelled her regular trip to London. She always looked forward to her trips, as they allowed her a vast change in social scene, and a chance to do a little shopping. As Thomas usually spent his time in the men's clubs and dealing with business, Arabella was left to herself and very much enjoyed the freedom from his company.

Her hands struck a sour chord, reflecting her mood perfectly. She turned her irritation from the cancelled trip to her playing and tried the chord again. Getting it right, she continued down the page, only to miss another note four bars down. She tried again, and again, and each time something else went wrong. She held up her hands to look at them and found them shaking. Try as she might, she could not stop their trembling. Angrily, she slammed them onto the keyboard. The resulting cacophony did not make her feel any better or more in control. She stifled the urge to tear the parlour apart, putting her temper in sharp check.

She sat before the piano with her hands in her lap, breathing carefully and slowly. If nothing else, she would maintain control of her temper. She looked up at the great clock in the corner of the study. Tea would be brought into her sitting room shortly. Taken out of the social circles, this was a ritual she refused to let slip, even when she must Tea alone.

Suddenly, she felt something heavy and warm descend upon her shoulders. She looked back and saw Thomas standing behind her, a loving look on his face as he bent and kissed her cheek. "Do you like it?" he asked.

She glanced down at the lace shawl he had wrapped around her. It was of exquisite workmanship; rich, thick lace of soft ivory which set off the cream of her skin and the colour of her eyes remarkably. It was the kind of wrap she might have bought herself if she had gone to London, and served her a sharp reminder that she had been left behind.

"It's Belgian," he said.

"It is beautiful, Thomas," she said flatly.

He sat beside her on the piano bench, his back to the keyboard, and took her hands in his. "I missed you," he said tenderly, stroking her long fingers. "I trust you are feeling better? Perhaps later we can take the sleigh out?"

"No. I do not feel like a sleigh ride today."

He brushed his hand across her cheek. "I know you miss riding your horse, but it would be too much of a strain."

The clock chimed four, rescuing her from any further displays of his affection. She untangled herself from his loose embrace and rose. "It is time for tea, Thomas."

She kept the shawl wrapped tightly around her, feigning a fondness for it. It would please him to think she liked it and a happy husband is easier to control. Even dogs need their bones.

Tilly brought the tea tray into the sitting room and set it on the table between the two of them. Making sure that everything was properly placed, the teapot handle facing her Ladyship, and the book of poetry beside the cup, she left the two of them alone in the room.

Arabella made ready to serve the tea, placing two lumps of sugar into her husband's cup before pouring. She lifted the heavy, silver teapot and brought the spout over Thomas's cup. It was a strain to hold it steady. She had to grip the handle tightly and concentrate to pour. Even so, she was unable to keep it from shaking ever so slightly. She was keenly aware of Thomas's eyes on her hands. It bothered her. Her hands, she knew, were no longer graceful and beautiful, but thin and unsightly. It was not admiration in his eyes, but pity, and perhaps distaste. As she poured her own tea, her focus having changed from pouring to her husband's staring, the pot slipped, her fingers no longer having the strength to hold it. Thomas's hands were suddenly on hers, taking the pot from her. Without a word, he filled her cup for her.

She looked up at him, and found him concentrating on choosing a scone from the tray. She deliberately picked up the book and began to read.

***

It was early December, and Thomas lounged on the settee reading one of his tedious journals of scientific theory as he smoked. Arabella sat across from him, a heavy rug thrown over her lap and a gold-edged edition of Macbeth resting open there. She arched her back after a moment, stiff from sitting so still for so long, looked across at her husband who was paying absolutely no attention to her. She watched him for a time, just staring until he reached over to the ashtray and put out what remained of his cigar. He closed his book and set it aside, picking up another one he had lain aside and began reading it.

Arabella looked down at her own book, without reading. "I find it curious," she mused, only mildly interested in the subject. Thomas only hummed questioningly in her direction, without looking up from his book. "... That we have yet to receive invitations to the Worthington's annual winter festival."

Thomas looked up. "What was that, dear?"

She sighed, "Invitations to the Worthington's have not come. I know the circumstances hardly call for it, but I find it exceedingly rude of Rosa not to at least ask." There was something in his eyes as he turned them away that told Arabella that he was suddenly very uncomfortable. He was hiding something. "They **are** having the Festival this year, are they not?"

"Yyess," he nodded uneasily.

She closed her book, catching Thomas making a sidelong glance at it as she did so. "And we have not been invited, correct."

Pride Goeth

"They have not sent us invitations, no," he answered in a very quiet voice.

"Why?"

He let the silence drag a moment, before forcing himself to answer. "I... I spoke with William Sr. last week. He asked if we would be attending and I told him we could not. Rosa will not be sending us invitations."

Arabella sat there, silent, letting her anger build to a controlled gale force before venting it on her husband. "You took it on yourself," she began slowly, "to tell them I did not want to go without asking me first?"

"Darling, you said yourself that you did not want to see anyone," he protested.

"It is not your place to answer invitations, Thomas!" she snapped. "You know absolutely nothing of social structure and etiquette! Do you realize how they will talk?! I will be the sole topic of the evening!"

"You do so love to be the subject of conversation," he mumbled.

"What?!" she screamed. Her book flew towards him. He barely dodged the missile. "How dare you insult me so, you intolerable, hateful man!"

"Arabella, I did not mean it in that way," he pleaded, getting up, but afraid to come too close to her. "I would never insult you... my love, my life...."

"Then why did you not say it louder; instead of mumbling beneath your breath as if I were not meant to hear it?!" she accused.

"'Bella, my beautiful..." he said in a soft, consoling voice.

"Do not patronize me, Thomas! I am not a child! As hard as I have tried to give those gossips nothing to talk about, here you go and practically serve me to them on a silver platter! I will not be pitied!"

"But, would you have gone to the party, if the invitations had come?" he asked, trying a different tactic.

She merely glared at him. "That is not the point, Thomas," she said sharply. "The point is that I should have been the one to turn them down. I can do it in such a way that if I changed my mind, it would not look bad. As it stands, should I be feeling up to it, now I cannot go at all without generating more talk, and that I cannot bear! You have practically told them that that Autumn fiasco at Margaret's was the last party I will ever attend!"

"Please, my love," he begged, throwing himself to his knees beside her chair and taking her cold hand, "I only thought.... I knew how much not being able to go would upset you, and I thought to spare you the pain of having to tell them yourself. I thought having the invitations in your hands would only upset you more."

"So you thought that by letting me think they had snubbed me I would be less upset?" she fumed.

"I did not think of it that way...."

"You never think, Thomas."

He bowed his head, kissed her hand repeatedly. "I am sorry, Arabella. I did not mean to hurt you. I would never knowingly make you unhappy."

She sighed, showing him that she was not entirely forgiving him. The clock on the mantle tolled nine. Arabella glanced up at it. Something on the mantle struck her as out of place. The painting was different. In place of her portrait, in its dark and mysterious beauty, was a garish piece of children playing in a bright flower garden.

She removed her hand from her husband's and stood up, crossing to the hearth. "Where did this atrocity come from?"

Thomas, still sitting on the floor, turned to face her. "Paris," he said dumbly, not knowing quite what to make of this sudden new turn. "I saw it in a London studio. They only delivered it this morning. They had this little Frenchman working on another very similar to that one. It's the newest thing. I had thought you might like it."

She half turned, looking down at him. "It is the most pompous, gaudy, unsightly waste of canvas I have ever laid eyes on," she snapped viciously. "And how dare you have it placed here, of all places?! Removing MY portrait for this... thing! I am not even dead yet, and already you are removing me from your life? Have you no respect at all for the dying?!" she almost screamed.

"Nothing of the sort!" he protested. "I had your picture moved into the hallway, where it can be seen better."

She turned to him fully. "What do you know of décor?! Of all the inconsiderate things you could have done! You have no sense of the aesthetic! To take all my painstaking hours of placing each and every work of art in this house where it is best..." she began to cough. "To callously undo...." The cough was harder, her breathing more laboured The strain of shouting was too much for her. Thomas was unable to rise fast enough to catch hold of her as she fell.

She barely felt him sweep her off the floor as he rushed her upstairs, yelling for the servants to send for the doctor as he went. She felt the bed rising up to engulf her in its softness and the darkness of a deep swoon grabbing hold. She reached up, grabbed hold of Thomas's cravat, and pulled him near, using her last conscious breath to hiss, "You, Thomas, will be the death of me yet."

***

Thomas sat quietly across from his wife at tea. He watched her as she read aloud, her back straight in her chair, her eyes still kindled with life and fire. To look at her, one would hardly know she was dying. She was still as beautiful and graceful as she had always been. A half-suppressed cough shook her breast. She ignored it and turned her page. Thomas used the brief interlude to speak up.

"Ahem, Arabella?"

Her eyes glanced at him over the top of the book. For a moment, he seemed to have forgotten why he had disturbed her reading and stared, lost in their brilliance. "Yes, Thomas?"

Quiet as she had spoken, her voice had a very jarring effect on him, snapping him out of his sudden stupor.

"Yes, I..." He swallowed his hesitation, deciding suddenly to be firm and in control, something he rarely felt around his wife. "A friend of mine will be joining us for dinner tonight."

She set her book down, folded it over meticulously and placed it beside her teacup. She waited, a faint flush rising to her cheeks, stared him down, waiting for him to crack beneath her gaze, expecting him to apologize and stammer as he explained himself as usual. Instead, he seemed to gather his courage further and spoke, more firmly than she was accustomed to being addressed by him.

"Yes. He is a very important guest and I would like you to look your best this evening. He will be spending the night." Arabella continued her intimidating silence. "He was a friend of mine from the university and I have not seen him for nearly five years." The weakness returned to his voice as he rambled on, trying to justify his decision.

Arabella lifted her teacup to her lips. She had won. There was no need to continue to pressure him, except perhaps to punish him for taking that tone with her in the first place. She held her eyes steadfast, delighting in watching his discomfort. He droned on, and Arabella stared without really listening. 'How dare he?' she thought. 'Bring a guest into my house, with me ill, without asking my permission first. And to inform me on such short notice!'

Something he said snapped her out of herself. Rather, the way he said it.

"He will be here at 7 o'clock," he said, using that commanding tone again. "Please see that you are ready."

Without giving her time to answer, he left the sitting room. Arabella watched him go, stunned to silence.

***

Arabella sat before the vanity, fuming while Tilly arranged her hair. 'Thomas has never taken that tone with me! He must be up to

Pride Goeth

something!' Suddenly, she heard a noise coming out of the woods. She turned her head to listen, pulling a lock out of Tilly's hand as she did. As the sound of harness bells became clearer, she rose and crossed to the window, drew back the curtains. The lock of hair dangled unnoticed.

It was cold here, with winter beating against the glass, and it burned her lungs. She ignored the irritation and looked down into the yard. The carriage that pulled up was elaborate, drawn by six stallions of exceptional quality and spirit.

"He is wealthy, this guest of ours," she muttered to herself.

"Oh, my," breathed Tilly, stealing a peek from behind her mistress. A piercing glare from her Lady and she shrank back timidly.

Arabella watched as her husband stepped up to meet the man who disembarked from that carriage. At this distance, it was difficult to see the man's features as he embraced her husband amid much back clapping. As they turned to enter the house, she let the curtain drop and sat down again before the vanity. She studied her reflection carefully for anything remotely out of place. She fingered the single curl that just brushed the top of her collarbone. Tilly moved to pin it up, but she stopped her. "Leave it," she decided and turned to add the finishing touches to her cosmetics.

She scrutinized her eyes, imagining them somewhat more hollowed than they were, adding a bit more powder to hide the shadows there. To her cheeks, she added a touch of blush to lend some colour to the pallor that seemed to deepen weekly. She sat back, turned her head first this way, then that, admiring her reflection.

"You are stunning, my lady," breathed Tilly. Arabella thought she heard a faint tinge of jealousy in the maid's voice and felt more satisfied with what she saw in the mirror.

"Humph, if our guest is anything like my husband, he'll be too blind to see the flaws. As it should be."

From downstairs she heard Thomas's voice ring out, still unusually forceful. "ARABELLA! Our guest has arrived!"

She slammed her fist into the table, causing the various jars and bottles there to jump. "How dare he bellow for me like a common servant!" she seethed. She turned back to the mirror, and forced herself to relax, and remain calm.

"Shall I inform your husband that you will be down shortly?" asked Tilly in a mousy voice.

"No. Let them wait," she said, smiling wickedly at her reflection.

Ten minutes later she stood at the top of the stairs composing herself for her entrance. She smoothed down the dark green velvet of her gown where it nipped in at her narrow waist, paused to lay flat a curling bit of ivory lace that graced the bodice and her long white throat. She kept her breathing deliberately shallow in an attempt to forestall any coughing that might arise from the exercise of descending the long staircase. If she was to be forced into playing hostess, she would play it to perfection. Thomas would suffer for it later. She began her descent. Ever the lady, she seemed to glide across the floor to where her husband and guest stood waiting.

A quick glance at her husband rewarded her tardiness, as he seemed much irritated and attempted to hide it. Only then did she afford her whole attention to the man presented before her. He was taller than Thomas, somewhat broader in the shoulders. His gold-streaked, light brown hair was fashionably combed, setting off his deep, dark eyes. His face was lean and handsome, no jutting features or unpleasing lines. The skin was smooth and unflawed, pale, an uncommon colour for a man, yet striking. His clothing was silk, a crisp, blinding white that seemed to give him more colour by comparison.

"Arabella, this is Nigel Baronet Hartfordshire. Nigel, my wife, Arabella March."

"Lady Arabella March," she corrected politely, as he stepped forward, taking her hand. She took note of the way he moved, fluid, no motion wasted.

His hand was cool and strong, not quite as soft as her husband's, not quite that of a labourer. And when he brought her hand to his lips, it felt feverish against his skin.

"At last we meet," he said, his voice firm, his eyes dancing across her face. "I am honoured."

She met his gaze boldly, unexpectedly curious. She had imagined him a weaker man, more like her husband. Not the potent noble who still had not released her hand. There was arrogance and supreme self-confidence in his eyes.

"Dinner is waiting." Thomas's voice was an unwelcome intrusion, forcing the pair to break off their mutual assessment. Where before Arabella had no interest in the man, she now felt an intense and burning curiosity.

Dinner was served in the great hall, not the smaller, yellow dining room where Arabella and her husband ate their regular meals. This room, which Arabella adored, was reserved only for guests and had not been used in quite some time. Thomas hated the pretentiousness of it, his wife loved that very aspect. Three places were set at one end of the long trestle table. Thomas sat at the head, with his wife on the right and his guest on his left. As soon as they were seated, Thomas picked up a silver bell beside his plate and rang it. Immediately, four servants entered from the kitchen, bearing a small feast that was quite above their usual fare.

"We have outdone ourselves, Thomas," she said with mild surprise, then looked at him with eyes that both questioned and accused. "We must have been preparing this for some time."

"Well, this was important to me, darling." He smiled, covering her hand with his own. "I wanted to surprise you."

"That you have," she stated coldly.

"I am glad it pleases you," he smiled, then bowed his head and began one of his long and tedious blessings.

Arabella stole a glance at the Baronet. She found him staring boldly, not even pretending to observe the blessing, unlike her. She watched as the tip of his tongue slid teasingly across the edge of his teeth. He smiled at her, an expression which appeared more hungry than pleased. The way his eyes flitted across her face informed her that he was attempting to unnerve her. She simply returned his smug smile with amusement. 'This man,' she thought triumphantly, 'is a Player.'

"Amen," finished Thomas at last.

"Amen," she echoed dutifully and raised her glass to her challenger.

The conversation began small and dull. Arabella remained quiet throughout the early portion of the meal, using the time to make a deeper assessment of Baronet Hartfordshire. Unfortunately, as well she knew, carrying on a truly stimulating conversation with her husband was impossible. Thomas was able to turn the most intriguing topic into something completely mundane. He was only interested in getting his thoughts across clearly and had no concept of the art of conversation. Finally, she wedged her way in, neatly cutting her husband out.

"So tell me, Baronet," she began, "what brings you to this desolate part of England?"

"Your husband and I have been corresponding for quite some time. He has spoken quite highly of you."

"He is my husband. He is expected to speak highly of me." They gauged each other, eye for eye, neither moving, neither blinking. Thomas was left out completely, much as Arabella had been moments ago.

He arched one eyebrow and continued, saying, "He said only that he had wed the most beautiful, most regal woman in the Empire. I had to see for myself."

He was baiting her. She willingly accepted that bait, taking the risk in order to uncover the gambit he had planned. "And?"

Pride Goeth

He leaned forward, conciliatory. "You were very poorly represented. A gross negligence on his part."

Dead end. Flattery was thrown out to mask his next move. She tried another tact. "Thomas and I have been married nearly six years. Why choose this particular time to 'see for yourself'?"

He leaned back, politely dismissing the topic. "Business. Nothing you would find interesting."and

"You would be surprised what I would find interesting," she dead-panned.

His gaze shifted slightly, the eyebrow cocking itself again. "Perhaps I might."

"So tell me," she said, picking up her glass, studying its ruby contents, "what do you do with your time? My husband tells me you two attended the University together. What keeps a young nobleman such as yourself busy?"

"With my current schedule, my days are mine to do with as I please."

The minute signs present in the set of his face informed her that there was more to what he had said than was directly apparent. "As it should be for a nobleman," she countered. "But what occupies your nights?"

The unspoken challenge hung in the air as Arabella rose, the men quickly following suit. She gave a slight nod of her head as she spoke. "You gentlemen have much to talk about over your cigars and brandy. I have been ill lately and I think I shall be retiring early tonight. I leave you two to your reminiscing. Good night, Thomas. Baronet."

"As you wish, my dear."

"It has been a pleasure, Lady March," the Baronet smiled.

As Arabella left the dining room, she was fully aware that the men were watching her. She held herself arrow straight, intent on showing them no sign of the physical weakness eating away at her. It was not until she had ascended the stairs and reached the room that she allowed free rein to the cough that had been building up within her chest. The staircase seemed to get longer and steeper as the weeks progressed, the brief exercise more and more of a strain. The fit passed, leaving her wheezing and breathless as she eased herself into her chair by the fire. She helped herself to a glass of the brandy on the pedestal table and relaxed, ringing for Tilly to come to prepare her for bed.

***

Arabella dreamed fitfully. She was standing on the moors near her father's house, the winter wind whistling around her, carrying the soft sound of singing past her. She listened, identified the melody as a Scottish ballad she had often heard across the moors in her youth. Slowly, the realization came to her that she was no longer asleep. The fire crackled dimly in the grate and a chill had crept into the room. She sat up in the bed, took note of Thomas's absence, and scowled. She lit a candle to read the clock and discovered it was nearly four in the morning. She rose, put her wrap on over her nightdress, and left the room. She slipped down the short hallway and descended the stairs. The flagstones of the main hall were freezing, numbing her feet even through her slippers. She paused at the library door, peered in. It was empty, as was the sitting room. From under the door, she saw a dim light in the study. She entered and found her husband sitting in his chair, chin on his chest and an open book in his lap. Furious, she spun on her heel and left him there.

Returning to her room, the sight of the empty bed infuriated her even more. It was not that she missed his company in the least. It was the fact that he was neglecting her that made her burn. He had not come to bed for several nights, preferring, it seemed, to spend them downstairs either drunk or reading, sometimes both. She stoked the fire, adding a few light logs to it, and stood watching it burn.

Pride Goeth

The heat of the flames inched into her blood, chasing away the chill that irritated her cough. She listened to the wind hammering against the eaves, to the pounding of her blood in her ears, to the hiss and crack of the pitch in the wood, and the popping of dying insects. She cocked her head a moment, listening acutely to the outside noises. Somewhere, she distinctly heard someone singing. It was a Scottish melody, the same one that had infiltrated her dreams and awakened her earlier.

She crossed to the window, and looked out. At first, she could not clearly see until her eyes adjusted to the dimness and located a figure by the carriage house. She let the curtain fall closed behind her and studied the figure. It was the Baronet, standing in the open doorway to the barn in only his shirt and stockings, singing to the winter's night like a man drunk or insane. "The man is absolutely daft," she murmured. She watched him in amazement, unafraid of being seen by him, secure in the knowledge that it was impossible from the barn. Yet somehow his dark eyes seemed to stare at her, never once wavering.

Breathing in the cold air at the window reawakened her cough, and she turned back into the room. Out of the corner of her eye, she saw him beckon with a simple wave of his hand. Arabella did not look back.

Amazed by his impudence, she crawled back into the warm bed, pulling the heavy coverlets close, and tried to sleep. However, the singing continued. She tossed and turned, trying to get comfortable. The melody died out, the song unfinished, and the only sounds she heard were the season and the fire. She saw him gesture again; the moment replayed in her mind unbidden. She got up and began to dress, all the while trying to reason why she was doing this.

It was biting cold outside, even through the heavy fur of her cloak; but the wind had died some and Arabella forced herself to cross the courtyard to the open stable door.

The inside of the barn was not much warmer, and only a single lamp was left burning. Arabella stepped inside and slammed the door closed behind her. "What are you trying to do? Kill my horses?!" she demanded of the darkness.

"They are hardy creatures," the Baronet replied as he appeared from the depths of a stall near the lamp.

She continued her tirade. "I have a mare ready to drop a foal any..." she let her voice trail off as he emerged from the stall. Having removed his shirt, his body gleamed in the dim light. He had a superb physique, firm and muscled like a field hand. His pale complexion lent him a statuesque quality much like a marble museum piece or a Michelangelo. She looked into his face, herself completely unembarrassed by his nakedness. His challenge was open, accompanied by an arrogant confidence in his total victory. Arabella's enraged attitude vanished as swiftly as she had summoned it, and she regarded him with something akin to disdain.

"Having a tumble with the kitchen wench?"

"Not at all. I am waiting for the lady of the house."

She smiled, not the blushed smile of a woman flattered to embarrassment, but the cold, cruel, amused smirk of a princess propositioned by a stable boy. "The lady of the house is taken."

"That may be," he sneered, "but this house has no lord. Or can you possible be satisfied with that cold, limp fish you call a husband?"

Now she was incensed. She would not have her private life discussed so casually by a virtual stranger. "I am quite satisfied with what Thomas provides me!" she hissed.

"Are you now?" His eyes narrowed, "Perhaps I overestimated you. I had believed you a woman of desires and ambitions too extreme to be satisfied by a weak boy like Thomas."

"If you hate your old school mate so much, then why did you come?"

"Oh, I don't hate him. He has provided me a great deal of sport over the last few years."

Pride Goeth

She began to regard him with more caution. "Why are you here?" she asked again.

"I told you over dinner. Business."

"What business? And do not try to brush me off with 'you are a woman, it would not interest you'!"

He smiled, "Oh, I am certain you would be highly interested in our business. You are an intelligent woman, not some flighty, empty-headed socialite. Your husband has offered to sell me the Northern Cross."

This news did indeed spark her interest. "How much of it?"

"All six hundred acres of it. I told him I would give him a decision tomorrow night."

"Why would he want to sell the property?" she asked, more of herself than of the Baronet.

"He has a talent for picking a loser," he smirked.

"Playing the track?" she asked, matter of fact. News of her husband's gambling neither surprised nor angered her. She had always known of his penchant for cards. He was actually a fairly skilful player, but there are always men who are better, luckier.

"Among other things," he evaded. He moved away from the stall, strode thoughtfully over to one of his stallions and began to stroke the broad nose. "He has acquired a few small debts and has to sell the land to pay them, or lose it altogether. He has offered it to me first, thinking that I will permit him to keep the house."

Arabella folded her arms. "I take it, his trust in you is misplaced?"

His eyes raked the length of her body. He smiled, saying, "I could be... persuaded."

She looked him over, amazed by his audacity. "I do not come with the land," she replied in a low, tight voice.

"Not as far as your husband is concerned, no. But just between the two of us.... You might even find the arrangement... pleasurable."

"I am not a broodmare to be passed about...." she began, seething.

"Oh, you most certainly are not," he rumbled, cutting her off. He walked around her slowly, in a tight, close circle, predatory. "You are an exquisite woman, beautiful and proud in the extreme, and wholly unconquered." He stopped just behind her, his voice so close she should have been able to feel his breath against her neck. "I can fulfil your desires...."

There was a damp warmth rising inside her body, and she did not like the feelings it evoked. She used anger as a defence and stood her ground as he moved again, approaching, her eyes warning him back. It was a warning he did not heed. "My, you are a bold cockerel, aren't you?"

He stood directly before her, looming over her. "Bold enough to bring a woman like you to your knees."

She glared up at him fiercely, "I did not think a man of your calibre resorted to rape."

"You misjudge my intentions, Arabella. I would not dream of taking you by force." His expression tightened then, became sly and hard. "I shall wait until you surrender."

Threatening to find herself overwhelmed by him, she turned away, breaking their eye contact and moved towards the door. Moving faster than she could have thought possible, he was there, barring her way. She was momentarily startled, but regained her composure quickly.

The smile was gone as he spoke, "If you should decide to inform your husband of what has transpired here, I am afraid he will not believe you."

"I don't need to go through my husband to deal with the likes of you!" she snapped, insulted by the insinuation of being dependent on Thomas for anything. "If I so desired, I could have you thrown out of here myself!"

"No doubt," he chuckled. His eyes seemed to doubt her, to dare her to try.

Determined to wipe the smile from his face, she turned and called for the stable boy. There was no answer from the hayloft. She raised her voice. "WESLEY!"

The strain of shouting made her cough again, doubling her over in an effort to breathe normally. When she recovered, her face flushed and head pounding, Wesley had still not climbed down from his bed in the loft.

"Are you finished?"

She turned on the Baronet, glared accusingly at him. He seemed thoroughly amused with himself. "What have you done with the stable boy?!" she rasped.

"Nothing," he shrugged innocently.

"Then where is he?"

"In town, at the farrier's," he answered, moving slowly closer. "Probably decided to spend the night there. One of my stallions threw a shoe this evening on your drive."

"Damned convenient of the beast, I would say." The hackles rose on her neck as he approached. She stood perfectly still, her body tensed for anything he might attempt. Her breathing was still ragged, her heartbeat irregular.

"Tell me, Arabella," he began, circling her closely again, "is it your illness that had you so short of breath? Or is it something else? Passion perhaps? Desire? ...Me?"

"Such conceit in a gentleman is not comely," she replied.

"Such hypocrisy in a lady is repulsive," he charged. She whirled to meet him eye for eye and found herself suddenly trapped by them, unable to speak or look away. "You are a creature of passion and fire. I dare you to deny it! To deny the need rising up inside your body, the desire only now beginning to rage and consume you. Desire that needs more than poor Thomas can give you." He did not raise his voice. He did not need to. There was a great deal of force behind his words that revealed more in its restraint than it could have vented.

Arabella stiffened her resolve, letting his words anger her rather than frighten, and broke his hold. "You have overstepped your position, Baronet," she hissed to his face, unflinching.

"Not yet," he growled.

"You have grossly underestimated me if you think I will be had in a filthy stable like some tavern girl trying to turn a coin," she snarled. 'The very idea!' she thought.

He pulled back, a devilish grin twisting his handsome face. "If you would prefer, we could go inside, to your husband's bed?"

She covered her shock quickly, smiling. "I find your audacity amusing, but it is beginning to bore me." Once more she tried for the door, again he kept her from it. "Let me pass," she hissed.

"Why?" he demanded in a mocking tone. "Where are you going?"

"I wish to return to my house."

To her surprise, he stepped aside. Feeling that she had somehow won, she left, returning to the manor without a backward glance.

Climbing the stairs took longer this time, and she actually had to pause mid-way to rest. She was winded, coughing and in pain as she finally entered her bedroom and bolted the door behind her, not caring one whit that she was locking Thomas out. Still wrapped in her cloak, she retreated to the fireside and poured herself a brandy to ease the dreadful throbbing in her chest.

"That would be nice, thank you."

She turned, and found the Baronet lying on the bed! She hurled the glass in his direction, but fell short of the mark. He looked over the edge of the bed at the shattered glass and sighed. "Such a waste of energy that would best be spent elsewhere."

"What are you doing in my bed?!" she demanded, just barely keeping herself from screaming as she tried to figure out how he had gotten past her without her seeing him.

"You would not come to me in the stable, so I thought this would be a more appropriate setting."

Pride Goeth

Her rage was barely contained, and fast approaching the point at which Arabella no longer cared to hold it back. "If you think I will come meekly to your bed... MY bed...!" she corrected.

He grinned wolfishly, "Yes, it is, isn't it."

"Ooooh!" she exclaimed and turned her back on him. She snatched up the decanter and filled another glass, drained it without pause. She faced the fire, beginning to feel the heat of it through her heavy clothing. Fever and exertion made it worse, but she was not about to remove even the cloak with the Baronet in the room. He would see it as an opening, and that she would not permit. Sweat began, making her clothes damp and her skin to glow in the firelight.

"You appear quite uncomfortable," the Baronet observed. "Would it not be better to remove...."

"I am quite comfortable, thank you!" she snapped, cutting him off. He just smiled at her as he lounged on his side, watching her. "And get out of my bed!"

Obediently, he rose, and Arabella observed that he had removed his stockings. He came towards her, fully naked and seemingly oblivious to the fact. She pulled the collar of her furred cloak closer. He reached out and pulled the cloak open again. "Don't be a fool. I can see the unnatural flush to your cheeks, your shallow breathing. I can sense the tightness in your chest, the dizziness just beginning to creep into your head, the sweat beading between your breasts." His voice was low, rhythmic: hypnotic.

Arabella listened, staring at him as if enspelled, but her hand was creeping back to seize the poker leaning against the hearthstones. Her fingers locked around it, and she took a quick step back, bringing it between them. He let go of the cloak and stood watching her as it fell to the ground, unthreatened by the gesture.

"You cannot seduce me, Baronet. If you want me, you will have to take me by force." She was very aware that, if he took her up on that, she was badly outmatched; but somehow, she did not think he would.

"I take nothing that is not freely given," he answered, much as she expected him to. "You will have to surrender."

She gripped the poker tighter, not wanting the tip to waver because of rapidly failing strength. "Then you have a long wait, Hartfordshire. An Engleton never surrenders."

He smiled, a vicious, knowing expression. "I wouldn't say that. Merrick surrendered quite willingly."

Arabella's eyes danced with a fire of their own, kindled apart from fever. "My brother," she began tightly, "died of a fever twenty-two years ago. He was barely eight years old."

The Baronet raised an eyebrow. "Did he?" He watched her carefully, a smile beginning to curl upward at the corner of his mouth in spite of himself.

Merrick was the only person Arabella ever truly cherished in her life. When he died, any genuine feelings she might have possessed for another human being died with him. To see this man mocking that death with such casual disregard made her forget any anger she had previously displayed or held in check. All else yielded before the deluge of complete and absolute rage. She swung the poker at him with all her remaining strength. At the point at which she should have made contact with his chest, there was nothing. He moved, so fast he seemed to vanish, and the force of her swing carried her around, connecting with the brandy decanter in a spray of shattered crystal. She turned back quickly, bringing the poker to bear again, but he was gone and the room stood empty.

It was a long moment before she set her weapon back in its place on the hearth and allowed herself to relax the smallest fraction. Her wrists were positively throbbing with the pain of holding the heavy poker. She looked over the room, rubbing them with trembling hands, convincing herself that she was alone again. She moved towards the bed, hesitated, picturing him lying so casually there, defiling her bed with his presence. Stifling a nervous gesture, she ripped the heavy quilt off the bed and sank into her huge chair, wrapping herself up securely. Shortly before dawn, she slept.

***

Arabella heard the door open softly, and the maid come in. Somehow the door had gotten unlocked. Tilly gasped. "My Lady!" she cried.

Arabella glared at her. Tilly began immediately to pick up the glass on the floor. The brandy had dried, leaving a long, dark stain, which Tilly wiped at in vain.

"I want a fresh decanter brought up this afternoon," she ordered, staring at the single glass that had survived, and began unbuttoning her bodice.

The door opened again. Thomas entered, looking somewhat more dishevelled than usual. He stopped, eyed the broken crystal, then looked up at his wife seated in the chair in a rumpled, front-buttoning day dress. "What happened?" he asked, his tone having lost all the previous evening's unnatural forcefulness.

"Nothing," she snapped, dismissing him. She rose, and crossed to the bed, shrugging herself out of her hastily donned clothes, reaching for her discarded nightdress.

"Arabella, what are you doing?" he asked, gazing somewhat longingly at her lithe, naked body as she slipped the nightdress over her head. "We have a great deal to do today."

"You can do it by yourself," she answered, crawling beneath the covers. "I slept very little last night and do not wish to be disturbed."

"Arabella!" he began.

She ignored him. "Tilly, leave that. Wake me at three. Thomas, go away." With that, Arabella lay down and pulled the covers close, shutting both of them out.

Tilly left immediately, bearing her tray of tinkling glass with her. Thomas remained. He stood watching his wife for a long moment before he, too, sighed and left.

***

"Mistress?"

Arabella opened her eyes. Tilly's hand once again touched her shoulder.

"Mistress, it is three o'clock," Tilly announced timidly.

Arabella sat up, looked about the room. The fire had not been rekindled, nor had the brandy been scrubbed from the floor, although the clothes she had left on the floor that morning had already been put away. Tilly opened the wardrobe fully and began to lay out her Ladyship's petticoats.

"Any preference, My Lady?" she asked.

"Anything but the green one," she sighed, throwing back the covers. She looked down at her legs, partially exposed by her gown. They seemed to take on a bony, gaunt appearance in her eyes.

Tilly broke Arabella's train of thought as she laid a soft lavender garment on the bed beside her. Arabella rose, allowing the maid to dress her, all the while staring at her exposed limbs, imagining them more and more withered and wasted.

She was rather quiet as she entered the parlour for tea, almost subdued. As her husband stood, she realized their guest was absent. She looked around the room.

"Has the Baronet returned to London?" she asked, not quite certain that this pleased her. Infuriating as the man had been, he was... interesting, and a most challenging conversationalist.

Thomas shook his head. "He left a note saying he wanted to ride through the Northern Cross," he answered. "He said he hoped to be back in time for tea, but I suppose he has discovered some interesting sidetrack and will not be making it back. He should return well in time for supper."

"I see," she said, easing herself into her chair. Thomas sat down again and gestured for Tilly to come and serve. Arabella watched hatefully as the maid poured, a ritual she had always reserved for herself and was now incapable of doing. Thomas's voice sliced into her thoughts amid the soft clattering of the teacups.

"After all, we are the landlords, and the boy was in our care at the time. It is only proper we are there for the parents."

She looked at him, the maid totally forgotten as she raised her cup to her lips. "Thomas, what in the world are you babbling about now?"

He gave a tight, impatient sigh. "The funeral, Arabella. For the stable boy."

Her cup landed on the saucer with a loud clack. "Wesley?" she asked. "Our stable boy, Wesley?"

"Yes."

"What happened?"

"Wild dogs, we suppose," he answered, drinking his tea with a sigh of pity. "They caught up with him in the woods and tore him to pieces last night."

"What about the horse? The Baronet's stallion?" she asked, her nerves suddenly on edge.

"Strangely enough, Nigel's horse returned to the stable fine. I guess the boy was an easier target. If the boy had only managed to hold onto the saddle, he might have made it. Nigel has suggested various traps and such for the pack. He has been very helpful and I think the villagers will appreciate him for it."

She sat quiet, sipping her tea thoughtfully.

"The funeral is this Sunday," he continued. "I think we should go."

"We shall see if I am able," she answered, her tone closing the topic for good. The rest of tea was spent in silence, the book beside the tea kettle unopened and Thomas did not seem to notice.

After tea, Arabella paced the house. She had given up trying to play the piano several weeks before. Her hands were simply unable to perform adequately. She was not in the mood for reading, as she discovered after perusing the library for nearly an hour before giving up the search. Nothing appealed to her. Finally, she sat in the sitting room with a small hoop, a fragment of linen, and an embroidery needle and tried to sew.

She used a simple pattern, just a jumble of flowers, but found it exceedingly difficult. She could not make the threads lay just how she wanted them to, could not seem to do the stitches she had seen her mother use that had always looked so nice. The cloth sang like a drum skin as she pulled the thread through, a calming sound that helped to ease some of her frustrations and soothe her nerves. She gave up on the pattern, and simply ran the needle in and out for the sounds that it made. It was relaxing if nothing else, until the thread snagged. The melody of the needle broke with the thread. She turned the hoop over and saw the massive knot on the other side. She tried untangling it, picking at it thread by thread with the needle, but it was hopeless. The needle, still attached to the thread, became more actively involved in the knot and was soon entangled as well.

Her irritation returned, and she seized the scissors, cutting the threads without regard for the fabric. Suddenly, she gasped and jerked her hand away. She looked down at her finger and saw blood running down in a thin rivulet onto the linen. The needle had stabbed into her finger and been ripped free when she pulled her hand away.

She put her finger to her lips, licking the blood away and sucking at the wound to ease the stinging. She re-examined the thin scratch, damp and pink, but closing. In anger, she threw the cloth down, scissors and all, and flew from the sitting room. Her dress hissed, brushing roughly against the banister as she stormed upstairs. Throwing open the door, she nearly tripped over Tilly, on her hands and knees, just putting away her scrub brush. She looked up, startled as the door slammed back against the wall and her mistress suddenly loomed above her. Arabella paused for a moment before the girl then ignored her and threw the wardrobe open. Her hands flew through the hanging dresses until they found the one she was looking for. She thrust the dark blue riding habit into Tilly's arms and turned her back to the frightened girl.

She looked down at the dress in her arms. "My lady," she stammered, "surely you aren't going out riding...?"

Arabella turned on her.

"Iiiit isn't safe," she protested meekly. "The dogs..., the weather.... ...Your health, my lady!"

Arabella snatched the dress from her, and threw it onto the bed. "I did not tell you to ask questions. Now, are you going to help me change or do I have to dress myself?!"

"Nnno, your Ladyship I... I'll help," she answered. Her hands trembled as she obediently began to assist her mistress out of her day dress and into the riding habit.

Once dressed, Arabella left the room, giving no further thought to the maid or her admonitions. She entered the stable with such clear purpose that the younger stable hand brought out her gelding without having to be asked. Arabella noticed that, while still wearing his blue livery coat, he had tied a black sash to his left arm. The older groom came forward as she waited most impatiently.

He bobbed his head to her, a gesture she barely acknowledged. "Ev'nin, Madam. Would you be takin' an hescort out with you this afternoon?"

"No," she answered curtly, taking the reins from the stable hand.

"My lady," the groom continued, "there have been reports of wild dogs...."

"So I have heard," she snapped, seizing the saddle by its edges and swinging herself onto it from the mounting block.

The old groom reached out and took the horse by the bridle. "At least think of the weather, Mistress," he pleaded, still trying to be diplomatic. He knew she was not well, and that this could not be good for her. The horse tossed his head, agitated by conflicting commands. "Sweet Jesus, you'll catch your death out there!"

Arabella seethed. "Sweet Jesus be damned! I am already dying!" she cried and struck his hand away with her riding crop. The horse leapt free of the stable doors and ran across the yard and into the woods towards the Northern Cross.

She rode hard, feeling the wind ripping into her lungs. It was an exhilarating ride. She thrilled in her absolute control of the beast, the tiniest shift would send him barrelling down another path, up another rocky slope. It had been months since she had been able to ride like this, her illness had simply not permitted it.

A sudden movement across the heath below her made her pause, her hunter blowing heavily. A chill seized her as she thought it might be the Baronet, then a flash of red tail banished that fear, replacing it with a fierce joy. She guided her horse down to that heath, hoping for another glimpse of the creature. She had no hounds with her, which made the thought of the fox hunt far more thrilling.

She caught sight of it again just as she stepped out of the woods, and spurred her mount into pursuit. The three of them tore off through the East end of the Northern Cross, flinging themselves over fences and through the underbrush. The fox avoided the river, to her surprise, and on occasion, when she lost sight of it, it would be found moments later, watching her. It seemed to be playing with her, realizing it was merely a chase and not a real hunt.

The light grew dimmer, as the winter day came to its close, and the fox finally went to ground. Arabella heard it, in the distance, yapping to others, or to her, but she was unable to see it. Breathing heavily, she turned towards her own den and allowed the horse to walk all the way back to the manor. She could feel her blood rising to her cheeks, her heartbeat pulsing in her temples. Her chest ached, cold from breathing cold air, but she felt good, alive. The fading light gave her skin a pale cast, and for the first time, she began to give thought to Spring, something she had been told she would not see again.

Pride Goeth

It was full dark when she rode into the stable yard. There were servants setting out torches, to light her way, though not yet actively searching for her. As she passed by them going to the stable, they began to wander in themselves, putting out their lights. She said nothing to any of them as she dismounted and went inside the house. To her surprise, neither her guest nor her husband was waiting for her. Supper was no doubt ready. Then where was everyone?

Tilly had a bath waiting for her when she came upstairs. She began fussing over Arabella immediately as she rushed to help her undress.

"Oh, my lady, how flushed you look! Let us get you warmed up quickly!"

Arabella ignored her chatter as she stepped out of the gown. She reeked of horse, and that was all that mattered at the moment. Easing herself into the water, she felt the heat envelop her body like a shroud. She had not realized how numb she had become until it touched the water. The wind had robbed her of her own body heat. Her throat was dry and hoarse, and her skin was paler than she had ever been. 'How can one's body be in such a deteriorated condition and still feel so alive?' she thought. 'I feel better than I have in weeks, and yet I know I shall suffer greatly for it later. Why does that not bother me?' "Tilly, pour me a brandy."

"Yes, mum," she responded weakly, setting her sponge down.

Arabella watched the girl closely as she poured. She was still fairly young, her cheeks ruddy, her skin like fresh cream, her rusty hair hanging in great curls that refused to stay bound. Tilly was a handsome girl, with a great deal of life left in her. Arabella resented that. She took the brandy glass from her, refusing to look at her again.

She took a deep swallow. She looked down at the glass in disgust. "Ugh! This brandy is half water!" She thrust it back at the girl, not caring that it spilled in the process. "Take it away and bring me back a decent lot!"

"But his Lordship.." Tilly began.

Arabella turned on her, raising her body half out of the water, eyes blazing. "My husband is not a Lord, do you hear me?! I am the *only* true nobility in this house, see that you never forget that! It would be most unfortunate to find yourself without situation in the Christmas months! Now go fetch some proper brandy!"

The girl dropped her sponge again and ran out of the room, barely managing to hold on to the glass. Arabella sank back down into the water and scowled. "The very idea!"

When Tilly finally returned, she found her mistress already out of the water and beginning to dress herself. Tilly put the decanter down quickly on its table by the fire and rushed to lace her Ladyship's corset. She picked up the dress lying on the bed, looked at it with an eye of disapproval, but said nothing. Arabella took note of this, but held her own silence. The dress was a bridal white of damask silk; the throat cut low in the French fashion.

As Tilly fastened the heavy drape of pearls around Arabella's bare neck, she asked, "Would my lady prefer her white tasselled shawl? Or perhaps the new Belgian one?"

Arabella did not answer. She rose, brushing past the girl as if she did not exist, and proceeded downstairs at once. Halfway down the stairs, she caught a sidelong glimpse of herself as she passed one of the many ornate mirrors. She was pleased with the image, regal, stately in the supreme. Her airs were completely spoiled, however, when, reaching the foot of the staircase, she saw her husband and the Baronet only just leaving the study. She stopped on the last step.

"Oh, nonsense," Thomas was saying, his arm around the Baronet's shoulders. "There is no way you can stay in that house in the condition it is in. You will stay here as long as it takes."

"If you are referring to the old Heathrow Manor in the Cross," Arabella said, pleased to hear her voice cut the air and silence the pair, "it will be several decades before our guest is our neighbour."

"My lady," the Baronet said, stepping forward to take her hand, and kissed it.

"You would be better off tearing it down and building a new one," she replied, gazing defiantly into his eyes.

"It will suit my needs," he answered with the tiniest arch of his brow. A faint smile formed.

Dinner went much the same as before, and this time, Arabella allowed herself to be excluded from the conversation. It afforded her the opportunity to further study the Baronet as her husband took up his full attention. Suddenly, she found herself staring into his cold eyes.

"And how was your ride this afternoon?" he asked, his eyes dancing his challenge, filled with the arrogance of his assumed and premature victory. "I thought I saw you as I was exploring, but I lost sight of you too quickly, otherwise I would have joined you."

She smiled tightly. "It was fine, thank you. I prefer to ride alone."

There was a slyness to his tone, ripe with multiple meanings. "Under current circumstances, I would think that very dangerous for a lady in your condition."

Before Arabella could retort, she felt her husband's hand settle on her own as he chuckled, "My 'Bella never lets anything stop her, not even her illness. If she wants to do something, nothing will stay her."

She pulled her hand free, grateful that the Baronet had turned to look at Thomas and could not see the tempest raging in her eyes. How dare her husband address her so familiarly in front of a guest, call her stubborn and bring up her illness all in the same breath!? Seething, it was all she could do to stand and smile tightly, excusing herself with a polite tone. "If you gentlemen will pardon me, there are some things my 'illness' will not permit me. I leave you to your cigars. Good night."

She did not acknowledge the two as they rose, and spun on her heel, storming out of the room. As she crossed the floor of the outer hall, she could feel the Baronet's eyes on her, mocking her. Behind her, she heard one of them mutter, "Damn fine woman!" but she could not be certain which of the two it had been.

***

Arabella opened her eyes to the semi-darkness of the room. A log rolled in the fire grate and settled, sparking and hissing as the sap was burned away. Small insects trapped within the burning wood whistled and popped as the flames reached their hiding places. She looked at the clock on the mantle. It was nearly midnight. And Thomas was not in bed. Stifling a cough, she rose, crossing to the brandy sitting beside her chair and poured a bit into a glass. She sat in the chair staring at the empty bed. She took a sip of the brandy. It was still weak. He seemed determined to take from her the only means of relief she had against her cough. Finally, she set the glass down unemptied, tied her robe about her, and left the warm chamber looking for Thomas.

He was in the parlour, asleep on top of the card table. The cards were scattered underneath him, some spilling over onto the floor amid several empty wine bottles. 'From Thomas's behaviour,' she thought, 'one would think he was the one dying. You do not see me moaning about, drinking myself unconscious.' Highly irritated, Arabella took a lap rug from the back of the settee and draped it carelessly over him. She then went to the cabinet and took out the brandy decanter, tasting it for full potency before tucking it under her arm and going back upstairs.

She stopped at the top landing to catch her breath, glanced back down the long staircase. She could easily have her things moved into one of the downstairs bedrooms and avoid this climb altogether, but that would be admitting defeat. Besides, to sleep on the same floor with the servants would be unthinkable. She turned back towards her room, flitting past the Baronet's half-open door as she went. She paused, having seen candles burning within, saw him with an open case on the bed, sifting through papers, half-dressed and not seeming

Pride Goeth

to care that the door was open. She moved on, not wishing to be seen peeking like some serving maid half-wanting to be caught.

She closed her bedroom door quietly behind her and set the brandy on the stand. She emptied the watered liquid from earlier into the fire and refilled the glass, stood watching the increased blaze as she drank. The strong fluid soothed her burning throat as it went down, silencing the cough rattling in her chest. Her body felt numb, cold, and weak. She knew she should not have gone riding, but she did not care. She had needed to vent herself somehow.

A sound from the door called her attention from her musings. She turned. There was nothing. She turned back to the fire and saw the Baronet sitting in her chair watching the fire.

"You, sir, have more audacity than a cat!" she hissed. He merely smiled. "How dare you enter my bedchamber in the middle of the night, half naked, and with my husband just downstairs?!"

Slowly, he turned to face her, his fingers steepled in front of him. "I dare a great deal to get what I want. However, you have no need to worry about Thomas interrupting us tonight."

She suddenly recalled the soundness of Thomas's sleep. "What did you do to him?!" she demanded.

"I did not have to do a damned thing," he chuckled. He gazed steadily at her as she sank into the chair opposite him. "Ah, you are such a spirited creature," he breathed. "I think I understand why your brother hates you so much. You are too much alike, and what he struggles so hard to achieve comes so easily for you."

She looked over at him. He was grinning broadly. "What do you know of Jason?" she accused.

His eyes narrowed ever so slightly. "I know a great many things about you."

She looked away again, jaw clenched tight, as were the fingers on the snifter's bowl. "Thomas talks too much," she said through her teeth.

"On the contrary, Arabella," her eyes turned sharply on him at his use of her Christian name, "I have merely done my research."

Arabella straightened her back, tilting her chin up in defiance, narrowing her eyes as the sudden realization came to her. "You did not come here for a visit with an old schoolmate. Nor did you come for the land you have so recently acquired. You came here for me, completely and totally."

"If it pleases your Ladyship to think so," he said smugly, gently pulling at the sides of his mouth with a forefinger.

"Why?" she asked, suddenly very calm. "Why now? You claim to have corresponded with my husband for years now. Why have you waited this long to try and take whatever it is you think you can get from me?" He did not answer. "Surely there are countless other women, of stronger body than I; who would fall over themselves to please you."

"But you are not 'countless other women', and I think you know this. Stronger bodies, oh yes. Stronger minds?" He trailed off, leaving the floor open.

They stared at each other instead of speaking, each trying to read in their opponent some weakness to exploit. At length the Baronet reached behind him and pulled something out of his collar, unfastening it from around his neck. He held his closed fist out to her. She hesitated, then reached out to accept it. He laid a small gold locket in her palm. She drew it to her, turned it over, and gasped. She glared up at him. "Where did you get this?!" she hissed.

He smiled, "Merrick gave it to me."

She stood, enraged. "That is impos...." a series of deep and biting coughs forced her to break off, weakening her so that she had to sit back down, her head pounding. When she regained some control, she tried again, lowering her voice, "That is impossible!"

"Is it?" he asked with an arched brow.

Pride Goeth

"I placed this locket in his coffin," she ground out. He merely continued to smile at her, never once blinking. "Who are you?" she demanded. "How do you know so much of me?"

"I am Nigel Baronet Hartfordshire. And a wise hunter always knows his prey." He rose, bowed, and took her hand. She tried to pull it away, but he held tight and kissed it. "I bid you goodnight, Lady March."

Her eyes followed him as he left the room. Even then, she was not entirely convinced that he was gone. For the second time since he had arrived, Arabella slept in her chair beside the fading fire.

***

Tilly woke her late. She opened her eyes and looked up at the clock. She narrowed her eyes at the girl. "Tilly, you have let me sleep half the day," she hissed.

The girl stepped back wisely. "You did not look well, my lady. His Lor... Mister March said to let you sleep in case your ride yesterday made you worse."

"How thoughtful of him," she said flatly. "And where is my loving husband?" she asked, slowly getting up. She did indeed feel worse but was not about to let the girl know this.

Tilly moved to the wardrobe, pulled out a day gown, and began to help Arabella dress. "London, my lady."

She drew up short. "London?"

"Yes, ma'am," Tilly answered without pausing as she tightened the lacing on Arabella's corset. "He said he had business to attend to there and would be returning in a few days. He asked me to tell you to see to his guest while he was away."

"The Baronet did not go with him?" she asked, refusing to acknowledge the need to cough, or the sudden tightening in her chest that had little to do with her consumption or the tightening laces.

"No, ma'am."

"Where is our guest now?"

Arabella felt the girl shrug as she tied off the laces and reached for the petticoats. "Most likely at Heathrow Manor. His carriage is gone."

Arabella finished dressing in silence. Her mind was in a fury as she sat before her mirror having her hair brushed. Left alone in this house with that man. The things he would dare now that there was no one here to hinder him. But then, such had been the case before. Thomas had been out cold and useless both nights. No, he would not dare more than he had already. Besides, he had said he would not use force, and she believed him. It would not only spoil whatever game he was playing but would be as much as admitting defeat.

And just what was his game? There were ways of finding out. Arabella rose and left the room the instant the last pin was in place. She entered the guest room without the slightest hesitation. Looking around the room, she saw the scattered evidence that her unwelcome guest was indeed still in residence. She moved to the wardrobe, opened it, and closed it again. She ran her hands over the empty dresser top, opened the bureau drawer, and found only blank paper, pen, and inkwell. Then she saw the satchel sitting unobtrusively on the chest at the foot of the bed.

Seating herself daintily at the edge of the chest, she opened the satchel and began sifting through the contents. It was all business papers, deeds, and debt letters. She read through some of them, then dropped them all back into the satchel, uninterested. A corner of paper in a side pocket caught her attention. She drew it out and read with renewed interest. It was a listing of all her husband's creditors, and all of them tied themselves neatly back to the Baronet. Suspicion began growing as she carefully put the paper back in its side pouch, where she found a small, leather-bound book.

She took the book out and opened it. It appeared to be the Baronet's journal. She turned the pages excitedly. This was a discovery! Much to her disappointment, none of it revealed his intentions towards her or her husband. It was concerned only with Thomas and his conduct and conversations at various London clubs over the past couple of years. Some of the conversations were put down in great detail and it infuriated her to learn that, the more intoxicated Thomas became, the more shrewish she was described. Refusing to read more, she snapped the book closed, slipped it back into its hiding place, and closed the satchel as she found it.

As she rose to leave, she heard the crinkled rustling and looked down. A small, folded piece of paper lay beneath the hem of her dress. 'It must have fallen from amid the papers,' she thought as she picked it up. Before putting it back, she could not resist reading it. It was in a meticulous script, handwritten in a curious brown ink. It read: To face immortality, one must first embrace death.

'Curious. I would not have taken the Baronet to be a religious man.' She set the note back inside the satchel and went downstairs for tea.

Arabella took her tea quietly while she read, periodically interrupted by spasms of coughing. Finally, she pushed her teacup away and leaned back in the chair. She did not touch the fresh scones, her stomach turning at the very thought of sweets. After a moment's rest, she rose, heading upstairs to read in her room. As she passed the door to the library, she overheard some of the maids gossiping inside and paused to listen.

"Did you 'ear the way the old lady was coughing? Tsk, tsk, she won't see Christmas that rate."

"Won't live out the week, you ask me."

Arabella identified the voices as Megan and Holly, and made a mental note to ensure their Christmas bonuses were substantially less than they were expecting.

"Won't be sorry to see 'er go, personally."

Substantially, she amended.

"Meg!" cried Holly, "you shouldn't talk like that! 'er death will destroy Mister March."

"Sigh, love is so blind."

"Well, I'm not blind. Did you see the Baronet last night?" asked Holly in a much more conspiratory voice.

Megan, too, dropped her volume. "Seen 'im? I've seen all of 'im!"

"Megan! You hussy!" Holly cried, but could not stifle the giggle that followed.

"Can I 'elp it if the man left 'is door open whilst he changed? I only caught a glimpse. I was too embarrassed to look longer. But I saw 'im putting money in his case. There must have been five or six thousand pounds in that bag!"

"Wealthy and 'andsome to boot!"

At this, Arabella left. She had no desire to listen to the Baronet's virtues being extolled by the serving maids. Still wheezing, she retired to her room for the rest of the afternoon.

Night fell. The book lay unread in Arabella's lap as she sat, immobile, staring into the fire, listening to the music it made. Suddenly, she saw herself dancing to that music and remembered it as a dream. She focused inward, letting her mind flow with the memory. It was a ball, a crowded dance floor in the midst of which, she whirled, a vision of elegance in a dress that rippled like the fire. She remembered happiness, a floating sense of freedom making her feel giddy.

Her partner was very good, a strong, easy lead. It was not Thomas. It was someone else, someone whose face she could not recall. She struggled to remember it, the spell of giddy enchantment beginning to slip away with her control of the situation. Unable to see his face, she tried, had tried, to disentangle herself from him; but the arm around her waist was like a band of iron. She could not remember his face, but she remembered his body, pressed improperly close as they danced. It was well-formed and broad, lean and hard, befitting a man of action. And it was cold. Being pressed so tightly against it seemed to steal her own warmth, made her breath short from the pressure, her

Pride Goeth

chest tight. She struggled, and her partner laughed. Looking into his eyes, she suddenly knew him.

It was the Baronet!

The party around them vanished, and they stood before the fire in her bedroom, her naked body moulded to his. In that instant of recognition, she banished the vision, consciously forcing from her mind the image of their limbs intertwined in such a passionate embrace.

As she tried to recompose herself, to banish the heated flush from her cheeks, there came a soft knock at the door. She glanced at the clock. It should be Tilly with her supper.

"Come in," she said, clearing her throat carefully, lest she begin coughing again.

To her surprise, it was not Tilly who entered, but the Baronet, bearing her supper before him on a tray. "Miss Tilly said you were not well. So I took the liberty of bringing your supper myself."

"How thoughtful of you," she said, studying him to read his motive, finding to her frustration that he could not be read.

"I hope you do not mind?" he asked, his voice indicating that it would not make any difference to him if she did mind. He set the tray neatly in her lap and seated himself in the chair across from her.

"Will you not be...." she began, unfolding her napkin.

He waved her off. "No. My hunger is of... a different nature."

She glanced up at him over her slim supper. "Still believe you can seduce me? Better men than you have failed attempts to cuckold my husbands."

"A woman such as yourself needs a strong man, not a weak, malleable soul like Thomas March," he sneered.

"I have had my fill of strong men, thank you very much," she snapped without looking up at him, cutting into her veal.

The Baronet leaned back, crossing his legs as he laced his fingers over his chest. "Ah, yes! The good Captain West. Your second husband. A rather churlish brute, wasn't he?" Arabella stopped eating and stared. "Not exactly a doddering old man." A look of feigned concern marred his features for a moment. "My dear Lady March, are you feeling well? You look a bit pale. Vapours?" He was grinning again.

Arabella forced herself to look away and resume eating. "I am certain you have a point to all of this?"

He made a nonchalant gesture, "Just your taste in men, really. Not very consistent."

"I did not exactly choose my first husband," she glared.

His grin broadened. "Yes," he murmured, speaking with the attitude of one who had been there. "Your brother, Jason, was responsible for that, I believe. Talked your mother out of her own preferences. Said that none of the other suitors was good enough for his 'Bella."

She hated being called 'Bella. Which was precisely why her brother never called her anything else. She made herself smile anyway. Her long-held suspicion that Jason had had something to do with her mother's decision confirmed. She chuckled. "He actually did me a favour. Mother had wanted me to marry Arthur Dalming, an intolerable old fossil, whom, I might add, is not only still alive, but widowed twice since with five children between the two wives. As it was, I only had to put up with Lord William for two years."

"To quote a certain lady I am enamoured of, 'How convenient'."

Arabella delicately wiped her mouth, "I would hardly use the word 'enamoured', Baronet." She carefully set the tray on the hearth and rearranged the rug on her lap.

"Ah, but you must admit, none of those men have ever satisfied you." His eyes focused tightly on her face as if trying to create a crack in her shield through which to force an entry into her mind. "There were either physically incapable or simply self-interested. For all your experience, you are a woman who has never known sexual satisfaction."

He said this as a man laying down a hole card, and when she failed to react as he desired, it seemed to frustrate and anger him. Arabella smiled contemptuously. "And you are capable of doing so?" He only stared dourly at her, trying to discover what had gone wrong. "Be serious, Baronet. Sex for a woman is not an act of pleasure, but a means of gaining something desirable; whether that be money, favour, position, love, security or power. In this, every woman is a prostitute. You, sir, simply have nothing which I desire."

He watched her thoughtfully for a long moment before he rose. "Very well," he said, as he kissed her hand, all traces of smirk gone from his face. "I bid you good night, my lady."

Tilly entered as the Baronet left and gazed over her shoulder at him as he walked down the hallway. "Tilly," Arabella barked. The girl gave a small jump and promptly closed the door, crossing to her mistress to help her to bed.

***

Arabella opened her eyes. It was past midnight, her bed empty and the room cold despite the fire. She was growing used to waking in the night and sighed as she turned on her side. Thoughts of going back to sleep vanished immediately. She sat up halfway, startled to see the Baronet standing at the foot of her bed, completely undressed, and with a pistol in his hand.

There was a short-lived burst of terror in her heart when she saw the gun. She had once told him that he would have to take her by force. Is that what he now intended? It made no sense. He stretched his hand out to her, holding the gun by the barrel, offering it. Hesitantly, she accepted.

"Do you know how to use this?" he asked. His voice was flat, all traces of earlier arrogance gone.

"Well enough not to miss your chest at this range." She held the gun tightly in her hand, not sure what game he was playing now. The gun was one of her husband's duelling pistols from downstairs.

"Go ahead," he said. "Shoot."

"Why?" she asked guardedly.

"There will be no question of your own honour," he snapped impatiently. "A naked man in a married lady's bedchamber? You were only defending your virtue."

"You really want me to shoot you?" she asked in disbelief. This felt wrong, out of character.

"You have told me I cannot win. I do not wish to live." Still, she did not fire. "I could come at you threateningly if that would make you feel more comfortable," he added with some irritation.

"Why not do it yourself?"

"I thought I would give you the pleasure of ridding yourself of me." He was impatient now, almost angry with the delay.

"How very thoughtful of you."

"So you have said. Now, will you shoot?" His fists clenched at his sides.

Without another thought, Arabella raised the gun and fired. Blood sprayed everywhere, splattered across the sheets as he was hurled backward and lay, unmoving, on the floor. The gun's report echoed through the house, bringing servants quickly banging at her door.

Arabella climbed out of the bed and stood beside the body. The ball had made a hole in his chest large enough for her to see his still heart and the white of his shattered sternum. His mocking eyes were still open and staring up at the ceiling with a shocked expression.

"My lady?!" came the muffled shout through the door, followed by a panicked pounding, when they discovered the door was locked.

She turned away from the gruesome sight at her feet and crossed to the door, the gun still in her hand. She opened it and faced the manservant there. Halfway down the hall, she could see a handful of the maids fearfully peering after him.

"My Lady? We... 'eard a gunshot," he stammered.

"Just remove the body," she snapped tiredly, opening the door wide enough for him to enter.

He just stood there. "Ma'am? Are you all right?"

"I am fine, oaf! Now, will you please come in and remove the body!"

He looked past her again, crushed his nightcap between his large hands. "Beggin' yer Ladyship's pardon. What body?"

"That...!" She turned, furious, to point out the obvious, and saw nothing where the Baronet had fallen. She stopped, staring in unbreathing shock, and slammed the door in the man's face. The pounding on the door instantly resumed.

Suddenly, the wardrobe door swung open, and the Baronet stepped out, wiping the blood from his chest with one of her silk scarves. The skin was as pale and unbroken as it had been before the gun had gone off. His familiar smirk was back as he crossed to her, holding out his fist. When she did not respond, he took up her hand and opened his fist into it. Numbly, Arabella looked down and saw the discharged bullet gleaming there, still hot.

Arabella was barely aware of being placed into her chair, and the gun being taken from her hand, barely aware that the pounding on the door had finally ceased. She looked up at the Baronet at last, his eyes gleaming with infinite patience. "What are you?" she asked, her mind suddenly very clear and sharp. "And do not tell me devil or angel, because I do not believe in heaven or hell."

"What does it matter what I am? I have nothing you desire." His entire manner had changed; still supremely confident, but more commanding and in undisputed control. He reached over and moved her braid from her heaving, half-exposed breast. "You are still a beautiful woman, Arabella," he said. "It would be a pity to see that lost."

She sat there, blinking at him, lips parted in stunned silence. He was gone, and she could not remember seeing him cross to the door.

***

When Arabella woke again, it was morning. She had not moved from the chair and blood still spotted her nightdress. So, she had not dreamed it. She got up, crossed to the wardrobe, and searched for the scarf he had used to clean himself with. It was not there. 'He took it with him,' she thought. Her mind worked furiously, the wheels spinning, going nowhere.

Tilly came in, startled to see her mistress up already. More subdued than usual, she dressed her distracted lady and began to unbraid and brush her hair.

Arabella stared at her reflection. 'You are still a beautiful woman,' he had said. Granted, she was just past her prime, but she had held on to her beauty far longer than other women her age, and even now, if the paleness and deepening hollows be ignored, there was a haunting attractiveness in her face. But in Arabella's eyes, those pale hollows could not be ignored. They served to remind her of what she was losing. Tilly stood behind her in full bloom of youth. The ten-year difference between the two women seemed magnified. 'It would be a pity to see that lost.' Suddenly, Arabella snatched up a perfume bottle and hurled it at the mirror.

Tilly drew back with a shriek, letting go of the brush still caught in Arabella's hair. The stool fell over as she stood, turning away from the dressing table in fury. As she whirled, she felt the brush dislodge and land solidly behind her. There was another squeal from the girl, but Arabella did not look back.

She stormed down the stairs, not even glancing at the mirrors along the wall. They had mentioned a correspondence, her husband and he. Thomas would have those letters somewhere.

She began in the study. Every drawer was pulled, sifted through, and overturned onto the floor. Every shelf checked, inside and behind every book. Cabinets were searched. Every possible hiding place she could think of was disembowelled, and the contents spilled out into the middle of the floor. Nothing. She moved to the parlour, leaving the fearfully whispering servants to emerge from the shadows and clean.

Pride Goeth

She looked everywhere, obsessed, no, possessed, by the need to find... anything. She even checked the piano case and its bench, scattering sheet music over the couch and chair, before thinking to search through the cushions. These, too, ended up on the floor.

Teatime. The grandfather clock tolled neatly, calling attention to itself in its dark corner. When Tilly brought in the tea tray, she found her mistress searching the clock case. She set the tray on the coffee table and left quickly. The tea grew cold waiting for her. The parlour yielded nothing, as had the study, and she moved on to the library. It, too, suffered the fate of the rooms before it. Yielding nothing, they were simply torn apart. Arabella came to a halt in the centre of the room, breast heaving, hair clinging to the sweat of her face and body. The library was a blizzard of discarded papers and books. She was breathing heavily, her body cold, almost numb, in spite of her exertion. A blackness began creeping in on her vision, smothering her. She reached frantically to grab hold of something and realized in horror that her arms had never moved. The blackness enclosed her seconds before the floor rose up to collect her crumpled body.

***

Arabella felt a warm softness all around her. This feeling being in direct contrast to the last sensations she could remember, she moved to sit up, opening her eyes to her fire-lit bedroom, and a hand on her shoulder forcing her back down. She looked up. The Baronet was at her bedside, muttering something about lying still. He gave an order to someone she could not see, who skittered off to obey. He adjusted the pillows beneath her so that she could sit up at least partly and stood there grinning.

"I did not dream...." she insisted, putting a hand instantly to her head to try and still the hammering there.

"No, you did not," he answered firmly.

She looked back up at him. "Then... what happened?"

He sat in a chair next to the bed. "The servants found you unconscious in the library shortly after seven, carried you upstairs, and Tilly dressed you for bed."

As her name was being spoken, the girl in question entered the room with a dark glass in her hand. This she passed to the Baronet carefully and promptly left. She never once dared to look at her mistress, but Arabella caught a glimpse of a bruise on the side of her face. The Baronet pulled a tiny envelope out of his coat pocket and opened it, pouring the contents into the glass and stirred it. He got up and stood over the bed. Taking Arabella's hands, he wrapped them firmly around the glass without giving her the chance or option of accepting it for herself. "Drink," he ordered. "This will ease the burning in your chest, and maybe," he added, "drown that dreadful frog in your throat."

Arabella bristled at that. She had not realized until he had mentioned, just how hoarse she was. Obediently, she drank. It was warm and spicy, a little bit bitter, but not unpleasant. It did, indeed, ease the discomfort in her chest and throat. "Why was a doctor not called?" she complained as she drank.

"Madam," he growled in exasperation, "it was all I could do to keep them from calling the constable."

"Why in the world would they need a constable?" she snapped, glaring at him over the rim of the glass.

"Because you were clearly maddened by your illness, and a danger to yourself and others. Fortunately," he grinned, "it just so happens that I am a doctor." She turned to face him, accusation on her lips. "Ask your husband," he countered.

She put the empty glass aside and studied him carefully. "What are you? Really?"

"I am very real. That is all you need to know for now." He pulled the covers up higher for her. He stood over her, looking down. "I don't think anyone has ever said this to your face, but... I doubt sincerely that you will live to see New Year's."

Pride Goeth

She ignored the prod, certain he had meant it to goad her into a depression from which he could manipulate her. But Arabella was already beyond that. She seized his arm. "How did you survive a point-blank pistol shot? You should be dead!" she hissed.

He pulled his arm free and drew something from his coat, holding it out to her. She looked down, saw a dagger in his hand. "Would you care to try again? Perhaps feeling the blade enter my heart will be more convincing...?"

She struck his hand away. "That will not be necessary," she snapped.

He put the dagger away with a self-satisfied smirk and left the room without another word.

Arabella stared at the closing door in shock. She made herself look away. It was just as well. His abrupt exit had kept her from asking questions she desperately wanted answers to, but was not yet willing to pay the price of asking. She sank back into the pillows and tried to rest, but sleep avoided her. Perhaps it was the medicine that kept her awake. It had most certainly driven all need to cough from her aching lungs. In fact, her whole body felt deliciously warm, mysteriously stronger. She curled her toes, then her legs, pulling herself up into a tight ball and stretching out again. She felt as if she had just come in from a long ride, all her muscles throbbing with a dull ache that felt so good, so alive.

She held her hands up before her face, flexed the long fingers. They did not seem so skeletal and frail now. Even the trembling was less pronounced. On impulse, she got out of bed, pulled her dressing gown on, and went downstairs. Bare feet padded softly across the stone floor to the heavy carpet of the parlour.

It was cold in the room; the fire having been doused for the night, but she barely felt it. She sat down at the piano, lifted the lid from the keys, and played for a long while: soft, quiet melodies that suited the hour. She was just barely aware of the servants peering in out of curiosity. It had been a long time since she had played, since she had been able to play. She played until her eyes ached from reading the music by candlelight. This time, when she returned to bed, she slept and did not wake again that night.

***

Arabella felt a hand on her head, smoothing her hair back from her face where her braid had come loose. She opened her eyes with a start, expecting to see the Baronet. It was only Thomas. At her reaction, he pulled back, a worried look creasing deeper into his face. He took up the hand nearest him and sat down on the edge of the bed.

"My love? How are you feeling?" he asked, thinly masking fear and sorrow behind a strained smile.

She met his eyes for a moment. From the look on his face, he expected her to have one foot already in the grave. She snatched her hand away with surprising strength and placed it over her eyes to block out the sun that glared off the window panes. "What time is it?" she muttered.

With a slightly trembling hand, he brushed his fingertips along her cheek. "Tilly said you were very ill last night."

"What time is it?" she asked in a stronger voice.

He sighed quietly. "Just after noon."

Tilly entered the room, a pair of pails balanced across her shoulders on a bar, and crossed to the small, side chamber where the bath waited.

"Make sure it is hotter than it was yesterday," Arabella growled, brushing aside both the covers and her husband as she climbed out of bed. Thomas's hands needlessly reached out to steady her and were also brushed aside. "I am not an invalid yet, Thomas. And I will not be treated as such."

He sank back down onto the bed and heaved a sigh of relief. Before entering the bath, she glanced back at him, and saw a smile on his face. He did not notice her observation, and therefore no longer tried to hide his feelings. His smile was pained but genuine. There was relief amid his sorrow, but at what? That it would soon be over? Or that she had suddenly exhibited more strength and physical control than of late? Still musing, she slipped into the side room where the tub was kept and allowed Tilly to help her out of her nightdress.

The water was steaming and Tilly made a face as Arabella eased into it, afraid she had made it too hot. But Arabella closed her eyes in pleasure and sank down 'til the water came up to her chin.

She looked up. Thomas was standing in the doorway, worshipping her. Arabella suddenly smiled, prompted by a deliciously wicked notion. She leaned forward as Tilly ran the soaped sponge over her back, moving into just the right position so that the lather ran over her shoulders, down her breast, to mingle with the water at a point just above her nipples, obscuring them neatly from view. She looked up at him without tilting her head, giving him a small smile, while her fingers unbound her braid. The heat of the water rosied her cheeks, the steam making her lips and eyelashes moist, her hands 'nervously' distracted. It was a look of coy innocence.

His face tightened, frozen in its expression of adoration. Arabella leaned back, and lifted her legs out of the water, resting her ankles neatly on the edge of the tub. Using her feet as an anchor point, she pulled herself towards them, sinking further into the water until she was totally immersed. Her hair fanned out like a living thing, gliding over her body, alternately covering and uncovering her treasures, exploring for itself.

Pushing away from the edge of the tub with her feet, she burst out of the water. Wiping the water from her eyes, she let them wander the length of her husband's body. She smiled secretly upon observing his physical response. 'Even dying and wasted,' she thought smugly, 'I can still evoke passion in a man.'

Thomas took a step into the room, his eyes dark with his desire. Arabella read his intent, and, with a small, forced cough, sharply curtailed it. His expression changed back to its usual frustrated sadness, his whole body seemed to sag under the weight of it as he turned and left the room. Arabella sent a few more, deeper coughs after him, although she had felt no real need for them.

She smiled inwardly as Tilly finished her bath and washed her hair. She was feeling better, yes, but not enough to put up with her husband's lovemaking. All traces of a smile, inward and out, were gone as she rose from the tub and allowed her body to be wrapped in a large, warm towel, and her hair carefully brushed and dried beside the fire.

Thomas was in his study when Arabella came downstairs. She quietly went into the parlour and sat before the piano. After a few minutes, she noticed Thomas's presence in the doorway behind her. Neither spoke, and Arabella let him watch. She played a soft, wistful melody she knew he would recognize. It was a memorial for lost loved ones, the song she had been playing when he had first seen her at the Wilkinson's New Year's Eve party, seven years ago in London.

She remembered when he had come up to her, leaned against the piano in the empty sitting room where she had secluded herself, and just watched her. At first she had been put off by his smitten schoolboy attitude, but when he had spoken, she saw something. It was in his eyes: genuine adoration. The kind of worshipping love that made a man easy to control, the kind that thrives on the poetic and thus is so easily blinded to the truth.

She heard Thomas's voice behind her, somewhere by the settee. "Do you miss him?" a smile in his voice as he repeated the first words he had ever spoken to her.

Thomas had known she was newly widowed, having asked a friend who she was, and had thought the melody was for her dead husband, and the child so recently miscarried. In truth, she had been thinking of someone else entirely, Merrick, her youngest brother, and not of the loss of a husband she had never loved or the child she had

Pride Goeth

never wanted. "Not at all," she answered, as she had seven years past. "Not. At. All."

He came up behind her, resting his hands on her shoulders, and bent to kiss her. He felt hot to her as he touched her, his body heat intensifying her own beyond endurance. Her mood bitterly mellowed, she turned her cheek towards him without looking at him and pressed the back of her hand against his chest as she stood. He did not resist as she moved away from him.

She crossed to her embroidery stand, idly running her fingers over the tangled threads. The pattern was beyond repair. She looked back at her husband, still watching her from the piano. A large patch of sunlight glared through the window, illuminating the place she had just occupied. She pressed her hand to her cheek. The fingers felt cold against her hot face. She had not realized she had been sitting in the sunlight. Perhaps that was why she felt so hot. Maybe an hour or so in a cooler spot would kill the feverishness she felt.

The grandfather clock in its nook began tolling four, and Megan brought the tea in. Arabella turned to watch her setting the things on the table and caught a glimpse of herself in the reflection of the clock's glass. How frail she looked. Still graceful, still beautiful, but so very frail. She looked away, seating herself on the chair across from the one her husband had moved to.

As Megan reached for the pot to pour the tea, Arabella dismissed her. Not daring to question, having heard much of her Ladyship's temper from Tilly, the girl left quickly.

Arabella poured the tea herself, aware of Thomas's eyes on her, waiting for some sign of weakening in her hands. Nothing spilled, nothing shook, and Thomas sank back to enjoy his tea quietly. Arabella picked up her book and began reading aloud in a firm, cool voice. "Tomorrow, and tomorrow, and tomorrow...."

The rest of the evening was spent reading quietly in the parlour. When dinner was ready, Thomas put out his hand to Arabella to help her up. She stopped, her hand in his. "Where... where is the Baronet? I just realized we have not seen him all evening."

Thomas pulled her to her feet. "I did not tell you? He moved out early this morning. In fact, his coachmen were loading the last of his things on the carriage when I arrived."

Her heart paused suddenly, and Arabella bristled, not knowing why. "He has moved into Heathrow already?" she asked, instantly angry with herself for the disappointed tremor in her voice.

Thomas shook his head in disbelief. "Why, I do not know. Surely our house is more comfortable than that wreck. But," he sighed, "if that is what he wants." He looked down suddenly, putting his arm around his wife as she began to slip from his grasp. He eased her back into the chair. "Are you all right?!"

"I...," she wheezed, "do not feel too much like eating dinner tonight. Go on without me."

He fell to his knees beside her. "What is wrong?!" he insisted.

"Nothing! I... just feel a little weak, that is all...." The fevered feeling was returning with a vengeance, draining from her body all strength. Her head throbbed, her chest felt constricted. She began coughing uncontrollably, gasping for breath. When she pulled her hand away, there was blood. She had felt so strong today, so healthy. Now, suddenly, it was worse than before.

Thomas lifted her up as easily as if she were a child, and carried her upstairs to bed. He undressed her himself, throwing her clothes in a corner in his haste, before yelling for Tilly and stoking the fire up. Arabella saw him standing silhouetted by the firelight, his arms up, fingers in his hair, his face frantic. Then he tore off downstairs, yelling at the top of his lungs for the girl. Arabella closed her eyes.

When she opened them again, she was lost as to how long she had slept. There were several more blankets covering her body than before, and she was wearing her nightdress. Thomas was in the room, near the fire. Though she could not see him, she could hear him breathing heavily. Probably dozing. She turned on her side, her hand

Pride Goeth

resting lightly on the pillow near her face. There was something underneath her fingers. Slowly, she lifted them, revealing a small envelope and a note. Quietly, trying to breathe very slowly and softly, she opened it.

"The medicine will ease your last days. ...I can extend them."

She slipped the note beneath the pillow with a trembling hand and finally gave vent to the cough swelling in her chest. She heard Thomas get up and cross to the bed. "Here," she rasped, holding up the envelope. "Medicine. Tilly knows how to fix it."

He took it from her hand hesitantly. "Where did you get this?" he asked.

"The Baronet gave it to me last night. I... I had stuffed it under the pillow for safekeeping."

"Why did you not tell me earlier? Instead of letting me sit here helpless...."

She cut him off with a glare, "How dare you lecture me, Thomas?! I have never seen you," she gave a stifled, half-cough, "so inconsiderate!"

"Please, 'Bella," he pleaded, relenting instantly, "lay back and rest. I am sorry. I acted without thinking. Now please!" Arabella lay back down, scowling still. "I will have Tilly get this ready for you." He paused long enough to press a kiss to her forehead before he dashed downstairs to find the maid.

She pulled the note out from under her pillow and read it again, stopping only to cough as she sat up. She leaned back against the headboard, feeling the weakness devouring her body. The progression of the illness had accelerated. '*I can extend them.*' So, he not only knew the secrets of immortality, but now he offered them to her. She reached out to the candle flickering beside the bed and placed the fragment of paper between her fingers and the flame. The note flashed into nothingness in seconds, the ashes cooling in the holder where she had dropped them.

The medicine affected her as before, easing the cough and returning some of her faded strength. But still, she had no desire for supper, and the note wore heavily on her. She sat beside the fire thinking for a long time, until Thomas finally went to bed and fell asleep watching her. The medicine indeed seemed to cure her, but as it wore off, it made her worse, speeding up the end instead of stalling it.

The note again. He had offered her immortality but had not named his price. 'Ahh, what price immortality?' she thought. *Better to reign in Hell than serve in Heaven*. She had read that once, somewhere. She leaned towards that philosophy, not that she believed in either place. 'And what of Thomas?' she thought, looking towards the bed. To spend an eternity with him would not be worth immortality.

She suppressed a yawn. She rose, put out the candles, and crawled into bed. Thomas stirred, but did not wake. She turned her back to him and settled deep under the covers, but sleep would not come. There was still too much on her mind. She closed her eyes, trying to will herself to sleep. A hand settled on her ankle. She opened her eyes to see the Baronet standing at the foot of the bed, thankfully clothed, resting his hand casually on her ankle as if he had been standing there a long time and just now reached out to wake her.

"Feeling restless?" he asked. The smile on his face gave another, more leering meaning to his words. She pulled her foot away, sat up.

"You dare to come here, with my husband asleep beside me?!" she hissed.

"Nothing to fear there."

"Shall I roll him over to make room for you?" she hissed sarcastically, gesturing to Thomas's still soundly sleeping form.

His grin broadened, eyes a-spark with the thought. "If you like." He leaned closer, making her draw back.

"What is it you want?" she snapped. "Are you trying to drive me into another fit of madness?"

He drew back, feigning innocence. "Not at all."

Pride Goeth

"You come in here, night after night, trying to seduce me. You ask me to kill you but have not the decency to stay dead. You provoke a physical collapse and then claim to be a doctor, giving me a medication which keeps me up most of the night, makes me sleep half the day, and, in spite of making me feel somewhat better, only makes me worse with each...." He stifled her ravings with a finger to her lips. She glared at him, pulled his hand away. "What the hell do you want from me?!"

"Your surrender." She opened her mouth to retort, but he cut her off with a gesture toward the window. "My carriage is waiting at the gate." He held up another packet of medicine. "Medication or cure, the choice is yours." He tossed the packet into her lap. "I will not wait for long," with that he turned and left.

Arabella lay back down, pulling the covers under her chin to shut out the cold. She lay there nearly five minutes, refusing to give in. She had wanted to know his price. He had just given it. She had given of her body before, in marriage, for the sake of wealth and prestige, but what were they when compared to immortality? What is a title compared to eternal youth and beauty? She rose, threw on her dressing gown and slippers, wrapped herself in her cloak, and went out to the gate.

The horses stood impatiently, blowing and pawing in the cold, and the driver did not acknowledge her. The Baronet opened the door from within, held it for her. She did not enter but stood there staring defiantly at him. He shook his head slowly, no trace of a smile on his face now. "You are not ready," he said.

"I am ready," she insisted.

The smile returned, but it was almost hollow. He gently lifted her chin, "On the contrary, my dear, you have entirely too much spirit left." With that, he closed the door, and the carriage drove off, leaving her staring furiously after them.

***

Sunday morning dawned cold and clear. Arabella was in a fitful mood, in spite of the medicine, and Thomas was hesitant to ask her to church.

"Would you rather stay home, my love?"

"No," she sighed, "It would be bad form not to go. After all, the boy was in our care at the time of death. I am well enough to attend the child's funeral. By the way, did they ever catch those wild dogs?"

Thomas shook his head sadly as he helped her into the carriage. "No. I have been told they killed a milkmaid while I was gone."

"I had not heard," she answered, shocked.

"I am not surprised," he mumbled.

"What do you mean by that?!" she snapped.

"Nothing, 'Bella. It is just that you have allowed no visitors for so long, they would not wish to disturb you with such horrors." The carriage lurched into motion and Thomas took her cold hand in his. For a moment, she was content to leave it there.

The funeral was long and unpleasant. The casket was closed, and the air was thick with wet sobs and whispered condolences. The church seemed to close in on her with the stale air of so many bodies. Villagers in their threadbare Sunday best crowded past the small coffin to lay branches and wreaths of holly and evergreen upon it.

Arabella ignored the impact her presence made on the congregation, muffled though it was by the reason of the gathering. Obviously, she had not been expected to attend. Well, at least this would still for a while the gossip that she was already half dead. She was aware of eyes upon her from the pews where the nobles sat but was determined not to let it bother her. On the short walk to the graveside in the churchyard, Rosa and William Worthington made a weak attempt at small talk while trying to avoid calling attention to Arabella's illness.

"How was London, Thom?" William asked in his usual boisterous voice, only slightly dampened by the occasion.

"Dull."

"Really, Thomas," Arabella injected. "It is only dull because you never do anything in London but business and your fusty old clubs. I never find London dull."

"It is the travelling alone that gets me," he explained.

"Hmmm, yes. Well, one gets used to it, I suppose." William was rewarded with his wife's elbow in his ribs. "Oop! Oh, sorry."

"Are they any closer to catching the dogs?" Rosa asked, deftly changing the subject.

"I am afraid not," Thomas sighed. "I only just heard about the village girl, the milkmaid. I suppose they will hold her services near the end of the week."

"Umm, yes," William muttered. "Still, today has turned out rather nicely. Good day for a funeral wouldn't you say?"

"There is no such thing as a good day for a funeral," Rosa hissed. "How could you say something like that in front of..."

Arabella was fed up, "Really, Rosa," she snapped. "I may surprise you all and live through this! That would put a crimp in your gossip, now, would it not?!" She grabbed Thomas's arm tighter and forced him to walk faster.

The interment went no better than the memorial, and Arabella insisted on leaving immediately afterward, not waiting to mingle and talk.

Leaving the churchyard, Arabella became strangely subdued.

"Arabella, are you all right?" His hand brushed her cheek. "Do not let that incident with Rosa upset you..."

"Thomas," she began, her voice hollow, tinged with the horror she was beginning to feel creeping up from within her. "Do not ever subject me to that again. Not even when I die."

"Arabella, do not talk like that!"

She seized his cravat and turned to look at him, "When I die, I want you to put me in the vault immediately. You can hold whatever kind of wake you want afterward, I just do not want to be there. I do not want anyone to see me like that. Not even you. Promise me, Thomas! Or so help me...!"

"I promise, love! I promise! Now, please, stop talking like this!" he begged, kissing her hands.

She relaxed, leaning back, and turned to watch the countryside as they passed.

By mid-afternoon, Arabella was feeling ill again and took herself up to bed. That evening Thomas brought up a bowl of broth and tried to force her to eat, but she could not stomach even that. Finally, he gave up and left it on the bedside table should she want it later.

She slept until nearly midnight, when her coughing woke her. She got out of bed, careful not to wake her husband, and poured herself a brandy. It did not help much. She sank into her chair and pulled a lap rug close around her.

The clock downstairs could be faintly heard chiming the hour. As the ringing faded, she began to hear another sound, outside. She looked up, listening. It sounded like harness bells. She set the empty snifter aside and went to the window. At the edge of the driveway, half obscured by the trees, she saw the Baronet's coach. She smiled to herself.

"One would think harness bells detrimental to sneaking about in the woods," she said quietly to the room behind her, expecting him to step from the shadows and answer her. No reply came. She turned and found the room empty. Miffed that he did not even have the decency to come up to her, she snapped, "Let him wait!" and went back to bed. A short time later, she heard the carriage trot off again into the night.

***

Thomas was just getting dressed as Arabella woke. "Where are you going?" she muttered.

He paused long enough to press a kiss to her forehead. "William Sr. has made arrangements for a group of men to go out and physically hunt these dogs down. The traps have yielded nothing so far."

"No one was killed last night?" she asked warily, coughing.

"Just some cattle, but enough is enough. It is nothing for you to worry about, love. I have to hurry, they are waiting for me. Oh, this came for you this morning," he laid an envelope in her hands. "Nigel sent it. Probably more medicine," he speculated as he shrugged into his coat, kissed his wife again, and left.

Hurriedly, she opened the envelope. Several packets of the medicine fell out. There was a brief letter in the Baronet's hand:

"My Dear Lady March,

These should last you a few weeks. I am sorry I cannot do more. I am returning to London. I have patients there who need me more.

Yours eternally,

Nigel Baronet Hartfordshire"

The letter fell from her hands. She became vaguely aware of Tilly collecting the small packets of medicine from her lap, but could not remember telling her to do so. Her mind was numb, unable to focus clearly. A glass was pressed into her hands, the contents warm. She stared into it without drinking. There were seventeen of these with the letter, and the days of her life were numbered with them. She was of half a mind to throw the glass across the room, but she was not quite that mad. She gulped it down quickly before her temper got the best of her.

***

Arabella sat perfectly still as Tilly did up her hair for dinner. She stared transfixed into the mirror. Her face seemed hollow and pale beyond the effects of cosmetic repair, her eyes unnaturally large. She ran her fingers along the breast line of her emerald gown, watched their reflection as they slid across the bright satin. This gown was stunning, displayed her figure well, what was left of it, the colour setting off her eyes like brilliant jewels. Those jewels, despite everything else, had not lost their lustre. They alone had not deserted her.

She rarely wore this gown because it set off her eyes above everything else, distracting from her other features. Tonight, for some inexplicable reason, she insisted upon it. She had been full of nervous energy all day, unable to sit still for very long. She had no patience for her sewing, which usually calmed her. She had spent an hour choosing a book to read, and in the end, put her choice back unopened. Thomas had not come in for tea, so she had drank alone, reading Twelfth Night aloud to an empty room. She had not touched the warm elderberry tarts, nor even finished her tea. Only now, in front of her mirror had she been able to calm herself.

Tilly finished her hair, and still, she sat there, hypnotized by her fading beauty. If Arabella had been a weaker woman, she would have wept.

A figure suddenly loomed behind her, hot hands descending on her shoulders. A kiss was placed with soft, burning lips against her throat. "God, Arabella, you are so cold," Thomas whispered. "Your skin is like ice."

"Like a corpse," she answered.

"Do not say that, Love," he moaned against her hair. "For the love of God, please do not say such things!"

She sighed, rose from the chair. "Let us go down to supper, Thomas."

"Do you feel like eating?" he asked, warmly surprised.

"Whether I do or not, we are going to sit at table like a civilized couple." She paused a moment, then, "I will at least try to eat something."

Throughout supper, Thomas complained of the long and fruitless search for the wild pack of dogs. He ate like a man half-starved, while his wife barely ate at all. She listened to him without interruption, without questioning, without really hearing him. She suddenly became very tired of sitting here listening to him. The calm she had painstakingly manufactured before the mirror had faded, replaced by an agitation she could not ease.

Pride Goeth

Finally, Thomas finished and retired to his study to enjoy his cigar. Arabella went into the parlour to try and read, but could not concentrate. She paced the house, inspecting corners she rarely went into, adjusting statuettes and baskets of dried flowers for the sake of something to do, for proof that she was still alive and moving. Her cough began creeping back, sporadically, and her fever. Her heart was beating rapidly, as if from extreme exertion. She stopped at the study door, looking in on her husband. He was asleep in his chair over some physics book. She turned away, went back into the parlour. She paused in front of the tall windows near the piano and stared out into the dark night. There was half a moon drifting in and out of the cloud cover, shedding a dim light on the cold, empty lawn.

The clock behind her tolled eleven. By tomorrow he would be gone, back to London, and the life she might have had gone with him. Might still have had if she had not been so stubborn last night. 'Mother always said your temper would cause you trouble someday. But when did you ever listen to Mother?'

The cold here by the window was bad for her, she knew. But she had been so cold all night that she no longer felt it, could no longer feel her body. It was as if she were already dead. All that remained was to lay her in that satin and rose-lined box.... Suddenly, barely aware of what she was doing, she left the window and swept through the sleeping house to the front door without bothering to get a cloak. She did not feel the coldness of the wind beating against her shoulders as she crossed the courtyard to the stable. She drew the door open, only vaguely remembering another night out here in the barn only a few days past.

Her hunter raised his head as she approached his stall, found her saddle and bridle draped over the stall door. She took up the bridle, grabbed his halter and slipped the bit between his teeth, pulling his ears through the straps and tightening it. The saddle was too heavy for her to lift, so she called for the new stable boy, asleep in Wesley's old bed in the loft. After a second shout, she heard movement upstairs and finally, a small, half-asleep figure climbed down the ladder pulling hay from his hair.

"Yes'm," he yawned, not bothering to cover his mouth. He was a few years younger than the previous boy had been, no doubt the best that could be done on such short notice.

"Can you saddle a horse?" she asked as it suddenly dawned on her that he might be here just to watch the animals.

"I think so, ma'am."

"Well then, do it," she snapped, waiting impatiently as the boy sleepily led the horse to the mounting block to saddle him.

Once the job was done, she did not wait to dismiss the boy, but mounted and rode out into the night. The moon barely lit her path as she galloped at a breakneck speed through the wood. It was biting cold out, but the wind felt warm against her fevered skin. In what seemed no time at all, the ivy-torn face of Heathrow manor loomed ahead. The fountain in front was empty and crumbling, choked with weeds. The shutters were falling, and the roof was in dire need of repair, outright missing in some places. The Baronet's carriage sat in the drive, the harnesses laid out awaiting the horses. There was at least one light on in the house despite the hour.

She dismounted on the steps and let her mount wander the lawn. It had not been her conscious intention of coming here, so why did she now find herself standing here knocking at his door? Before she could reclaim her senses completely and leave, one of his servants answered.

"Yes?"

"Lady March, to see the Baronet," she managed to cough out. He gestured for her to enter. The house was barely warmer than outside.

"Wait here, please," he said. "I will go and inform the master you are here."

She stood in the foyer, trying to collect her thoughts, to fathom what it was she had come here for and how to phrase it to her best ad-

Pride Goeth

vantage. She was clearly flustered; she had never been so out of control of things, out of control of herself. It was a sensation bordering on madness.

The servant returned. "He is waiting in the study, madam," he said and gestured down the hall. He did not wait to guide her but went up the rotting staircase without another word.

She waited a moment to get herself under control, then walked down the hall to a lighted doorway. The Baronet was seated behind a desk, his back to the fire, writing. He did not acknowledge her presence. And, after a moment of this, she spoke.

"Am I ready now, Baronet?"

He smiled without looking up. "No. As I said before, you have entirely too much spirit left."

"I thought men liked spirited women," she snapped coldly, choking a cough.

"Only for the purpose of conquering them. I sincerely thank the late Captain West for leaving that intact. You have been most entertaining, but, no, you are not yet ready."

"I am dying, Nigel!" she rasped, her nails digging into the door frame as she held herself steady.

He paused in his writing, looked up at her. "Rather," he drolled, calmly re-inked his pen, and went back to his papers.

"Damn you, Hartfordshire!" she screamed. "Damn you to hell and back again!" she choked. Her breath caught in her throat, forcing her into a violent fit of coughing which left her weak and gasping on the floor.

"Are you quite finished?" he asked calmly. She glared up at him. He was leaning back in his chair watching her with an amused smirk on his face. "Ask me again, 'Bella," he whispered. "Crawl to me on your hands and knees and ask me again."

Fury smouldered in her breast, threatening to burst her heart with the pressure. Her head throbbed and her throat burned from coughing, and her strength was all but gone. Still, she reached up and grabbed the door-jamb, using it to pull herself to her feet. He did not move to help her. Unsteady, but on her feet, she took the few yards between the door and the desk slowly, stopping in front of the grinning jackal. With every ounce of strength remaining, she slapped him.

The grin remained. He shook his head sadly. "Again, you are not ready." With that, he rose and left the room.

Arabella sank onto the couch and beat out her exhausted frustrations on the musty pillow. Her pride or her life, her choice was clear cut, but no less difficult to make. Finally, she rose from the couch and went in search of the Baronet. The rest of the house was dark, and she had no desire to risk the rotted staircase. She decided to wait in the carriage. Obviously, it was being made ready for his use this evening. Eventually, he would be there.

She went outside, noticed that the horses had been hitched, but there were no servants in sight. She opened the carriage door and stepped in. To her surprise, it was not empty. The Baronet sat across from her, watching her from the shadows.

"I will have your horse tied to the back of the carriage and take you home."

"I did not come here to be sent home," she snapped, sitting opposite him.

"Indeed," he smirked. "What have you come here for?"

"You know exactly what I have come here for! One way or another, I will not survive the night!"

"You are quite right," he said, the smile fading for an instant. He shook his head, "If you had stayed home and taken care of yourself and taken the medicines I gave you, you might have lived another week or so, but as it is...." He handed her a small dagger. "So do it then."

She hesitated, trying to read his face for some clue to his intent. Then she remembered the note she found in his satchel, To face Immortality one must first embrace Death. If this was the way of it, then

Pride Goeth

so be it. Defiantly, she drew the blade across her wrist, watched the bright line of blood spring forth.

The Baronet's hand grabbed hers, and, with a growl, pulled it close to him. Startled, she watched as he bent his mouth to her bleeding wrist and raked his tongue across the wound. Her hand released, she examined her wrist in shock. There was a thin pink mark streaked here and there with smears of blood, but no wound. "I know what you want, and you know what I want. Without it, neither of us gets anything," he growled.

Struggling with her pride, Arabella slid the knife behind her back, beneath the row of satin-covered buttons, and cut the dress open. Angrily, she pulled the fabric away from her body, slicing the corset up the front, kicking the heavy skirts to the floor, and exposing herself to his mocking eyes. "There! Do you see anything in this age-withered and disease-wasted body that you could possibly desire!?"

"It was never your body I was after. It was your mind. Your body, handsome as it is, was never more than a pleasant extra."

He came closer, laid a hand on her bare thigh. "Can you feel that? The heaviness of your own cold body, death creeping up on you even now?" She turned sideways, pressing her back against the side of the carriage, feeling the weakness overcome her. "You were right, 'Bella, you will not live long without my help. See Christmas? You won't see morning!" He bent closer, whispering. "You cannot feel your own limbs, and the numbness keeps creeping higher, working its way to your fevered brain." Suddenly he seized her ankles and pulled her towards him, laying her out flat on the seat. "You are a dying woman! Can you not feel it?" he hissed.

"Take... what you... want...." she rasped, feeling a terror seize her as she ceased to feel his hands.

"I do not take, I give," he answered shortly.

"Please, Nigel.... I..." she fought with the words, her pride trying to stop what her heart would scream if it could. The burning in her lungs was beginning to fade, her heart pounding frantically to stave off the chill entering her chest in its place. "I surrender," she whispered, turning her face away from him and closing her eyes.

"Look at me," he snapped. She obeyed. "Say it again."

"I surrender."

"Louder."

"I ... surrender..."

The darkness in the carriage was deepening quickly, her heart slowed as he pressed something cold and wet against her lips, she drank as he bade her and the darkness receded. His mouth replaced the unknown vessel as he eased his body across hers. Where his cold hands touched her, she could feel warmth stealing back into her body. The burning in her belly that she had felt in the stable that first night returned in force, and this time she yielded to it. His ardent kisses roved across her body with more expertise than any of her husbands could have dreamed, awakening sensations she never imagined existed. Seventeen years of sexual frustration culminated in one furious moment, overwhelming her in a wave of passion unlike anything she had ever felt in her life. Unbidden, she found herself wishing she had given in sooner and not insisted on her stubborn games.

The act left her weak and trembling; but, just when she thought it was over, he began again, moaning against her throat as he kissed her there, building her up to a point of tension so fierce and sweet she would have screamed for relief if she could have found the voice. This time it ended with an explosive release.

Somewhere beyond the warm, hazy after, she heard Nigel's soft, husky voice teasing her, "Tell me, little 'Belle, did you gain something desirable?"

***

Arabella woke in her own bed, rather late, feeling very warm and satisfied. Thomas had already risen, and she was alone in the room. She thought for a moment, suddenly remembering the madness of the

Pride Goeth

night before, her wild ride, and the carriage with Nigel. The Baronet, she corrected. Somehow, even in her thoughts, she could no longer call him that in contempt. Was this love?'No!' she snapped at herself. It was self-satisfaction with a business transaction gone well. Tonight he would come for her and she would be made immortal. Tonight was her last night of 'life'. And tomorrow she would be free, free of illness, free of weakness, and free of Thomas. From there she would be awakened to a new life, unable to succumb to disease, death, and age. How she knew this, she did not know. He had not told her per se. But the thoughts were there in her mind, empirical and unquestionable.

She rose, worried suddenly what the servants might say about her ride of the night before and of her coming home in a ruined dress at such a late hour. Although, she did not remember the trip home, only the passionate embrace in the carriage at Nigel's doorstep. She opened her wardrobe looking for the green dress, intending to do something with it, but it was not there.

Tilly entered the room, setting aside towels and scents for her lady's bath. "Afternoon, 'mum," she said brightly.

"Tilly," Arabella began, "where is the green dress I wore yesterday?"

"I don't know. I put it away last night."

"Who dressed me for bed?" she asked, frustrated.

The girl hugged the towels to her, suddenly afraid her mistress was beginning another fit of madness. "I did, 'mum." She hesitated, "Is her Ladyship feeling all right this mornin'? You were fevered something awful last night. Shall I make some of the Baronet's medicine for you before you bathe?"

"No. I feel quite all right this morning," she smiled. The gesture must have alarmed the girl, as she leaned away.

"It's almost one, your Ladyship," she whispered.

"Well, then, by all means, let us not keep my bath waiting."

Arabella felt better than she had in years. The limbs her illness had thinned seemed to have fleshed out overnight, restoring her to her prime. She was in a good mood and it was not long before the rest of the house became aware of it. When she came sweeping into the parlour in a dark red dress, Thomas forgot all about the groomsman standing in front of him.

She smiled facetiously at him. "Thomas, Harold is waiting."

The groomsman bobbed her a cheery good afternoon, and Thomas got back on track. "Yes, yes, of course. Take him now."

"Of course, sir," Harold said, bowed to Arabella again, and left.

She crossed to her husband's chair and placed herself in his lap. "So, what was that all about?"

"Oh! Your horse. He somehow got out last night and threw a shoe. Harold was asking to take him to the blacksmith. By the way, the mare dropped her foal this morning. A strawberry-coloured filly. Would you care to go out and see her?"

"Hmmm, maybe later."

"Are you feeling all right?" he asked, grabbing the hands that had been playing with his cravat.

She untangled herself with a smile and pulled it loose. "Well enough," she purred.

"'Bella, it is the middle of the afternoon!" he frowned, trying to look indignant, but she could feel his reaction against her thigh and would not be swayed.

"So?"

It did not take much coaxing before he carried her upstairs and laid her upon their freshly made bed. He fumbled with the fastenings of her dress, pulling off one of the buttons in his haste. His lovemaking was clumsy and inefficient, his kisses leaving her body wet and uncomfortable. He was an improvement over her first husband, to say the least. A sixty-seven-year-old man is not exactly an ideal sexual partner for a seventeen-year-old girl. And her second husband, although more skilful than Thomas, always managed to make her feel helpless, a feeling she despised above all things. However, none of the men she had known could compare to the sensations of last night.

As she allowed her thoughts to wander in that direction, tendrils of memory-invoked feeling came creeping back, weak, but enough to carry her convincingly through her present coitus. As she lay in his exhausted arms, she felt the pain of unfulfilled passion begin to sour what had begun as a pleasant mod. She rose almost immediately and crossed to the bath, slipping into the tepid water that had not yet been emptied, scrubbing herself furiously.

When she finally climbed out and wrapped a damp towel around herself, Thomas was already getting dressed. She pulled herself into a clean shift and rang for Tilly. When the girl arrived, she was quiet, saying nothing about the rumbled bed and the missing button as she helped her Ladyship into another dress. Without a word, Tilly gathered up the offending garment and carried it downstairs to mend.

Arabella sat before the mirror, admiring herself before touching up her cosmetics. Lines she had thought grossly exaggerated now seemed barely visible, even without powdering. Perhaps it had been the fevers, and the now arrested disease that had her seeing herself as more wasted than she actually was. The mind can play terrible tricks on one. True, she had lost some weight, but she was far from a bony hag. She looked closely at her eyes in the newly replaced glass, looking for flaws. Only clear brilliance glittered back. She saw a glint of defeat there, as well; a hint of surrender and submission. She dismissed it completely, for the time being. Later, maybe, she might regret what she had done, but for now, it was not defeat she saw, but a complete and total victory over Death and Age.

Thomas came up behind her, admiring her reflection even as she did. "Up to seeing that colt?"

She made herself smile at him, glancing up at his reflection with a coy expression, "I thought you said it was a filly."

He laughed. "So I did. So I did." He held out his hand for hers and guided her from the room.

The stable was much warmer than she remembered it from the night before. But then, she was now attired in a heavy, fur-lined cloak, which she had neglected last night. She eyed the stable boy as he stood holding a pail of warm mash for the new mother while she ate. He glanced up at her, nodded his head, and looked away. If he remembered saddling the hunter late last night, he gave no indication. Perhaps he thought he dreamed the whole thing. He had been more than half asleep when he came down.

The filly was hiding behind her mother, peeking from underneath her belly. She looked rather silly. Arabella laughed quietly and offered the mare a bit of dried apple. The filly crept over, sniffing with interest. Arabella offered her the empty hand and smiled as the foal began licking her palm. She stroked the soft, downy nose, running her hands down her neck and legs. "She feels sound... for a winter foal."

"Right as rain, 'mum," chimed the boy. "Horse doc sawed her this mornin'. Both of 'um's gonna be fine."

"A strawberry roan, though, Thomas?" she asked. "And long-legged. She get that from the sire?"

"Yes. He was nearly eighteen hands, if you remember."

"How can I forget finding that red monster in the south pasture? Do the Whitby's still have him?"

"I think so." He glanced down at his watch. "Hmm, they should be setting up for tea. We should get back inside."

With one last caress to the foal, she allowed Thomas to take her back to the house. After tea, she got up from her chair, moving closer to the fire, she sank gracefully onto the settee and picked up her sewing. She was fully aware that Thomas was watching her carefully, but said nothing. Perhaps he was watching for signs of fatigue, a weakening in line with her behaviour of the last four weeks. If so, he was disappointed.

Pride Goeth

After several hours, he looked up from his book and smiled across at her as she was re-threading her needle. "Now that you are feeling better, Love, perhaps you have given some thought as to what you want for Christmas?"

She let her hands fall limply into her lap, still holding the needle and thread. "I had not, really. I had been under the impression I would not live that long. But now...," she eyed him sharply, gave a knowing half smile, "Now I feel I will outlive you."

He laughed quietly, "Seriously, 'Bella. What would you like? Anything at all."

She thought a moment, then, "A new horse. A smart, grey Arabian like Rosa is always going on about. I want to ride it to church Christmas Eve to show those stuffy gossips that Arabella March will not succumb."

"I think I saw some for sale when I was in London," he mused. "I'll see."

At that point, Megan came in to announce supper. It was a small, quiet meal in the yellow dining room, intimate and close. The food was good, but somehow it did not taste quite right to Arabella. She ate more than she had of late, and the food felt heavy on her stomach; the wine, too thin. But she smiled her way through the meal, fully aware of Thomas's eyes on her. At last, she sat back, laid her napkin beside her plate, and watched as Thomas played nervously with his, looking for all the world like a schoolboy debating on stealing his first kiss.

He cleared his throat. "I... can do without my cigar for one night," he stammered, added quickly, "if you are feeling up to it?"

She only smiled her response, rose from her chair, and preceded him upstairs. He was more careful this time, unhurried. The results, however, were the same. Arabella's mind drifted midway to the body of another lover, and, consequently, sensations returned that were again left unsatisfied.

As Thomas fell asleep, Arabella rose, threw the blankets across him, and rang for her maid. Throwing on a dressing gown, she left the bedroom and waited in the hallway. The moment the girl appeared on the stairs, Arabella gave her her orders. "Fix me a bath and be quiet about it. My husband is asleep."

"Yes, my lady," she replied in a whisper and rushed off to heat the water.

No sooner was the bath filled, Arabella dismissed the girl. "That will be all for tonight, Tilly," she said, sinking deep into the water, cleansing from her body the touch of her husband's hands and lips, the inevitable fluids. She lay there soaking until the water cooled, then dried herself and slipped into a nightdress.

She stood beside the bed for a long moment watching Thomas sleep. 'I could have made poorer choices in a third husband,' she mused. She left the bedside, not feeling the least bit sleepy, and poured herself a brandy. Setting a second glass out, she sank into her chair to wait for Nigel. She watched the fire as if hypnotized, barely aware of the passing of time, the fire dying down slowly.

The curtains stirred by the window. She looked up, and saw a figure standing there, shrouded by the thin draperies and the pale moon. She smiled, drank, rolled the glass between her palms. The figure took a deep breath, smiled back. "So," he asked, amusement clear in his voice, "how was he?"

"No better than usual."

"Better than I?"

She suppressed a laugh. "No one can meet those standards." She set the empty glass aside.

"Are you ready?" he asked, never moving from his place by the window.

She rose, crossed the room to his side, looked up into his eyes, and met his gaze, all defiance gone. She merely waited patiently, like a child, innocent, eyes full of wonder and expectation. For several minutes neither one said a word. He seemed to study her, to try and

Pride Goeth

divine some rebellion or resistance in her. Then, "Will you never take what I give?" she asked softly.

His hands reached up to caress her shoulders, pulling loose the ribbon holding her gown closed. It slid to the floor, baring her body to him in the cold moonlight. He released the pins in her hair and watched the dark locks spill down to cover her breast. Slowly, he brushed them away, drawing aside the black curtain to expose those curves to his eyes and fingers.

She reached up to open his white shirt. He caught her hands tightly. She looked up into his face as he pulled her body against his chest and suddenly felt herself falling. His ankle swept her feet from beneath her and his body bore hers to the ground. His lips covered her mouth as he moved his hard body against her.

She ignored the coldness of the floor, focused only on what the body above her was making her feel. All her thirty-four years seemed to culminate in this one moment in time. Everything passed before her. None of it mattered. Three husbands, three lifetimes ago it seemed. None of them had tried to make her feel this passion, this sweet, soaring agony of anticipation. Her first had been incapable, clumsy and old. Her second had not cared, his own pleasure and her submission were all that mattered. Her third, well, he was simply unskilled, weak. Arabella was beginning to sweat, her body in flames, her breath ragged. The cold stones beneath her were baked with the heat of their bodies. She needed, and she needed now. Her hands reached for him, pressing his head harder to her breast. Her thighs tensed beneath his. A single lithe movement pulled himself between her and inside. She clung to him as a darkness began to envelop her, closing out the moonlight until all that remained was a single beam piercing through her eyes to her brain. There was a sudden shock to her system, waves both hot and cold flooded her body and drained slowly away. Pleasure and pain seared through her, simultaneous and inseparable, equally sweet. All feeling receded with the light, each following a peak of sensation too sweet for words, too intense for long endurance, until at last all she could feel were his lips against her throat. His burning kisses were her last sensation of heat; his soft, moaning words, her last awareness of sound. "To die, to sleep, 'tis all the same."

***

She was swimming in a limbo of darkness and dimmed sensation. She was aware of the bed beneath her only by the movement of another beside her on it. Hands reached out of time to touch her, hot hands that burned. A voice suddenly called out, a word that was unintelligible and repeated often with a growing sense of panic. Time flowed weirdly in this dark ocean, lights flickered on and off like candle flames, near and far. A shrill cry echoed across the water, indeterminate shapes crowded around her and were suddenly cleared away just as she was on the verge of being able to see them. Hands placed themselves on her face, her wrist. A head was lowered to her breast and raised again. A fog was suddenly pulled over her, pressing her deeper into the dark waters. A voice sounded above her, clear and sad. It was Nigel's voice. "I am sorry, Thomas," she heard. "She's dead." A single outcry of anguish followed her into the void.

***

Arabella opened her eyes and found herself surrounded in a dark haze. A ravenous hunger consumed her, burned in her veins. She put out her hands to guide her forward and found her way blocked by a wall just inches from her face. Suddenly the wall moved, and a blinding light pierced through her closed eyelids. An arm went around her waist, pulling her out of the darkness, pressed her back against something solid. Something cold and hard was placed in her hands. It was shaped like a brandy snifter and felt full. She brought it to her lips and drank as if mere liquid alone could satisfy the hunger driving her.

Strangely, the fluid seemed to strengthen her, staunching the gnawing hunger. The arm holding her up loosened. She opened her eyes, found herself in a torch-lit vault beside an elaborate, open coffin. Looking down at the empty glass in her hands, she noticed a thin red film coating it. She paused to identify the taste in her mouth. Blood.

She jumped back, throwing the glass from her, and turned into the arms of the Baronet with a small shriek. She tried to pull away, but he held onto her with a strength unlike that of ordinary men. "What have you done to me?!" she demanded, horrified by what she had just consumed, and with such relish.

He merely laughed. "I gave you what you wanted. I made you like me."

She struggled to loosen his grip. "No! This is not what I.... Let go of me!"

He pulled her closer, crushing her against him. "Oh, no. I will never let you go." He stared deep into her eyes, savouring the horror and broken defiance rising up within them as the implications began to sink in. "Body and soul, Arabella," he purred. "Now and Forever, you belong to me!"

THE END

The Saga of the Blood Eaters: The Wolves of Vinland

A.J. Jensen

In the days that followed the exile of Queen Gunnhild, daughter of Gorm the Old, wife to Eric Bloodaxe, Mother of Kings, and sorceress of some renown to her homeland in Denmark, thirty thanes of Harald Fairhair set out to send the wicked woman to dine with the Nifhiem in Hel. They rode the waves to Jutland to seek out the hall of Eric Bloodaxe. There, on the rocky shores, they were met by Bloodaxe's thanes in a mighty battle. Many strong men found their way to Valhalla that day.

When the battle was done, nine of Fairhair's thanes remained. Though all were injured in some fashion, they set out to finish their task. The Nine were Arne Truelson, Bjorn Halfbeard, Erland Alfson, Havelok the Bold, Njal of Westberg, Magnus of the Grove, Knut Risberg and his kinsman Ivar.

When the Nine entered Bloodaxe's hall, they were caught up in foul magic bonds. Struggling with all of their might, they found themselves no match for the Witch Queen Gunnhild. After much consideration of her captives, the witch decided not to send the Nine on to the next world but to instead curse them to walk in the shame of their defeat.

For the blood they spilled, the Nine were cursed by the witch in a ceremony of fire, forced to drink the boiled blood of their fallen brothers mixed with strange plants. Evil, ancient bind-runes were carved into their backs. The witch's curse left the Nine a life that would not end, no matter how grievous the wound or how many moons passed. They were cursed to find no satisfaction in drink or food except for blood.

The Nine were then nailed by their hands and feet to the hull of their own ship and set on a course towards unknown seas. The Nine suffered the pains of any man, but death would not take them.

After many days of being battered by the sea, the men discovered they could escape their bonds by ripping free of the nails. They bled greatly, so much a man should die, and yet they lived.

The Nine, now free from death, turned the ship back to their homeland and told Harald Fairhair their tale. Wishing no curse upon himself, Harald Fairhair cast them out.

For fifty years the Nine moved from clan to clan, kingdom to kingdom, land to land, selling their blades to jarls and kings alike, then quickly moving on, lest their curse be known. The Nine drank from the necks of their foes, the hunger for blood causing their eye teeth to grow until they were sated. Their curse, by design or happenstance they knew not, caused them to grow in strength and speed in battle until no man could stand before the least of them.

In the fifty-first year of their unending life, the mighty warrior Bjorn Halfbeard was surrounded in battle by twenty men. Though he killed many, he could not fight his way clear. A blade fell across Bjorn's neck and his head tumbled to the ground. The Nine discovered how they might die as they became Eight that day.

The heartbreak of losing a brother weighed greatly upon the Eight. When news of a new land across the sea reached them, they put aside their weapons, weary of fighting, and set sail for Greenland in Erland Alfson's longship called Blood Dragon. The Eight lived quietly in the hills, fields, and fjords surrounding the Eastern Settlement with their thralls and their thrall's children for thirty years before this telling begins.

This is a tale of the Eight, and I attest these words and deeds to be true. As I, Arne Truelson, along with my cursed brethren, Erland Alfson, Havelok the Bold, Njal of Westberg, Magnus of the Grove, Knut and Ivar Risberg, was there to live this tale and carry the burden of walking among the living still.

ᛒᛚᛟᛞ ᛞᚱᚨᚷᛟᚾ'ᛋ ᚠᛁᚱᛋᛏ ᛏᛖᛚᛚᛁᚾᚷ

It was rare for me to venture down the slopes to the sleepy village of Hvalsey, but the winter had finally released its grasp on the fjord. Everard, my most trusted thrall, had seen a blood-red sail in the harbor and come running to let me know. He had heard my tales of Blood Dragon's sail since he was a child. I couldn't resist the opportunity to see my old friends. The Eight had scattered over our 30 years in Greenland to avoid any trouble that might arise from our eating habits. I longed for a sense of kinship again, if only for a brief time.

Hvalsey sprang up as the farmstead of Thorkell Farserk, uncle to Erik the Red, whose own estate was up the next fjord to the north. Traders, whale hunters and fishermen were frequent visitors when the weather allowed and, on this fine day, there were three boats pulled up on the beach. Erland's ship, Blood Dragon, was easily twice the size of the other two and stood like a sea wyrm seeking a meal on the shore, its fanged head searching for blood. I was surprised the old ship still sailed, to be truthful. Seeing it brought back many memories.

The sounds of the wind and sea were colored with the sounds of village life as I approached the twenty sod houses that made up Hvalsey in those days. A smith pounded metal, a child cried, men and women went about the day's business. I could see a few men unloading baskets from Erland's ship, but none were known to me. Though I had drunk the carefully drawn blood of Eveard's daughter before I left home, the smell of so much blood around me caused my stomach to protest and I could feel my teeth. This is why we live apart.

I heard Njal's laughter long before I saw my brothers. Njal was a man of such size we often jested of his mother's relationship with the Frost Giants of lore. A good-hearted and humorous man he was, but I had seen him slay hundreds in battle. He swung his odd two-handed sword as if it were a dagger. A terrifying sight to behold.

I found my brothers in front of the longhouse used for trade, pretending to enjoy the mead they drank with a large group of men, boasting of their conquests. "Hail Erland, Hail Magnus and Hail the stinking giant!" I shouted as I drew near.

"Arne! Come wallow in my stench!" Njal pushed through the others with ease and wrapped his massive arms around me. I gagged and coughed in jest. When he released me, Erland and Magnus each embraced me in turn.

"Erland," I said, "You look well and your ship looks well and your crew looks strong. Tell me of your adventures."

Erland handed me a cup, "Dear Brother, we have been on a long voyage and only arrived this morning. We sailed west to Vinland! See the grapes here we have brought all the way from Hóp? We wintered there where the land stays green. Knut and Ivar joined us and remain there. It is a beautiful land!"

Njal threw his arms wide, "Fish, brother! Salmon so big I fear they might swallow me whole! Truly a land blessed by Odin's own hand!"

We laughed and talked for hours, each telling tales of rough seas, bountiful lands and beautiful women, though ever careful to keep our curse hidden from those around us. It was truly a blessing to be reunited with them.

When the sun dipped towards the horizon, Magnus, the smallest and brightest of the Eight, put his hand on my shoulder. "It is truly good to see you Arne, but I fear we must speak of serious things as well. Will you walk with me up the beach?"

"For certain, Brother, let us stretch our old legs." I said. We set off away from the small crowd of men and thralls. We walked in silence until we passed the last sod house in the village and made our way down to the rocky shore.

"We are far enough from prying ears, Magnus, what troubles have you?"

"You know of the Skraelings that live in Vinland?" Magnus asked.

"I have heard tales of strange beings, dark of skin like Moors who ride boats of hide, but not much more than that. A whale hunter who came through last year boasted of fighting with them, but he was drunk enough I could not discern the truth of it."

"Yes," began Magnus, "the Skraelings are few in the north of Vinland but their numbers grow as you travel south. In the wintering ports in the north, where the weather is as hard as here, a few men have learned a little of the Skraeling speech and trade coin and tools for food. I had seen none until we went to the far South, nearer to Hóp. There, the Skraelings are of a different sort. A different clan, perhaps, I know not their ways, but I have seen their savagery."

"You would know savagery, Magnus! Tell me, did you fight them?"

"I did not, but as we sailed from Hóp, we traveled from outpost to outpost and found many had been attacked by Skraelings over the winter. Men and women both were left dead in the snow. The Skraelings had bound and tortured many of them, the women had been violated before their throats were cut, the men were felled by arrows from afar or clubbed in the head. The children were just gone. The brutality of it was stunning to the thralls that have not lived as we have."

Wolves of Vinland

"This is grave news indeed." I said. "You are here to spread the word and raise enough men to end the Skraeling threat?"

"That was Erland's plan at first, but we turned back to Hóp to warn Knut and Ivar and the two dozen others there. When we arrived, we found the beach littered with the dead."

"And what of our brothers?" I asked with a heavy heart.

"Gone. We do not know, but none of the pieces on the beach seemed to be our brothers. We searched the surrounding forest and the banks of the river, but saw no sign of either men or Skraelings."

"Pieces? They were cut to pieces?"

"No, Arne, they were ripped to pieces. This was different than the other settlements. The men at Hóp were not bound and tortured as we had found in the colonies to the north, they were torn apart. I once saw a man who had been killed by bears and this reminded me of that. We found tracks, Arne, tracks of wolves the size of plates. Fenrir himself may have left these tracks, if there were at least five of him. Mortal men could not stand against such things."

"Ah, so that is why you are here. We are not mortal men."

"For certain," said Magnus, "We came for you first and then we will gather Havelok and Sten and travel back to Hóp to find our brothers together or avenge them. Will you sail into battle once more?"

I didn't hesitate for even a heartbeat. "My arm is still strong and my sword is still sharp. When do we sail?"

"Go home and make ready tonight, we sail on the morning tide. Bring no more than three thralls, strong men if you have them, we'll feast on Skraelings until we find our brothers." Magnus smiled and I could see his eye teeth grown long and sharp in the fading light reflecting off the sea.

A.J. Jensen

The wind was crisp and the sky was clear as we rowed off the beach, freed by the tide. I took this as a good omen for our short journey north to find Havelok and Sten. Six men of Hvalsey with business to the north joined us and we were able to man all thirty oars, making good speed to where the fjord opens and the sail could fill. Erland called for the sail as we cleared the wind-blocking mountains. The dark red sail, embroidered in black, filled my heart with joy as it filled with wind.

"Your thralls, Arne, do they know how to fight?" Njal asked as he rowed next to me.

"They know how to farm and they know how to fish, Brother, but they have never held swords as far as I know. The largest one there," I nodded to my thralls rowing in front of us, "is called Aleyd. He has a keen mind and has swung his axe at wood since he was old enough to lift it. The other two, Jaro and Frix are brothers and would surely defend each other if needed. I chose them because they are strong enough to feed on and still lend a hand at the oars."

Njal looked back to Magnus, "What say you, Magnus? Will the six of us be enough to take on the Skraelings and whatever beasts they are in league with?"

Magnus shook his head as he rowed. "I do not know, Brother. The tracks at Hóp were a mess. I wish Arne had been there with his skill at reading signs, but I am certain there are at least five of the beasts and many Skraelings. The Skraelings were able to defeat many men at other outposts, but they were not warriors and they certainly were not Blood Eaters. The beasts are the unknown."

Njal broke the somber mood with his bellowing laugh, "I have trained many dogs and was killing wolves as a child. We have nothing to fear except the anger of the gods if these are indeed Fenrir's children!"

"I hope you are right, Brother. I hope you are right." I said.

Wolves of Vinland

It was swift travel with the sail and oars, out of the fjord and up the next. Havelok and Sten shared an estate with a well-built longhouse above a small cove, halfway up the fjord to Brattahlid. We reached the shore below the estate by mid-day. Standing atop the rounded mound of the longhouse, surrounded by the smaller mounds of thrall houses and sheep, stood the tall figure of Havelok.

Havelok's bellow echoed across the fjord, "Hail Sten! Come see what filth Njord has cast upon our shore!" Then he ran down the side of the longhouse towards us.

Erland, having secured the sail as we approached, leaped to the prow and stood next to the magnificently carved dragon's head and leaned out, clutching one of its fangs in his hand and raised the other in greeting, "Hail, Havelok! We came for your women, but see now that none would have you!"

As the keel touched the beach, Erland leaped off and ran up the bank, meeting Havelok with an embrace.

Sten emerged from behind the longhouse, soot stained from working the forge, and waved to us as we disembarked.

When we all gathered together, we sent our thralls off to enjoy a meal while I and my brothers sat around a cold fire and shared our dark news with Sten and Havelock. Our brothers agreed to join us as swiftly as I had and set about gathering supplies and choosing strong thralls to accompany us on the voyage. Erland called for an inspection of the ship before we undertook the crossing to Vinland and I joined him in the task.

"I have not made this crossing, Erland, how long will we sail?" I asked as we inspected the rigging.

"The spring winds will push us north as we cross the sea and, Njord willing, we should see Helleland in a week, then we travel south past Markland to Vinland. Hóp is beyond the island by a half day. If we do not stop long and the wind doesn't fail and the thralls stay strong, a little over two weeks should see us to Hóp."

"We'll want new rope on this side." I said. "I have heard Helleland and Markland are much like here, is that so?"

Erland looked out to the sparse grassland and rocky beach. "Helleland is more bleak. Just rocks and waves. There are harbors to shelter from bad storms but many will eat a ship as soon as keep it safe. No one stops there unless they must. Markland is more like here when we see it, but has more trees the further south we sail."

"Speaking of ships, how is it that Blood Dragon still sails after all these years?" I asked.

Erland ran his hand along the gunwale like he was caressing a lover. "Blood Dragon is as immortal as us, yes?" He smiled. "In truth, she was out of the water for twenty years and Knut, Ivar, and I have replaced most of her. I went clear to Iceland to find the wood to do it. That was before anyone knew Vinland was there."

"I forgot Knut and Ivar are from a family of shipbuilders. I find myself forgetting much of life before the Witch."

"It has been a long time, Brother. We went to Vinland after seeing lumber others brought back. Knut has an idea to build a proper shipyard in Vinland. Some of the outposts have people that can help fix a ship, but none that could build one completely. I think they have grown bored with only thralls, sheep and Blood Dragon to care for."

I smiled up at Erland from the last of the rigging that needed work, "In truth, I'm bored of sheep as well. We have been here in Greenland a long time and a new voyage to a new land with a worthy enemy has me hungry, Brother. When we find Knut and Ivar, I think I may join them in Vinland."

"I am thinking much the same. I know Magnus would like to see if his bow can shoot further than the Skraelings' and Njal is a wanderer at heart. The Eight together again, in a whole new land. What a thing that would be."

"We are done here," I nodded to the rigging, "I am going to go help gather the rest of the supplies so we can leave at first light. No need to wait for tide here. Let's put Greenland to our backs and go help Knut and Ivar build a new world."

A strong northwesterly wind set Blood Dragon to flight across the waves. On the sixth day of the voyage, Helleland rose from the sea like a stone wall and we turned south. We sighted many whales and seals in the water, but the shore was barren. Two more days found us sailing past Markland, which did indeed look very much like our home in Greenland with grassy hills and inlets, though not as steep walled as the fjords. I spotted a herd of animals that looked like deer but were not.

On the ninth day of our voyage, the grassland slowly turned to sparse woods and, by the tenth, the trees blocked any sight of the ground. Here we stopped at an outpost Erland knew of, up an inlet marked with a rocky island that looked like a sea bird trailed by six chicks. We were well-met at the landing by the outpost's leader, a woodsman and carpenter called Torben, and four men who led us down a trail to a wide meadow where seven stout wood buildings stood in a circle. Six men and five women lived here and provided safe harbor, some metal work, and carpentry to passing ships.

We shared some mead with the people of the outpost and they shared their hearth and fresh meat with us. We sat together and discussed the slaughter of the outposts in Vinland. "Tell me, Torben," Erland asked, "Have you had problems with Skraelings here in Markland as well?"

"We are not friends," began Torben, "but we are not enemies either. When we first built this outpost, there was some misunderstanding about our intentions and theirs, but we trade now. They have a small village where a river meets the inlet not far from here. My wife, Dalla, has a gift for words and can speak some of the Skraeling tongue."

Dalla was a tall, strong woman who ran the outpost as much or more than Torben, as is the way with such places. "What would you know, Lord Erland?" She asked from where she sat across the fire.

"Have the Skraelings here sought to fight?" asked Erland

"No. Their village is little more than a few huts. When we first arrived four summers ago, they were just building their own outpost, so I don't think they see this as their land."

"Would you take us to them so we might learn something more of their ways before we must confront the Skraelings in Vinland?" Magnus asked.

"I think the Skraelings may misunderstand if your ship pulls up on their beach. Tomorrow is the day they usually come with meat to trade so, if you stay for tonight, the trading party should be here early in the morning."

"It would at least give us a better idea of what we may face" Njal offered.

Erland looked around the fire, and each Blood Eater nodded in agreement. "We will accept your hospitality for the night then. Our men could use a night ashore to rest for the next part of our journey."

Torben rose from the log he sat on, "You are welcome, but I must ask that you do not put us in danger with our local Skraelings. They are not many but they are skilled hunters and I only have thirteen here to fight once you sail away. If that is understood, you may make camp here."

"We will not start a fight." Erland assured him.

ᚢᛘᚢ

We made camp close to Blood Dragon. We Blood Eaters were careful to feed off our thralls where the people of the outpost could not see. The thralls shared food and drink with Torben's people and all retired to our make-shift beds early, weary from our travels and knowing more lay before us.

Wolves of Vinland

Erland, Magnus, and I rose with the sun and met Torben and Dalla just as the Skraeling traders broke through the trees on the far side of the meadow, carrying large skin bags laden with meat. We were unarmed and not wearing armor, so as not to frighten them. Njal, Sten and Havelok stayed in the trees behind us, ready for battle should it prove needed.

The Skraelings were all male and dressed in skins, cleverly cut and tied with rope. Their skin was much darker than ours and their bodies were small of stature and lean. I was reminded of a man I once met from the far Caliphates whose skin and body was about the same. They did not strike me as formidable warriors, though two of the group carried bows and all had knives and odd hand axes about them. When they spoke with Dalla, their words were like nothing I had heard in all my years fighting as a sell-sword from Norway to the land of the Byzantines, the Visigoths to the Vulgas and everywhere between.

With their strange words and many gestures, they struck a trade with Dalla and they exchanged their goods. Dalla pulled aside the leader of the Skraelings and waved us to join them. "This is Innick," she told us, "he leads the clan here. What would you know from him?"

Erland and I both looked to Magnus, as he is a man of uncommon intellect. "We would like to know all we can of the Skraelings of Vinland. Do you have the words for this?"

Dalla raised an eyebrow, "I will try, but we may need to find simpler questions." She turned to Innick and found a few words to say and pointed to the south. Innick was clearly wary of us, but he spoke his words back with more pointing.

Dalla looked to Magnus, "Innick knows there are people to the south, but he is calling them unworthy or he might mean they are bad. He is saying the same word for when they find a trade offer unsatisfactory."

"They are not the same Skraelings?" Magnus asked.

Dalla spoke to Innick again before answering. "No, they are a different clan, I think. Innick's clan came here from the North. When we first met, they had seal skins instead of deer skins as they do now."

Erland asked, "Does he know anything about wolves?"

"I don't know their word for wolves, but he must know of them. There are wolves in the woods here. Not the giants of which you spoke, just wolves like you would see in the old lands."

Magnus walked to where the women were unloading the bags of meat the Skraelings had brought and returned with an empty bag and a half-burned stick from the fire. "Arne, can you draw the tracks of a wolf?" He spread the skin bag on the ground and checked that the charcoal would leave a mark on it.

"I think so," I replied and took up the stick. I drew a wolf track as best I could and looked to Innick and pointed to it. "Wolf?"

Innick nodded "Mahigan."

"Dalla," Magnus said, "please ask our friend if he knows anything about very large wolves."

She nodded and pointed to my drawing and spoke to Innick more but kept shaking her head to his responses.

"He's telling me that some wolves are small and some are very large and wants to know if you want wolf skins in trade. I don't think he understands."

"Innick," I said, still kneeling over the skin. I pointed to the track I had drawn and said "Mahigan." I drew a track five times larger, "not mahigan." He looked at me then to Dalla and she laughed at his words.

"He wants to know if your head is sick. This is too big."

Erland chuckled, "Arne, your secret is out."

Not one to give up, I turned the bag over and drew the outline of a wolf then a man standing next to it and then another wolf, as tall as the man. "Mahigan," I said while pointing to the normal wolf. "Man," I said while pointing at the picture and then to myself. "Not mahigan."

I pointed to the big wolf and then drew a line from the big wolf to the man and struck out the drawing of the man.

Innick looked thoughtful for a moment and then his eyes went wide. "Uitiko." He turned to Dalla and spoke rapidly with many gestures until he saw her confusion and slowed his tongue.

"I think he is saying these Uitiko are bad... ghosts, maybe?" She said a few more words to Innick. "It doesn't make sense. He is saying they make people dead and that they are wolves and they are people. Does that mean anything to you?" She asked us.

We looked to each other but none could make sense of it. Magnus tried a different approach. "Innick, Uitiko." and pointed to the south.

Innick looked where Magnus pointed and started to pull his bow from his shoulder but Dalla stopped him with a calming gesture before speaking some more with him. He nodded understanding, let go of his weapon, and they exchanged more words.

"I explained the Uitiko are many days walk to the south and over the water. He knows of them, but he has never seen one. He keeps repeating that they are bad and they do bad things and make others do bad things. I don't think he knows anything more."

"We already know where they are and that they are dangerous. I fear we have learned nothing and delayed our journey," said Erland.

"We have a name for them at least," Magnus said as we watched Innick turn and speak to his companions. After a moment, Innick returned and handed each Erland, Magnus, and I small leather pouches on string they had pulled from their necks.

"He says this is magic that should keep you safe from the Uitiko, though he doesn't know for sure."

Magnus slowly pulled a dagger he had concealed at his back and handed it to Innick in turn. "Thank you, Innick." Erland and I did the same for the other two that had gifted us their pouches. Dalla spoke our words of gratitude and the Skraeling left the way they had come.

We pushed Blood Dragon out into the water not long after, rowed out of the inlet, and raised the sail. I looked in my new leather pouch to find a bundle of three different leaves that smelled of warm spices. I tied the pouch around my neck as the Skraelings did, then stood to watch the forests of Markland pass.

ᛒᛚᚨᛗᛁᛟ ᛁᛟᛏᛗ ᚨᛉᛋᛏ ᛦ ᚠᛉᛉᛉ ᛗᛏᛞᚠ ᛒᛉᛗᛚᛉᛁ

Two days past the outpost, the mountains of Markland fell into the water and Vinland rose out of the sea in front of us. The winds pushed us hard and a storm chased Blood Dragon across the water. Seeing we would not outrun the storm, Erland called for us to aim for Vinland and add our strength on the oars to the sail. A cold rain pounded into our backs by the time the keel hit sand. Here at the northern tip of Vinland was one of the outposts that had been attacked by Skraelings. Erland and his crew had burned the bodies after discovering the foul deed a moon before. The buildings still stood, so we made use of them.

We sent the thralls to the smaller buildings to take shelter and claimed the largest building, a carpenter's workshop, for ourselves. The smell of freshly cut wood still lingered in the air and we found plenty to build a fire to dry ourselves and our gear. We each slipped out to check that our thralls had found dry shelter and feed, but soon gathered back around the fire.

"It's been a long time since we all sat around a fire together," Havelok said.

"Not all of us." Erland stared into the flames. "Knut and Ivar should be here."

"Brother," Njal placed a hand on Erland's shoulder, "We will find them. I am certain they are sitting around a fire, fat on Skraeling and wolf blood, laughing at us for missing the battle."

Sten laughed, "Knut has always been fat. You would think a hundred years of eating nothing but blood would slim a man." He rose from the fire and walked to the doorway. "Rain will stop soon, I think. How much further until we reach Hóp?"

Erland finally looked up from his contemplation, "If the weather turns by morning, we will reach Hóp by mid-day tomorrow. It's on the mainland, not here on the island."

"Do we have a plan for when we reach Hóp?" I asked.

Sten laughed from the doorway. "Have we ever had a plan more complicated than kill the enemy until they are dead?"

Havelok stood and stretched his back, "It will be dark in an hour. I'm going to go make sure Blood Dragon isn't going to float off with the tide. Arne, lend a hand?"

"For certain, I haven't tried drowning in the rain yet as a test of the curse." I chuckled.

"I think the rain has stopped." Sten said, turning to look out. "In fact, I think some of the thralls are already on the... Oh. That hurts." Sten fell backwards, revealing an arrow shaft sticking out of his chest, right through his immortal heart.

We all stared in surprise for what seemed an eternity before Erland screamed, "Arm yourselves! Skraelings!" We all scrambled to our weapons. Magnus had his bow strung and arrow to cheek with preternatural speed. He loosed two arrows into the night and was rewarded with a thump and a scream. Few mortal men could draw his bow and I had witnessed him pass arrows clean through a man's body many times.

Erland leaned out from the door. "I count fifteen coming up from the beach. "Arne, with me. We will protect the thralls. Magnus, get some high ground. The rest go meet the Skraelings. Go now!" And he ran left to where the outpost's other buildings stood.

Havelok snapped the arrow in Sten's chest with the broad side of his war axe as he passed. "Come, Sten, you can nap when we're done with the day's chores."

Njal reached down and effortlessly lifted Sten to his feet. "So lazy. Let's go have a drink, shall we?" Njal stepped out of the shop's doorway and took an arrow in the shoulder. He stopped, ripped the arrow out and dropped it. He lifted his enormous two-handed sword and let loose a war cry before charging off in the direction the arrow had come from. I was surprised the Skraelings did not flee right then, but they kept coming, arrows landing around us. I rushed out and followed Erland.

I rounded the carpenter's shop in time to see Erland hit the first door so hard it exploded inward, startling the thralls that had been tending their own fire and eating. "We are under attack, arm yourselves and gather with the others." He didn't wait for them to comply before speeding off to the other buildings.

I stopped where the path between the carpenter's shop and the buildings further back from the beach narrowed. I stood in the path, facing the direction the Skraelings would come and waited. I saw Magnus reach the top of the building we had just left and launch arrows into the dying light.

Three Skraelings stood where the grass met the sand, shooting arrow after arrow at Havelok and Njal bearing down on them. Havelok went towards the Skraeling on the left, so Njal went right and Magnus put an arrow through the center Skraeling's head. The two remaining archers, either courageous or stupid, kept firing arrows as fast as they could. Havelok reached his target first, knocking the bow aside with his first swing of his axe and burying the axe in the Skraeling's guts with the second.

Njal didn't bother with two swings as he reached the last archer, he simply swung his sword in a wide arc, cleaving the Skraeling in two without even slowing as he passed. He hit the wide beach and screamed again, drawing the attention of two more. They charged at him at the same time, swinging heavy-ended clubs. Njal speared one through the chest and took the second's club to the head.

The second Skraeling swung to hit him again and Njal let go of his sword and snatched the club away. He threw a punch at Njal, despite being half the man's size, while screaming into his face. Njal flipped the Skraeling's own club in his hand and struck him in the temple, caving his skull in and dropping him dead in the sand. He hit him twice more to be certain anyway.

Havelok met three more before the remaining Skraeling got off the beach. He lowered his stance as they came at him and swung three times, leaving three more dead. The remaining seven split between Njal and Havelok and raced across the grass towards the buildings.

The fastest Skraeling was met by Sten, standing in the open, holding two short swords. The Skraeling raised his hand axe and dove at Sten, who simply stepped to the side and shoved a blade into the Skraeling as he sailed past. He spun away from the next and removed a leg from the third. Magnus took two more in short order, arrows hitting so hard the Skraeling were hurled backwards by the force.

The last three managed to get close enough to the shop that Magnus had no angle to hit them and rounded the building, still sprinting. I raised my sword and took the first in the belly, but the second tackled me before I could turn to face him. I used my strength to shove him off and then drove my sword through his chest, pinning him to the ground. I turned to look for the last Skraeling just in time to see Magnus leap from the roof of the shop, land behind the Skraeling, grab his head and snap his neck.

Magnus looked at the three dead Skraeling at our feet. "That was," he paused, "unusual."

I nodded at him, "I have never faced anyone so fearless in the face of being so over-matched. I expected Njal's bellowing to drive them back to their boats with their tails between their legs."

Sten joined us, "They didn't even hesitate as their friends died around them. They look like men, but they don't act like men."

"Hail Arne!" Njal called as he and Havelok approached. "Everyone okay? Have you ever seen such a...Agh!"

The Skraeling who Sten had shortened on one side lunged out with a blade and sank it into Njal's calf as he walked past. Havelok swung his axe and took the Skraeling's head from his shoulders. "Bastard!" Njal yelled as he pulled the stone dagger out. He picked up the head by its long black hair and hurled it into the night.

"That, Brother," I said, "Is something I have never seen before."

We called to Erland that the battle was done and then started gathering the bodies to burn, helped by the thralls carrying torches to ward off the darkness. Erland and Sten, having pulled the rest of the arrow out of his chest, walked out into the night to make sure no more Skraeling lurked.

Njal was the first to try the blood of a Skraeling, "It's gone cold already and it tastes of something strange."

"Strange how?" I asked.

"I don't know. Maybe they were very drunk? That would explain why they showed no fear. Try it and tell me what you think."

I reached down and took some blood onto my fingers and tasted it. "I see what you mean. I don't know what it is. Maybe Skraeling's just taste like that?"

We left the mystery for another day. Erland and Sten returned an hour later, having found no sign of more enemies. We decided to post a guard in case more arrived and the rest of us retired to our bedrolls to sleep what was left of the night.

Morning came with a breath of frost across the land. Once all were stirred from slumber and the thralls had eaten, we returned to the beach. As the thralls made Blood Dragon ready to sail, we inspected the dead Skraelings closer in the daylight. They all bore red painted markings on their faces in patterns of dots and lines we could not decipher any meaning from. Their clothing was well tanned leather and was several layers thick on their chests. Magnus believed it was meant to stop arrows and confirmed the idea with one of their two bows that were still usable, though it was not effective at close range. We gathered their weapons and took them with us as we did not have enough swords to arm all of the thralls.

The Skraeling's boats were long and narrow, much like the faering boats favored by fishermen for their speed and maneuverability, but made from sealed skins, stretched over wooden frames. The boats were light enough that two men could easily lift them and each looked able to seat six Skraelings. We carried the boats and set them atop the pile of bodies, before setting them on fire.

I watched the black smoke blowing away as we backed Blood Dragon into the sea and pointed her to the West. The wind was against us, so we sailed north and south to gain what we could and all rowed. Markland was on the horizon to the north and Vinland was soon left behind as we crossed a large bay towards the mainland and the river that marked the location of Hóp.

We passed an island before half-way and Erland pointed to where another outpost had been, before the Skraelings had attacked it, killing all. "If we sailed north and west from the island," Erland explained, "we would find a mighty river that cuts deep into the land. Knut, Ivar, and I rowed up it a full day before turning back to Hóp and never had trouble with depth. If we can find them and defeat these Skraelings and their wolves, I would like to see how far it goes."

"Uitiko," I reminded Erland. "The Skraelings at the outpost seemed certain they were not just very large wolves."

"Bha," Erland spat over the side, "wolves or Uitiko, it doesn't matter. We will find them and kill them and be reunited with our brothers."

We sailed on, pushing further south and west. With three hours of daylight left, we reached land. Erland gave the order to drop the sail and half of our number rowed while the other half watched the shore for any sigh of danger. I saw eagles and deer and trees bigger than any I had seen since we left the old lands, but no sign of Skraelings. "I see why Knut and Ivar decided to build ships here," I said to Njal at my side.

"Deeper in the forest, the trees are even larger. Many would take me a year to cut through with an axe."

"The beach there ahead," I pointed, "is that where we stop?"

"Yes, you should be able to see the hall we started to build over the winter, but we left before it was finished."

"Where? I don't see even the beginnings of anything."

"Burned, I think. See the scorched ground atop the rise? There were six houses and a workshop there when we left to find you. The Skraelings must have burned everything."

Erland turned from where he stood at the keel. "When we reach the shore, we Blood Eaters will get out and search the area. The rest of you will head out there and wait for our signal," he pointed to the center of the inlet. He then looked to his his most trusted thrall, "Drustan will take command of Blood Dragon. If we wave you off, head back to the mouth of the inlet and make camp there where the trees are thin on the south bank. Stay close to the ship and set guards."

Drustan secured his oar and stepped up beside Erland. "I will serve as always, Lord Erland."

When the keel approached the rock strewn beach, Erland called for a stop and we jumped from Blood Dragon into the shallows and made our way ashore. The six of us watched the tree line for moment and, when nothing revealed itself, we separated and began to survey the area for any signs. A month of weather had cleared any footprints from the beach, but the charred bone remnants of the people who died here were scattered about and small animal prints were everywhere.

My brothers circled the perimeter of the clearing where Hóp had stood, so I walked straight towards the top of the rise, watching the ground closely. I found the stone foundations, scorched by flames, but little else of note. I stood atop the largest rock I could find and slowly turned in a circle, scanning the surrounding tree-covered hills and mountains further inland. I had not seen so many trees in decades and my sorrow over my missing brothers warred with my awe of the land around me.

I turned back towards the sea, seeing Blood Dragon holding position out of bow range from the shore. Erland's thrall, Drustan, stood tall, waving his arms. When he saw that I was looking at him, he pointed off to my left and then held up one finger. I dropped from my perch and sped down the gentle slope towards where Drustan had pointed. Njal was near the tree line in front of me, so I angled towards him. When he saw me coming, gave me a questioning look and then turned back towards the trees and pulled his sword from the sheath on his back.

I reached Njal and whispered to him, "Drustan saw something in the trees here from the ship."

"I see nothing, Arne."

Spotting a game trail, I put my finger to my lips for silence and pulled my own sword. I crept down the trail as quietly as I could. Njal took up position behind me, but stayed in the open, much too large to move as quietly as I through the brush. Not twenty paces in, I heard movement in front of me and took cover behind a large tree. The noise resolved into footsteps as they got closer.

I waited until the steps were next to the tree before launching myself around it, swinging my sword hard at my target. The man ducked the swing with incredible speed and dove into me as my sword sunk into the tree. I tried to roll as I fell backwards, but his strength prevented it. My back hit the ground, driving the air from my lungs.

"Arne?"

Njal came crashing through the brush behind me but came to a skidding halt before he crashed into us. "Ivar?"

Ivar stood up from his position on top of me and held out his hand to help me up. I took it and let him pull me to my feet and then pull me into a fierce embrace. After a long moment I said, "Ivar, how many times are you going to crush me today?"

He finally released me and took a step back. "How are you here?"

I looked at his ragged clothes and dirt streaked face. Leaves and twigs stuck out of his hair and beard. "I came to tell you that you need a bath."

Njal came around me and wrapped his massive arms around Ivar. "We found you, Brother! When we couldn't find you after the attack, we went to Greenland to fetch Arne, Sten and Havelok to avenge your death."

Ivar looked down at himself. "I appear to not be dead. Knut still lives as well. The Skraelings and their monsters are on the other side of the mountain there and have him bound."

I put my hand on Ivar's shoulder. "Brother, we are here now. Let's gather the others and figure out a plan."

ᛒᛚᛟᛟᛞ ᛞᚱᛖᛗ ᚦᛖ ᛗᛁᛋᛋᛁᚾᚷ ᛘᛖᚾ ᚨᚱᛖ ᚠᛟᚢᚾᛞ

We left the woods and called out to the others to join us. After warm greetings all around, Erland waved the thralls to bring Blood Dragon to the beach so that Ivar might feed and regain his strength. When Ivar was finally sated after a month without blood, he told of the last month's events.

"It started two days after Blood Dragon sailed," Ivar began. "A group of men went into the woods to cut trees for the construction of the hall that morning and never returned. Knut and I set off just before dark to look for them while the others set a large fire so the tree cutters might see it if they were lost. We went towards the mountain just there," Ivar pointed to a jagged peak to the west.

"There is a grove of trees the right size for the hall an hour's walk that way. We found the missing men's tracks not far into the woods and followed them up the slope all the way to the grove. When we arrived, we found a few recently cut trees, some of their gear, and a few axes scattered around, but no sign of the men. It was fully dark by then and we had just lit a torch when the wind shifted. We both scented blood further up the slope."

"You scented the men?" asked Magnus.

"Not as we smell the blood in men, spilled blood. Knowing then that something bad had happened, we set off towards the smell. We spotted a few Skraeling arrows stuck in trees and realized the men had been attacked. We snuffed out the torch quickly, in case the Skraeling were still near, and separated a dozen paces before moving on, drawing our blades."

Erland turned to Havelok, Sten and I, "We have seen signs of Skraelings nearby but had no contact with them. The men would not have thought they were in any danger."

Ivar nodded before continuing, "When we found them, it was clear they had been ambushed. A few had been shot with arrows, but all were beaten and hacked with axes. Three were struck hard enough to crush their skulls. Only one man had used his axe to fight back, as near as we could tell. It was not the remnants of a battle, they were slaughtered. Nine men had left that morning and all nine found their end there.

"The bodies were cold, so we put little effort into searching the area for Skraelings before turning back to share the grim news with the other men. We decided to follow the stream back to the outpost, so that we could wash the blood from our hands."

"There is a stream here?" I asked.

"Just past the tree line a few hundred paces there, Arne." Erland said. "It flows from the mountain, through a narrow chasm."

Ivar continued. "We followed the stream down, discussing how we might face the Skraelings. We could just make out the signal fire here when we first heard the screaming from below. When we realized the outpost was under attack, we began running to help. Knut fell behind as we ran and that was the last I saw of him that night. I was less than a hundred paces from the beach when a massive creature leapt over the stream and slammed into me from the side. It was a wolf, but one the size of a horse. I got to my feet and spun to face the monster. I expected it to attack right away, but it paced side by side, taking my measure. I stood with sword ready and waited for it to attack, but it just stared at me, saliva dripping from its fangs. What it didn't know is that I have fangs as well.

"I bared my fangs at the beast, ready to battle fang to fang if I had to. I heard a deep howl come from the outpost and realized the beast was keeping me from helping the men and there was more than one. I took my eyes off the beast to look upstream for Knut and the monster leapt at me. I turned back in time to run my blade deep into its shoulder, but it grabbed my leg in its jaws. It pulled my leg out from under me, lifted me up in the air, and shook me from side to side, ripping the muscle. I tore my sword out of its shoulder and it flung me away. That is the last I remember of the night. I woke up in daylight at the bottom of the stream's chasm. My right leg was a mangled mess and my hair was crusted in my own dried blood.

"Unable to walk, I crawled through the stream to where it enters the river and found a branch there to help me stand. Making my way here to the beach, I found blood everywhere and a still burning pile of bodies."

"Oh, dear Brother." Njal said quietly. "We piled the bodies we found here. We searched for you and Knut. We sent them on to Valhalla just before we sailed away to get help. I'm so sorry, brother."

Ivar looked confused. "You came back?"

Erland answered, "We came to warn you of Skraeling attacks at the other outposts. All three in Vinland, and one, just across in Markland, were attacked. They killed everyone. We saw no signs of the Uitiko there, only here we saw their tracks."

"Uitiko? Is that what the wolf monsters are called?"

I answered, "We met a Skraeling clan leader in Markland who gave us the name for them. Though not much more."

"Four days," said Magnus. "You must have been unconscious for four days in the stream. I, too, am truly sorry. We must have been just over the horizon when you came back."

"How could you know?" Ivar said with a shrug. "I have lived and I have learned much. Finding myself alone, I waited, knowing you would return eventually. Three days after, the Skraelings returned without the wolves, the Uitiko?" he looked to me and I nodded. "My leg was still weak and they were many. I am shamed to say I hid in the woods and watched them burn everything we had built here."

Magnus placed his hand on Ivar's shoulder. "There is no shame in not fighting a battle you can't win, brother."

Ivar didn't look convinced. "A week after, my leg was well enough to travel and my need for vengeance strong enough to kill all of them. I followed the Skraeling's trail up the mountain and over. They have a village on the west slope. I hid in the woods and watched for the rest of the day, planning my attack. It soon became obvious there were just too many to attack head on, so I kept watching.

"When night fell, the males gathered around a fire in the center of the village and sang and danced. When they finished, the wolves emerged from the huts closest to the fire. There were five of them, one limping where I stabbed it. They all sang again and danced some more until a group of female Skraeling came bearing jugs that were passed around. After they all drank in turn, the ceremony was over.

"The next morning, I watched a group of four Skraeling with bows leave the village and start walking towards where I hid. I let them pass, then followed them up the mountain. When they were far enough from the village that nobody would hear them scream, I killed them. I was weak from healing without blood, but they were still no match for me up close. I drank from one, but his blood made me ill.

"Five Skraeling set out the next day, I presume to find the four I killed, and I killed them as well. I tasted one and it was the same as the first. We could live off the Skraeling, I think, but it would not be pleasant."

"Did you see the Uitiko again?" I asked.

"I did not see them until another week had passed. I had killed twenty Skraeling by then and knew when the wolves appeared they would hunt me. I made my way back here, well ahead of them, and swam to the other side of the river. I stayed in a cave there until yesterday. I came back to kill more Skraeling.

"Last night, they did their ceremony again and I saw Knut. He was bound to a litter, his own sword jammed through his chest. They cut him over and over while dancing. My rage at seeing Knut treated thus almost made me charge in and take my chances with the Uitiko and the Skraelings. I held off only to come back here and grab an axe for my other hand. That's when Arne tried to take my head."

"Your head is too big to take anywhere without a cart and horse," I jested.

"How many Skraeling are in the village?" asked Magnus.

"I don't know for sure, but I would guess around seventy that would fight. The females carry weapons sometimes and there are young ones. When they aren't dancing with the Uitiko, they go about life as any people would, though they only venture into the woods now in larger groups."

"The Uitiko are only there when they have the ceremony?" asked Sten.

"That is the only time I have seen them. They come from the huts around the central fire and go back to them after."

Magnus looked thoughtful. "So if we attack the village as Ivar planned, we face many Skraeling and five Uitiko. I think we could handle the Skraelings without much trouble if we move quickly and hit them at sunrise."

"Are we just stealing Knut back or are we killing all these vermin Skraeling and their dogs." said Havelok?

"I am happy to kill those that killed our men here," I said, "but do we kill the females and children?"

Ivar spit on the ground. "I say we paint the village in their blood and make new coats of their Uitiko."

Njal stood, "I say we get Knut back and let come what may. We have battled these Skraeling and, though they are fierce and show no fear, they fall as easily as any man. We are Blood Eaters. We are warriors. Some call us monsters, but I will not kill an entire village, even of Skraelings."

"I know you want vengeance for what they have done to your kinsman," Erland said to Ivar, "but Njal is right. Knut still lives, thanks to a long dead witch. Let's focus on getting our brother back and let the Norns decide who dies at dawn."

ᛒᛚᚨᛜᛞ ᛁᚺᛏᛖᚱᛋ ᚠᛖᚱᛋᚢᛋ ᛋᚴᚱᚨᛖᛚᛁᛜᚷ

We spent the rest of the light preparing for war. Though many years had passed since we last preformed the ritual of readying ourselves to face an enemy, the motions came to me almost without thought. I sharpened my sword, though it was already sharp. We planned to approach the village quietly, at first light, so we left our chain mail behind and chose our leather armor instead.

We all fed from our thralls for the added strength, then sent them off in Blood Dragon to the beach at the river's mouth. Most protested and begged to join us in battle, but the Blood Eaters stood firm. Our pact with the thralls was to defend them from all harm. They live peaceful lives with every comfort we can provide in exchange for just enough blood to sate us and keeping our curse to themselves.

Armored and armed, we followed Ivar into the woods and up the slope of the mountain. Ivar held a torch in the lead and Havelok lit our path from behind. We stopped before we might be spotted from the west side of the mountain and waited for the sun. We sat on a few wind felled trees, passing the night with tales of our time apart and resting in turn. We did not speak of the Uitiko, but all had eyes and ears on the darkness around us.

The patch of sky we could see through the trees finally showed a hint of light. We rose, checked our weapons, and set off towards the village. The mountain blocked the rising sun behind us, but there was just enough light to see where we stepped. Ivar signaled for us to halt and we gathered close together.

"Another dozen paces and we will be able to look down on the village. We should split up here and take different paths, I think."

Erland and Magnus walked to where the path began to drop steeply into the village and looked down. They whispered back and forth for a while before returning to the rest of us. Erland looked each of us in the eye, "Njal, Sten and I will circle to the south and attack from the flat ground there. Havelock, Arne and Ivar will attack from the west. Magnus will work to the north where there is a huge boulder from where he can cover the center of the village with his bow. Knut is near the center, still strapped to a litter as Ivar described. We can't count on him being able to fight once we free him, so whoever gets to him first needs to cut him free and flee with him back this way. If we can take him without a fight, we will. If we are challenged, kill whoever stands in your way. Any questions?"

"If we get him and flee, we'll probably be chased. The Skraeling must know these woods well. What then?" Havelok asked.

"We are faster than Skraelings. Move fast." Njal said.

"And what of the Uitiko?" I asked.

"I do not know. We are Blood Eaters. We will find a way. Let's go." Erland turned and set off to the southwest, Njal and Sten following.

I put my hand on Magnus' shoulder. "Shoot well, Magnus. Let's go get our brother."

I lead us down the path towards the village. We made our way down in the dark, trying to keep as quiet as possible. When we reached the treeline surrounding the village, we stopped and waited.

I counted twelve huts from our position, but more were out of sight. Seeing no movement, I crept forward and into the village, aiming for the center as best I could. I stopped and listened for movement as I passed each hut, but only heard snoring from one. The brightening sky pushed me forward. With two huts left between us and the center of the village, I caught movement to my right.

The skin door of the hut next to us was pushed aside and a Skraeling stepped out. He looked at us, his eyes went wide, and Havelock planted his axe right between them. The Skraeling fell to the ground with a meaty thump. A female spoke from inside the hut, likely asking her mate what had happened. Ivar sheathed his sword and drew his dagger before pushing past the door and into the hut. The female inside started to speak again but was cut off by a wet gurgling noise. By the time Havelock freed his axe from the twitching corpse, Ivar emerged and nodded for us to continue.

We reached the hut closest to the central open area and stopped again. The very center of the village held a large fire pit, embers still glowing from last night's fire. Knut was on the opposite side of the pit from us. His face was caked in dried blood, but I could make out bits of hanging skin and bone beneath. A sword stood tall, plunged through his chest and deep into the ground. He was naked, covered only in blood and shredded skin. I gave up caution and rushed to his side.

It wasn't until I put my hand on his chest that I was certain he still lived. The curse we bear keeps us alive but does not spare us pain. He must have felt every blade that did this to him. I knelt down and set to work, cutting the thick leather straps holding his arms, legs and neck. He didn't stir at all, but his chest rose and fell in ragged breaths. I had only finished one leg and arm when a scream rang out from my right.

"Ivar, time to earn our pay." Havelock said, taking up a position to defend me while I kept cutting the straps.

"I don't think we have time for cutting," Ivar said, taking position on my other side. "Can we carry the whole thing?"

I looked over the litter, "The only thing holding it here is Knut's sword." I reached up from where I knelt and grabbed the hilt. "Sorry,

Knut. This is going to hurt." I yanked the sword out of his chest. His eyes flew open and locked with mine for a heartbeat before he passed out again. "Havlock, grab the other end, quickly!"

We snatched the litter up and took no more than a step before Skraeling started pouring into the opening from all directions. Ivar stepped in front of us and held his sword high, menace pouring off of him. The Skraeling stopped well out of sword range. "Who wants to die first!" Ivar screamed at them.

I looked back at Havelock and he nodded, setting down his end of the litter and pulling his axe from where it hung on his back. I set my end down and drew my sword. We stood ready, but the Skraeling just stared at us. I counted thirty, all armed with clubs and their hand axes. None wore leather chest pieces like the Skraeling that attacked us in Vinland, but those had been ready for battle, not just waking up for the day. I could hear fighting coming closer to us from my right, but it was a long way off still. We would have no help from the others.

The largest Skraeling I had yet seen, nearly as tall as I and muscular, stepped from one of the huts close to us. The other Skraeling parted for him to pass. When he cleared the last of them, I could see his left arm was injured, bound to his side. He surprised me by speaking in our tongue. "I am Amaqjuaq. Put down weapon or die."

Ivar took a step towards him. "I am Ivar Risberg, this is my kinsman you have harmed. Let us pass and I may let you live."

Amaqjuaq tilted his head and sniffed towards Ivar. "I know Ivar. It scream name," he motioned towards Knut on the ground. "Know smell. Kill many people. Hurt me," he looked at his left arm. "You die."

Amaqjuaq's face contorted like his skull had turned to liquid and he dropped to his hands and knees. His body shaking, he screamed out in pain as his skin split open down his back, revealing dark gray fur beneath. The Uitiko emerged from Amaqjuaq's skin, somehow bigger than the skin should have been able to contain.

We watched, mouths agape, as the Uitiko raised his head, at the same level as ours he was so big, and howled out across the village. It was answered by more howls from the woods around the village.

Ivar turned back, looked at me, and smiled, his fangs grown long. Turning back to the Uitiko, he screamed out a battle cry of his own. He brought up his sword above his head and was about to leap when Amaqjuaq fell to the ground with a yelp, one of Magnus' arrows lodged in its side. Another arrow appeared, pinning his head to the dirt. The beast kicked twice then lay still. The Skraelings screamed and charged.

Ivar took the first to reach him easily with his sword and then stepped back, swinging wildly as the mass of Skraeling hit him. I jumped to his left and fended off the clubs and axes raining down. I quickly lost ground but turned so Ivar and I could fight back to back. I spared a glance towards Havelok where he stood over Knut, holding his own against a few Skraeling that came at him. I did not count how many Skraeling we killed in the storm of blood and severed limbs. I took a hand axe to the shoulder and many club blows, but we stood strong.

More of the Skraeling entered the village center as we fought, and I began to worry they would never stop coming. Ivar stumbled back into me and I saw a hand axe lodged in his chest and another in his side. He was bleeding everywhere, as was I. Swinging my sword wide, I created some space for us to retreat towards Havelok. looked south and saw Njal charge into the rear of the Skraeling attacking us, Erland and Sten on his heels.

Njal screamed and cut down Skraeling after Skraeling, body parts flying in every direction as he headed straight for us. The Skraeling backed away at last, when he reached us, wanting no part of the storm coming down on them.

Erland joined us around Knut, "Time to go, brothers. Can you carry him?" Erland looked at our wounds.

Ivar pulled the axe from his chest with a scream and took a big breath. "I can carry him with help."

I couldn't speak, I was so tired, but I picked up one end of the litter and nodded. Ivar grabbed the other and we pushed to the East. The Blood Eaters fell in around us, Njal leading the way. The Skraeling that were left stood back and let us pass, though rage still showed on their faces. Erland came up beside us and looked down at Knut. "He will heal in time. I saw one of the wolf beasts dead, did you slay more?"

Havelock answered him, "We didn't kill that one, Magnus did. We did not see any others."

"We killed two of them," Erland said, "they do not die easy." I glanced back and saw his lower left arm was flopping, barely attached at the elbow. I had seen the deep claw marks down Sten's back already.

"At least two left." Ivar said through clenched teeth.

Arrows started falling around us as we left the village and entered the woods. An arrow hit me in the back and I fell, dropping the litter. Sten helped me up, snapped off the arrow and took my place carrying Knut. I took his place guarding our left and we started forward again.

"Move faster!" Havelok screamed from the rear. I looked back and saw four Skraeling with bows, taking aim from the edge of the village. Havelok had at least six arrows in him already. We reached the steep path leading up towards the mountain and began the climb as arrows started landing around us. One hitting poor Knut in the shoulder, though he didn't react.

I looked to the top of the steep trail to where it leveled out and saw Magnus there, arrow to cheek. He let fly four times and the arrows stopped falling around us. "Those were my last arrows," he called down to us. "Move!" He shouldered his bow and drew his short sword and waited.

I looked back towards the village. Many Skraeling stood looking at us, but they did not advance. We reached Magnus and he took the lead up the mountainside as we made our way back to the beach. When we crested the slope and began to descend down the east side of the mountain, Erland called for a halt.

"Magnus," Erland said, "You are the fastest, and uninjured. Will you run ahead, down the river bank, to fetch Blood Dragon for us?"

Magnus nodded, "I will. Keep your eyes open, Brother. We may not be done with these Skraeling yet. I saw at least twenty leave the village to the North from my perch. They may have circled around to trap us." He walked over to Havelock. "May I borrow these?" He grabbed one of the arrows sticking out of Havelock and yanked it free.

"Agh, Bastard! Havelok cried. Magnus snatched the others out of him to matching cries.

"You whine too much, Brother," Magnus grinned. "I would fetch you a nursemaid, but I have a boat to catch."

"With all your speed then, Magnus." Erland nodded to him and watched as he darted away through the woods with the grace and speed of a stag.

We trudged on through the woods, making the best speed we could. The sounds of the woods mixed with the smell of the sea as we neared where the outpost had stood. Every part of me ached from wounds and fatigue and none of my brothers looked much better off. Though we did not age, it had been a long time since we fought any battles and I wondered if we would have fared better fifty years ago. I was about to say as much when a low growl sounded somewhere close behind us.

We all spun and drew our weapons as one of the Uitiko stepped out of the trees and onto the path behind us. Havelock raised his axe and screamed at it, but it stood its ground. I heard a rustle in the brush to my left and looked in time to see another, running low and swift past me. I turned to follow it just as it leapt and hit Njal in the side, riding the big man down into the brush beside the trail. I raced to help, hearing yells and chaos behind me as the other Uitiko attacked.

I cleared the brush and turned to see the Uitiko on top of Njal, sinking its teeth into his shoulder. I swung my blade down on the beast's back and it dug in, but not deeply enough to sever its spine. The Uitiko dropped him and spun around, my blade flying from my grip.

I pulled my knife as it lunged at me, stabbing it in the side with the woefully inadequate blade as it bore me to the ground. It bit my arm deeply as I tried to defend myself and I lost the knife as well. It spit my arm to the side and lunged in for my neck. Everything moved slowly for me as I realized the Uitiko would take my head off with its teeth and my never-ending life was about to end. I was just trying to decide if I wanted that or not when the Uitiko stopped. It made a strange hacking sound like something was caught in its throat and stepped back off of me. It shook its head back and forth and whined before vomiting on the trail.

It looked back at me and growled, preparing to attack again. It did not see Njal's blade swinging down to land close to where mine had on its back. Unlike my pathetic hit, his blade carved clear through the beasts spine, stopping somewhere in its guts. Njal kicked it in the head and I heard its neck snap as its body fell in two pieces.

"Bad dog!" Njal screamed at it before kicking it again. He looked back down the trail to where the others stood, staring at him. "What?"

"Nothing, Brother," Said Erland with a chuckle. "The other one ran off that way," he pointed to the north. "Do we chase or let it flee?"

"I see Blood Dragon coming." Havelock said, pointing past me towards the sea. "I say we let it go."

"We can always kill it later." Ivar said with a shrug.

"Arne," Njal turned back to me. "What did you do to that Uitiko? Do you really taste so bad?"

"I don't know." I said. "It went for my head and I thought I was done."

"The pouch Innick gave you. It worked," said Erland. I reached up and grabbed the pouch I had completely forgotten about.

"Who is Innick?" asked Ivar.

"A Skraeling I owe my life, Brother."

We made our way to the water and began cleaning our gear and our wounds while we waited for the ship. When Blood Dragon reached the shore, the thralls helped us, binding wounds and offering blood for strength. Knut finally stirred as we lifted him into the ship, but he could not speak until he healed more. The thralls took turns, cutting their arms and holding them over his mouth, but it would take many days to bring him around and he would surely have nightmares from his ordeal.

We loaded the gear into the ship and rowed back off the beach. "I say we make for that island we passed on the way here and rest for a while before deciding our next step," Erland said from his place at the keel.

We were a stone's throw from shore when the Uitiko stepped out on the top of the rise where the beginnings of the hall once stood. The brush on the north side of the clearing moved and a large group of Skraelings stepped out, all armed with bows. Magnus dropped his oar and picked up his bow, swiftly stringing it. The Uitiko howled from the hilltop and started towards us.

Knowing we could not row out of Skraeling bow range before they could shoot, we scrambled to snatch up shields from their holders on Blood Dragon's side. "We will have to get out and fight them. If we move fast, they may not get many arrows in the air," said Havelock.

We readied ourselves as the Uitiko approached. Magnus took aim at the beast and waited for a sure shot. When it was nearly to the beach, the Skraelings all put arrow to cheek. The Uitiko howled again and started to run towards us. The Skraeling, in almost perfect unison, turned and released their arrows, hitting the Uitiko with all of them. We stood watching as a few walked up to the Uitiko to make sure it was dead. When they decided it was indeed no more, they turned to us and held up a fist to their chests before turning and fading back into the trees.

Thus the Eight were reunited and the Wolves of Vinland met their end. I attest these words and deeds to be true as I, Arne Truelson, along with my cursed brethren, Erland Alfson, Havelok the Bold, Njal of Westberg, Magnus of the Grove, Knut and Ivar Risberg, was there to live this tale and carry the burden of walking among the living still.

ᛏᚺᛖ·ᛖᚾᛞ

CASEFILE: THORNEWOOD

S.L.Thorne

TO WHOM IT MAY CONCERN:

In late 1987, I purchased an old manor in Northern York, UK known locally as Antwood-Thorne. It is a little run-down, but one would expect a 500-year-old to have a few bags and wrinkles and wonky plumbing. Antwood-Thorne had lain fallow for nearly three decades, maintained only by a single housekeeper and her groundsman husband and a trust that was nearly two hundred years old itself. The trust was running out, and the new head of the firm maintaining it had decided to offload it.

Enter me: American lottery winner.

I had big dreams, an intense need to explore my English roots, and 235 million US burning a hole in my bank account. I love old buildings, every damp nook and cold cranny and historical scrap of them. And let me tell you, this place... this place had Addams Family stamped all over it.

What began as a labor of love has become an obsession and, after discovering what I am about to reveal, I have begun to understand a great deal more than I should about the darker corners of the universe. Let me tell you, some things one should just let lie.

The house is of the kind that makes the weird seem normal. You ignore strange noises, like scratching in the walls, yet make no attempt to

CASEFILE: Thornewood

rid the place of rats. It seems to breathe like no place I have ever been in the US. And then there is the old lady; who is creepy fast, silent as the tomb, and stronger than her aging husband, I suspect. Her husband will not enter the house at all. Once Mrs. Tudbury assessed I planned on living there, she gave me more warnings than I could remember, and rules about What Could Not Be Changed. The paintings were part of those rules.

They are all well done, but... they all have this element of the macabre or bizarre that tweaks your brain even before you consciously notice it. And They are Not To Be Moved.

I tried once. There's this painting in the library of a reverse mermaid (a woman at a window with the head of a goldfish. At least I think it's a goldfish) and I find it very disconcerting. It's like an omen or a ...prophecy of something wicked soon to come. I moved it to a lesser-used room. The next morning it was back in its place.

I tried again, only to have it back by dawn, only this time the frame was duct taped to the wall.

Then Mrs. Tudbury, who had not been in that wing since reconstruction began and had not been informed of the incident, politely reminded me that the paintings were to be left where they were. Only to be removed for cleaning or repairs, but were to be put right back when it was done.

Eventually, I tried hiding it in the attic... which is where I found a stack of boxes containing hundreds of notebooks and files and learned a part of the house's history. I had been told most of its provenance, including the additions, but what I had not been told was that before it had a brief stint as a Destination Hotel in the late Forties (after having served as a place for a good many of the children sent out to the countryside during the war), it had been Antwood Asylum. What I found were the records of the patients during the fifty or so years it had served the mentally unbalanced or the just socially unacceptable. (apparently, that happened more often than not during certain eras).

Yes, I read through them, the ones that were still legible. Time was not kind to them. They are all horrifying in their own way, but this one... this one disturbed me and intrigued me and may very well be the end of me.

S.L. Thorne

I have transcribed the journal as best I could. In interest of maintaining the integrity of the document, I am using two different fonts. It seems the doctor's handwriting deteriorated as time passed, and he had begun going back to scribble comments to his prior notations. These notations are in *Adgreement Signature*, and placed as close to where they were scrawled as I can manage. [*My own commentaries are in Baskerville, italicized and so bracketed.*] There is also a third handwriting, in a different pen and hand, as if someone else were running commentary on the doctor's commentary. These are printed in *Adine Kirnberg*, a font which closely approximates the neat, deliberate hand.

The original is in a safe deposit box in a hermetically sealed document sleeve to protect it from further degradation. But here you are with the only other copy.

READ AT YOUR OWN RISK!

S.L. Thorne

Casefile: Abigail Merideth, Lady Thornewood
1 April, 1821

Patient is a young woman, married, 3 months shy of 18 years. Dark brown hair, dark blue eyes, fair skin with a haunting countenance. *Or would it be more appropriate to say haunted?* It should also be noted that the patient is the wife of Chester Wilde, and the only child of Colonel Arthur Thornewood (deceased), and the only grandchild and heir to the late Whitby, Lord Thornewood, recently deceased. (Connection to the woman's madness?)

Husband claims that she evinced normal grief patterns after the death of her grandfather, her only remaining relative, until this past March, when her whole demeanour changed. She left off her mourning and began to behave as she had prior to the old lord's death. Lady Thornewood had been observed laughing at odd moments, carrying low tone conversations with shadows. She had even began to paint again, painting a portrait of her grandfather in the solarium. Although unhealthy, her husband was willing to ignore her fixation upon her dead relative for a time, except that she took a sudden turn for the worse a few weeks ago. A servant observed her huddled in the shadows in a corner of the library in an urgent whispered conversation with no one. When the lady saw the servant, she promptly changed her manner, and ordered the servant about their business.

According to her regular physician, Lady Thornewood suffers from weak constitution and has to be carefully watched, lest she over exert herself or become exposed to one of numerous (and possibly dubious) irritants that produce asthmatic reactions. Due to this, her husband informs me, her grandfather made certain she was never out of someone's sight, and the woman has come to depend upon this so heavily that, if she is ever alone for more than a minute, she gets nervous. These last weeks have seen a drastic change in this, in that she has actively sought solitude. Always, when the servants find her, she is hiding somewhere, whispering. When found, she ceases all conversation and adopts a guarded manner. Fearing she was hiding something, her husband eavesdropped instead of revealing himself and listened to her holding a rather one-sided conversation with the shadows, calling it "grandfather".

My initial assumption is a grief-induced dementia consisting of delusions and a mild case of paranoia. As Lady Thornewood is in a highly agitated state at the moment, I am having her sedated, restrained, and observed for the time being. I will conduct a thorough interview with the lady in the morning and hopefully begin to properly diagnose the problem.

2 April, 1821

Having spent a large part of the morning with Lady Thornewood, I believe my initial diagnosis to have been correct: mild dementia, with auditory and visual hallucinations. Cause: her inability to handle her grief. Prescribed Treatment: reason therapy combined with a serum to eliminate the hallucinations, and therefore any validity to her dementia.

Though she was still very languid in manner from the sedatives, (Nurse C. informed me she was still prone to resistance this morning) she appeared lucid enough. She was ever the lady. She insisted that there was nothing wrong with her, that her husband was just trying to get rid of her. When I asked how she knew this, she informed me that her grandfather had told her so. He'd overheard her husband's conversation with one of his hunting friends. When I informed her that her grandfather was dead, she smiled, (a slow, charming, knowing smile) and said, "I know that, and you know that, and HE knows that, but Grandfather apparently doesn't care. I need looking after and he has come to realize Chester just isn't the man for the job."

I informed her that her stay with us will be brief and that it was all just formality. She must remain with us for her physical health if nothing else.

I have had her sent to the west ward, where she can observe some semblance of freedom, yet be under constant surveillance. This will enable us to observe how her dementia affects her under quasi-normal circumstances. She is to be treated as befits her station, even given paint and canvas, but she is still a patient.

CASEFILE: Thornewood
3 April, 1821

We have come to an agreement, the Lady and I. I have told her to consider her stay a holiday for her health. If she cooperates with us, she just may get out of here all the sooner. She has agreed, and we began today with a long talk about her life at home and why she feels certain that her grandfather has come back from the dead to be with her. We have also agreed to a withdrawal of the sedatives. After this second interview, I have come to the conclusion that it may take us some time to relieve her of these delusions. They are very deeply seated. I have given instructions to begin the serum treatments this afternoon. Perhaps, after a few weeks of this, she will cease to have these hallucinations and we can begin serious treatment.

4 April, 1821

Apparently, the lady is highly sensitive to heather bloom. I have given orders for the patch just south of the garden wall to be mown immediately. It took us some time yesterday to discover the source of her sneezing fits and respiratory distress, and even then she still required sedation in order to be able to sleep at all. Minor setback, but one we will overcome. I have conferred with her regular physician and gotten all the information he has on her condition. Perhaps we can take care of her body as well as her mind. At least this way we will not have any incidents with chemical sensitivities.

I have prescribed a sulphur bath for this afternoon, perhaps that will help clear her lungs a bit. Also, I am having her moved for the evening to one of the interior rooms. I have explained that she will have to be locked in for her own safety considering the location (near the violent ward), but until the air has cleared from the heather she will have to remain in a secure internal environment. I cannot have another attack like yesterday. Surprisingly, she seemed to believe me, though she was mistrustful at first. Her willingness to trust me gives me hope for her condition. Perhaps her paranoia is due to the reactions her delusions have earned her, which would be a perfectly logical response, and gives me hope for her.

5 April, 1821

Lady T. took a violent turn for the worse last night. Because of the location, no nurses are allowed on the ward after hours and none of the orderlies enter the cells, so no one checked on her until the nurse went in to fetch her out this morning. She was found huddled on the floor in the corner behind the bed, half frozen and blue with cold. She was wide-eyed, panting, and unable to speak. When the nurse touched her to move her, she snapped aware as if she had been sleeping with her eyes open. She resisted at first, but then cocked her head as if listening to someone, then reached out her hand and allowed Nurse C. to take her from the room to her previous quarters where she calmed down somewhat and began to fuss about her appearance. (I shall have to look into the temperature issue of that ward. I cannot have the patients freezing to death in the night because the furnace cut out, even if they are criminally insane.

Upon physical examination, she has irritated her throat to the point of laryngitis, apparently from screaming. We had to conduct our interview via paper and ink. I have included my questions in the transcription here of our conversation, though her original paper is in her medical file:

Lady T: They were everywhere. The voices. I could feel them, hear them, everything but see them. Pawing at me, clawing, screaming, howling, yelling.
Doctor: What did they want of you?
Lady T: Some of them, nothing, just the torment of me. Others help, escape, remembrance. Faced with this, how can one stay sane?
Doctor: So you are insane?
Lady T: No. But leave me in that room another night and I will be.

Should have listened, should have listened!
[this was scrawled across the whole of the above transcript.]

I have compared her handwriting with that of a letter written to her regular physician (he was so kind as to leave all records he had of her with me for the time she is in my care) and this choppy, nervous script is a far cry from her usual flowing hand. Whatever happened last night terrified her greatly. Whether that was only the normal shrieks and noises of that particular ward or something new within her head has yet to be deciphered and the only way to discover this is to eliminate, one by one, possible stimuli.

9 April, 1821

The hallucinations are only growing worse, and I have been forced to increase the dosage of the serum. At first, the voices came only in the night, far more softly than that first night in the criminal ward, which led me to assume it merely her interpretation of the general, incoherent noises of bedlam. A nightly dose of laudanum fixed that easily enough. *IDIOT! I was just too thick to understand, and now... it is too late* Now, however, the voices have begun to pursue her even in daylight hours and she is becoming increasingly more distressed. The voices are no longer just her grandfather, and some are less than benevolent.

One of the orderlies has begun to mutter about her being devilled, or possessed, which is understandably upsetting several of the staff and patients. If he persists, I will be forced to let him go. I myself do not subscribe to such nonsense and will not have it hindering the recovery of any patient or the advancement of the science as a whole. As it is, what sane person wants a madhouse for a neighbour? I do not need religious nonsense making matters more difficult than they are at current.

Thankfully, Lady T. does not view her voices as devils, though she says some of them do 'devil her so'. She claims they are the ghosts of the asylum, but I no more believe in these ghosts than in that of her grandfather. I have noted one difference between the original hallucination and these new ones. She only sees her grandfather, she cannot see the others; they are merely voices near her and this fact makes me concerned. It is a sign of chronic lunacy which is far harder a matter to deal with than mere grief-induced self-delusion.

I am also beginning to worry about her physical health. She has been mostly chair-bound the last few days, not just due to the sedatives, but physical weakness and a general malaise. Her body is perpetually cold, almost corpse-like and, indeed, there are times when passing her in the ward, and even in the sunlit gardens, when a chill draft seems to find her no matter where she is put.

Thankfully, there have been no recent lung fits or asthmatic episodes since I had the field mown. As it looks like she may be here longer than first anticipated, I may have the heather pulled up by the roots, so that we do not have to secure her in the deeper wards again. I like having her in a sunlit place. She is far too pale as it is and the brightness will perhaps drive away the melancholy that she keeps so carefully hidden. Should the serum fail completely, I may have to resort to harsher methods. I will need her husband's permission for that.

I will give the serum another two weeks before asking. I would hate to have to take the drill to her.

12 April, 1821

I have had some marginal success with the new formula, adding the smallest infusion of prussic acid and strychnine to the serum. It is too early to tell if it is working or if she is simply not speaking of matters to hasten her release. I may need to try an incomplete sedation and interrogation to know for certain. I discovered last fall, quite by accident, that a partially sedated patient is more apt to answer questions put to them, and far more truthfully. Further experimentation with this has generated very positive results, with some patients saying things which are not necessarily known to them on a conscious level. However, it does not necessarily work on every patient. Although, some do have a tendency to spout complete nonsense altogether.

13 April, 1821

A very disturbing session with Lady T. I am convincing myself slowly that there may be no recovery for her. Shame.

We began the session as I had anticipated; the patient was incompletely sedated and put to bed. As the session was to take place within the patient's private room, and in deference to her social rank, a nurse was present at all times. I sat by the bed as she tossed and turned uneasily for several minutes before I began to read from the list of questions I had diligently prepared the night before.

It began simply enough, as I said. I asked her if she could hear me; she said yes, etc. established communication and asked if she was alone.

CASEFILE: Thornewood

She said no. When asked who was with her, she said my name and Nurse C., using the third person which told me she was successfully in the susceptible state I needed her in. When I asked if her grandfather was there she said no. For a moment, just a moment, I began to hope that she was healing. Then she said, "He is trying to fight the others off."

Troubled by this, I asked her who else was with us. She said no one for the moment, but that the others were just beyond the door. I spent several minutes trying to get her to tell me who these others were, until she suddenly gasped, and grabbed at her throat as if she were strangling. When Nurse C and I bent over her to try and discern the trouble, she seized my throat in a vise grip beyond the strength of a woman and growled in my face in a very masculine voice "Is this what you wanted to see, Doctor Troglodyte?"

She simply laughed as we tried to pry her fingers from my neck: an eerie, deep laugh I swear I've heard before. The temperature in the room dropped easily thirty degrees and then she went limp. We took prompt advantage of her laxity to apply the restraints to her, remaining diligent should she suddenly snap out of it, or it be a ruse altogether.

She came around only after prompting, and when asked why she attacked me, she seemed genuinely unaware of the act. Possible double consciousness? I refuse to believe possession. However, I have had a frightening realization. There was only one inmate who ever called me Doctor Troglodyte, a violent psychopath named Talbot Fitz-Warren who died six years ago due to a strychnine overdose. There is no way she could have known this.

He told her, that's how, or he was her... He's still here. Dead or not, the bastard is still here!

How she came to this knowledge is a mystery, *not anymore!* though it may be possible someone else on the ward knew and whispered it to her.

My interview from there was pretty useless. I only got from her the story of how her grandfather came to her weeks after his death before she began struggling against unknown assailants, screaming at them, turning her head in a drugged attempt to shake off something. Nurse C.

FANG

thought it kinder at the time to fully sedate her and leave the questioning to another session. She was right, of course. Still, it bothers me....

But was she, really? Did we do the child more harm than aid with our kindness?

I really must look into the temperature in her rooms. It seems to be perpetually freezing in there.

29 April, 1821

A patient in the west ward hung herself this evening. A tragedy, of course, just when I thought we had cured her melancholia. I had set up an easel in the day room for Lady T. so she might continue painting, hoping that the images will give me an insight into her psyche. The latest one seems to have been what set Cassandra off. It is of a young woman standing at a window, but the young woman's features are more than vaguely fishlike, and there is an angel standing in the shadows watching her. Sight of the painting seemed to have stressed Cassandra into a nervous fit, but she calmed down the moment the nurses noticed. We found her hanging out the window with her bedsheet around her neck. She had tied it to the foot of her bed. It may or may not have been an accident, as the sheet was wound around her hand as well as her throat. Either way, she'll be buried in the asylum lot. She had no family.

I am worried, however, how Lady T. will take the news. She had become close to the girl. Granted, she treated her as one would a small child, but that was all that Cassandra responded to. Thinking of her in those terms may make it harder for the lady to process this death as well. I am considering telling her that the girl was moved to another facility, or that she was released into the care of a long-lost relative, but I am not certain she will believe that. I have, for the moment, forbidden any of the staff to speak of the matter or answer any questions regarding Cassandra. Perhaps this will head off any further trouble. *God, I was such a fool!*

CASEFILE: Thornewood
30 April, 1921

    I am appalled that one of my staff would go against my direct orders. Apparently, someone (I have not yet discerned who) informed Lady T. of Cassandra's death. During our conversation today, she looked dead at me and asked when I was going to tell her about the girl. I skirted the issue, but she kept on the subject, insistent. "I know she is dead, that she tried to escape the other night by climbing out the window, but that someone, whoever it was that drove her to flee (and she won't tell me who) *I think I know. God, help me, but I think I know!* twisted her up in the sheet so that she hung herself instead. You know how Cassandra is: if it disturbs her, she clams up. And you were going to tell me when?"

    Just like that, mostly in one breath. She is very hard to deny. I decided that candour was the best approach and told her flat out that I had felt it best she not know as I did not want to delay her healing process by adding another "ghost" to her repertoire. She only smiled at that and said "ghosts come and go as it please them, not us. If it were that simple, I would not be here and you would not be sitting there, contemplating eavesdropping on my nightmares. Do you want me to tell you about them?"

    She then went on to describe the most horrific scenes which caused Nurse C. to go completely pale and nearly faint. Nurse later insisted that the scenes which the lady described in such detail were straight from the darker pages of the asylum's history. Pages unwritten that only the witnesses could have known. Nurse C has been with the asylum for more years than I have breathed and seen much. I find it disturbing that a woman who lived through those events with relative composure would fall to pieces at their retelling. She insisted that Lady T. told the stories *as if she had been there.*

    It worries me that she may begin to listen to these voices, giving in to the decadence and antisocial behaviours they promote. It is fortunate for her that her husband did not take her to St. Mary's. They would surely have attempted an exorcism by now.

15 May, 1821

Things have not been going as hoped. The serum is apparently not working, despite variations in formulation. (One such variation resulted in convulsions, to my frustration) Lady T. insists on continuing her delusion that she hears voices and sees the ghost of her dead grandfather on a regular, conversational basis. Whenever I think I am making progress, she just smiles enigmatically and nods like I haven't a clue. *Because you don't, you jumped up lob-cock! But you do now*

20 May, 1821

I grow worried about Lady T. Her prognosis does not look good. She grows paler by the day and is prone to fits of weakness and lethargy, often confining her to a wheeled chair or bed altogether. Ironically, it seems she grows more beautiful even as she begins to look more like one of her ghosts.

It also bothers me that her husband has visited only once since her committal and that only to ask *me* how she was, not to see her at all. This, I fear, will only re-surge her paranoia, though it begins to lend weight to her earliest claims that he was merely attempting to off-load an unwanted heiress and keep her wealth. Wishing to make certain of her situation (in case his behaviour be the cause of her retreating into a delusional state) I have had private conversations with some of Lady T.'s staff. According to them, prior to her mental breakdown, the two were absolutely inseparable, a storybook romance. Now, Lady T. has even gone so far as to claim she has seen her husband riding the moors with another woman, not far from the asylum. I do not know whether I should believe her and I am not privy to the social circles which would allow confirmation. Her servants will not say.

As her stay will undoubtedly be longer than first anticipated, I have ordered Henry to begin pulling up the heather by its roots rather than deal with the consequences of regular threshing. I have even authorized him to pay tuppence to some of the village boys for their aid in the task.

CASEFILE: Thornewood
21 May, 1821

Lady T. has become aware of the complete removal of the heather and reasoned the significance. She is furious. She explained that she is of no harm to herself or anyone regardless of whatever delusions I may think she has (her words, not mine, and I have not used that term in her presence. Somehow I begin to suspect she is reading my casebook).

[*In a very different, flowing, almost feminine hand in violet ink. Perhaps watercolour?*]

Very likely, dullard. Though I hadn't at the time, someone was... and you had been very naughty!

When I tried to placate her, she jerked down the sleeve of her dress to expose an alabaster shoulder marked with deep gouges and snapped that she was in very real danger here, not only of actually losing her mind but physically as well. *And it's all my fault!*

*Maybe not **all** your fault. You didn't create them, only locked me away with them.*

She has been keeping this from me and Nurse C by virtue of private bathing. (This oversight will be immediately corrected.) When I used this as proof that she was a danger to herself, she flew into such a rage she had to be restrained. She actually tried to walk out of the asylum. She led the attendants on a right merry chase (for a frail lady, she is clever and quick). I have ordered her removed to a padded cell and strait jacketed until such time as she can restrain herself without medication.

26 May, 1821

A mistake perhaps? Haste on my part? I do not know.

Lady T. was found this morning in such a state we took her for dead at first. Her skin was almost blue and though Nurse's breath showed clearly in the chill air, Lady T's did not. We did prove her to be breathing when they moved her.

I ordered her moved into a warm bath immediately to bring up her temperature. If we are not careful, we may have her death on our hands due to winter fever. I have spoken to the caretaker about the heating system, but he insists there is nothing wrong with it.

Another horrifying discovery: when Nurse C. got her warmed up in the bath, she noticed blood in the water. At first, she thought it to be women's blood, but the volume became quickly too great for that. It was then that she moved the Lady and discovered that her back has been laid open by several wounds of an unknown cause. The jacket and room were searched thoroughly for any possible source of these wounds and none were found. Furthermore, there is no evidence upon the jacket, either tears or blood, that she sustained injuries of this severity. I can only assume the cold kept them from bleeding until her body was warmed up enough for the blood to flow.

The only possible explanation is that someone entered her room while she was sedated, removed her jacket and dress and did this to her, waited until the cold did its work, and then redressed her. But this is almost as impossible, as those set to watch and guard her are my most trusted.

Ha! Ha! Ha! Are they really?

She has been bandaged and dressed very warmly: wool stockings and gloves, even indoors. Her lassitude is greater than before, perhaps, understandably, from blood loss, so I have prescribed a special diet of blood thickening and enriching foods (beef hearts, kidney pies, a broth of organ meats and rich red wine, and boiled liver)

27 May, 1821

The Lady has slipped into an actual melancholia to the extent that she must be spoon-fed to get her to take interest. She will not speak.

I have attributed this to the beginning of the normal grief cycle, so I have assigned one of the younger nurses to attend her around the clock. We shall simply take care of her body for now. Perhaps the serum has done its work. I will begin it again in half doses in two days, to be certain the hallucinations do not return. And, with any luck, in a few weeks or a month, she will have grieved enough and come to terms with her loss and walk away from this place whole again.

I have sent Lord T. word that I believe her to be on the road to recovery and ask that he perhaps plan to visit her next week, to be there for her, to support and console her in her loss.

30 May, 1821

Her grief seems to be taking a dramatic, slightly unhealthy but understandable course. To my great frustration, Lord T. has not made the time to see his wife at all, in spite of several messages sent in entreaty. Expenses are paid regularly by a solicitor in town who is apparently in charge of managing her trust fund, but beyond this, the new Lord of the Manor has taken no further interest in his wife's well-being. His wife may very well be dying of a broken heart, and he is out hunting and enjoying the season. (I have had confirmation from Henry that Lord T. *has* been in the hunting parties that have recently been seen crossing the asylum property)

2 June, 1821

Just when I think she is starting to strengthen and possibly come out of things, she slips again. I have had her moved to the outer courtyard during the afternoons to take the sun. Her skin is a deathly pallor, almost waxen in its texture and nearly translucent in nature. She is beginning to look like a lovely statue that has been well polished by centuries of caresses. Even painting in the sun does not seem to heighten her colour.

She has begun to paint angels. Is she nearing death? Does she believe this? I have asked but the only answer she will give me is "Death walks the halls here nightly. Death is nearing me." Again, there is this fishy woman, a sort of reversed mermaid, in her paintings, watching the asylum walls under the shade of a twisted tree whose bark is not unlike that of a man… Her psyche seems to be likewise twisting even as she slowly stops talking. Her speech is now rare and cryptic. In the past she refused to allow me to sit with her at tea, insisting that she only takes tea with friends; but now she no longer objects to my presence at such times, though when I join her she does not drink no matter how I coax.

Her hands tremble now, and the medications seem to have no effect on her. The poppy juice I have ordered added to her tea has kept her increasing nervousness to a manageable level, and allowing her to continue to paint provides her a focus. I have cut back on the serum's dosage, testing the waters to be sure that the hallucinations are gone. Nurse C. has dared to suggest that some who claimed to have seen Christ or the Virgin Mary were sainted and not committed. I do not believe in either and told her as much. If she wishes to continue to work here, she should mind her opinions and allow the doctors to do the thinking.

6 June, 1821

I fear that her madness is becoming deep-seated. She has been heard speaking to nameless voices in the night. Following up on reports from one of the night nurses, I visited the hallway outside her room at half-ten last night. I indeed heard voices from within the room, one clearly Lady T's drug-slurred, tired voice, and two others, one slightly effeminate but male, the other female. When I entered the room, there was no one else there and the lady had fallen silent, though she was looking at me, clearly awake. The delusions are so strong that now she has begun to speak for the voices to give them substance in her mind and the mind of others.

9 June, 1821

Today is the anniversary of Lady T's birth. She is eighteen today. Tragic. She is a truly beautiful woman, in spite of her rather unhealthy pallor. She looks more and more like a ghost every day. *If only...* My morning interview yielded no results whatsoever. She would not even acknowledge my presence, just continued to paint what I can only describe as an Ophelia, or a Juliet in the tomb. Which it is she will not tell me. Though the fingers applying the brush do their work with sufficient skill, the rest of her trembles and she is more white-lipped than ever. In fact, her lips were tightly pressed together as if she were fighting not to say

CASEFILE: Thornewood

what she was thinking. I am considering the partial sedation session again tonight. Maybe that way I will get some answers.

I visited Lady T a second time this afternoon. This time in response to the staff. Apparently, something she said sent one of the other inmates running through the courtyard in tears. I may have to discipline the attendants for handling her too roughly, as, when I got to her, she was beginning to bleed from her nose and slightly from one ear, though I could find no evidence of blows or cause. She was staring straight ahead and babbling constantly. What little I understood of what she was saying sounded like threats. At one point, she looked me in the eye and told me that I should pay more attention to my patients as people and not as subjects and that I should beware of too readily prescribing rat poison as cures. Then she laughed at me. I ordered her restrained and put somewhere she could not hurt herself but could be observed constantly.

She did not fight the strait jacket, but continued to whisper to the orderlies as they worked. One of them grew very upset and, I understand, went home within the hour on some excuse. As Nurse C. was wheeling her away, muttering something about the jacket being unnecessary, Lady T smiled enigmatically and said that she should be patient, that she would be running this place in all but name inside of thirty years. Imagine that, a woman in charge of an asylum! And Nurse C. at that! Why, she has to be in her fifties now if not older. In thirty years she won't be able to take care of herself much less an asylum. I will watch her carefully for any signs of insubordination. Find an excuse, if I must, to let her go. I will not be undermined in my own asylum.

10 June, 1821

I cannot believe this! We have lost her! This morning, when the shift changed, Harold, the orderly who was set to keep an eye on her was face down in her room, dead, and Lady T was nowhere to be found. There is no possibility of her escaping without help and I have to wonder if perhaps she somehow persuaded someone to help her out of her situation. The predictions she spent all yesterday making are having a profound impact on both staff and residents. Though no one else is unaccounted for, the staff will all be questioned thoroughly by me.

I cannot report this, as I have no proof she has escaped. In fact, there is no way she could have on her own power, as she has been so weak the last few days she had to keep her palette on her lap instead of holding it. I can only assume she is somewhere still within the walls of the asylum. If I report to Lord Thornewood that I cannot find his wife, the stipend he has left us for her care will dry up and we cannot afford that right now. And, at the moment, her presence is something of a draw for more than charity cases.

Either way, I cannot allow this to get out. *Get out, get out! I want to GET OUT!* [*again scrawled across the page*] Her husband never checks up on her, and only requests progress reports when the payment is due. I am certain I can make something up. It should be easy to predict the direction her psychosis was taking her. I will worry about his visits if one ever occurs. Until then we shall scour not only the grounds but the asylum itself. For the next few days, no inmate will be given walking privileges. All will remain in their rooms. We have to find her before something happens to her and I have a dead lady and a scandal on my hands.

At the moment, only Nurse C., Brutus(who found the body) and myself know that Harold is dead. I have ordered him buried in the cellar. If things get out, we can claim Harold kidnapped her. Brutus will not talk, as I have discovered (ironically, due to something Lady T. said yesterday that I overheard) that he has a criminal record. He has been warned that any attempts to tell anyone what has happened here could easily result in his getting blamed for everything and ending up on the end of a rope. He merely grinned and said that he did not get where he was by ratting out. I shall keep an eye on him, but, for the moment, we are safe. Still, I must find her.

12 June, 1821

No luck so far. I cannot continue to put off treatment of other patients forever. If I do not find her soon I shall have to assume she is either kidnapped and in another's care or lying dead somewhere. For the time being, the records will show that she is in a padded cell under Harold's watch. If someone else finds her before we do, then it shall be stated that he kept her absence a secret from us. I am not worried about this journal doing anything more than providing explanations should the truth get out, as this is my personal casebook and no one has access to it. I keep a separate file on patients with less personal commentary and more technical wording for the necessary scrutiny.

Like I said, you had been very naughty!

14 June, 1821

Scotland Yard came by today. Wishing to see Lady T. Apparently, it seems that Lord T.'s mistress was found slaughtered in the master's bed last night, right next to him. He swears that his wife hacked her up. I am afraid I actually laughed at that point, and had to explain that it was, in my professional opinion, impossible for Lady T. to have harmed anyone, as her physical condition prohibits it. Nurse C, at this point, came in and stated that if the officers would like proof that Lady T. was in fact still safely locked away she would be happy to take them to see her.

I was angry at first, but with no choice but to follow her lead, went with the gentlemen to the padded ward where she allowed them to peek into a door window and surprisingly, walked away satisfied. I peered in the room myself and saw that Nurse C had arranged another lady patient of similar hair colour and size to be propped, sedated and half curled up in a corner to masquerade as Lady T. Had I not known better, I myself might have been fooled by a casual glance. I must commend Nurse C's ingenuity. Thankfully, she has not seen fit to gloat or bring up the subject since.

As I rejoined the investigators from the Yard, I discovered that they had been talking to a few of the inmates and staff, and there are some who claim to have seen the lady. After they left, I investigated myself and several inmates and night staff claim to have seen Lady T. wandering the halls at night, still in her nightdress, often in the company of another woman. When asked which woman, some of them shrug their shoulders, but one person pointed out a figure in one of Lady T.'s displayed paintings. The one that usually appears vaguely fishlike, though they claim she had no aquatic features at all.

I will eventually get to the bottom of this.

No, it has gotten to the bottom of me! Ripped me, gutted me, shredded me nightly. Each night she comes and sucks me dry and laughs as she plays in my head! I can no more touch her than a ghost but I know she is cold flesh and dead blood!

How does it feel to be one of the mad, Doctor? Delightful, isn't it?

THE END

SPECIAL ACKNOWLEDGEMENT

I especially wish to thank the two people who I invited to join me on this little excursion when I thought I did not have enough on my own to justify this volume.

Mae Baum: who jumped at the chance with a laid-by piece of delightfully twisted darkness. A tale of torment and sacrifice. Thank you. Hopefully you'll join me again, should I decide to do another one.

A.J. Jensen: who rushed to get his piece ready for me when I gave him a two week deadline. (My fault, wholly, for deciding to do this last minute.) Honestly, I'm glad I waited. 'Cause it's really good. I can't wait to see how he's going to 'make it better', when he puts it into a whole novel!

**Other Books By
S.L.Thorne**

Love In Ruins
The Speaker
Mercy's Ransom

The Gryphon's Rest Series:
Lady of the Mist
The Gloaming

SHIFT Books 1 & 2
Stag's Heart
Dragon's Bride

All Available in hardback, paperback and ebook
at:
Thornewoodstudios.com/books
or
Amazon.com

Read More by Mae Baum:

Mae Baum – Fantasy

Monster of Winter

The Benton Betrayal (included in Renegade City anthology)

Writing as Cali Mann - Paranormal Romance

Shifter Island
Uncursing Her Bears
Finding Their Mermaid

Thornbriar Academy series
Lost
Found
Bound
Saved
Bloody Lucky (a Thornbriar Academy side story)
Beautiful & Deadly (Boxset)

Misfit of Thornbriar Academy series
Infiltrate